marriage, friendship, loyalty, and the nature of theater and art flow through every sentence. A one-sit read, I promise!"
– Nadeem Zaman, author of *The Inheritors* and *Up in the Main House and Other Stories*

Praise for
Romeo and Juliet Keep Their Eyes on the Prize

"Fans of Evanston writer Richard Engling's 2023 comic novel about Chicago theater, *Give My Regards to Nowhere*, will be delighted to learn that he has written a follow-up. The rollicking sequel...continues the adventures of Dwayne Finnegan, the sometimes brilliant, sometimes hapless, artistic director of the Psychedelic Dream Theater, as he struggles to mount a fresh production of theater's most famous romance. Naturally, comic obstacles abound."
– Maria Carrig, *Evanston RoundTable*

"A welcome return of the beleaguered yet indefatigable Dwayne Finnegan. Dwayne once again leads his fractious theatre company into an unparalleled adventure. As the bard well knew, there is no romance without tension, and tension abounds in this excellently written and twisty caper. Engling's years in Chicago's storefront theatre ensure that, no matter how complex life on and off the stage becomes, the events are always exquisitely believable. It's funny, yes, and engaging too, but also wise and moving."
– Liam Heneghan, author of *Beasts at Bedtime*

ALSO BY RICHARD ENGLING

Body Mortgage

Antigone and Macbeth: Adaptations for a War-Torn Time

Visions of Anna

Give My Regards to Nowhere

Romeo and Juliet Keep Their Eyes on the Prize

A Dwayne Finnegan Novel

Richard Engling

Polarity Ensemble Books

The characters and events in this book are fictitious. Any similarity to real persons, living or dead, is coincidental and not intended by the author.

Polarity Ensemble Books
www.polarityensemblebooks.com
Cover design by Laura Boyle

Also available in audio and ebook editions.

ISBN 978-0-9776610-9-1

Printed in the United States of America

Dramatis Personae
(in order of appearance)

Angela Monica Guiseppelli , fifth grade teacher, wife of Dwayne

Dwayne Finnegan , artistic director of the Psychedelic Dream Theatre

Madeline Forthright , author of *Keep Your Eyes on the Prize*

Reginald Camper , artistic director of the Goodman Theatre

Orlando Gunn , handsome actor playing Romeo

Ingrid Baardsen , blonde Viking executive director of the Psychedelic Dream Theatre

George Aleister (Aleister) , Dwayne's oldest friend, a successful psychiatrist, and author of *The Soul in Grief*

Barry , the bartender at the John Barleycorn Memorial Pub

Joan Dunam , stage manager, board member of the Psychedelic Dream Theatre

Coco Nesbit , gorgeous diva actor playing the Nurse

Tom Collins , Dwayne's creative partner from *Titus Andronicus*; fight and dance choreographer playing Mercutio

Melinda Prentice , a pretty young ingénue playing Juliet

Wallace Proctor , veteran actor playing Lord Capulet

Eric , an executive at Image Imagination, a commercial video studio

Ry Joodey , guitarist, music director, playing the Prince

Peaches Brown , bipolar costume designer for *Romeo and Juliet*

Chaz Ackersley , P.R. man, gambler, divorced, Dwayne's old friend

Uncle Bull , Coco's uncle, loan shark

Bonnie Ackersley , Chaz's ex-wife, lawyer, brilliant red hair

Rockwell Nesbit III (Rocky) , Coco's father, playing Lord Montague

Jayden , handsome young Poet in the Schools, working with Angela

Raymond Green (Green) , manager of the Playhouse

Dan Darwood , leader of the Indigenous Connection Church

Armageddon and **Pearl** , Dan Darwood's priestesses

Yvette Nesbit , Coco's mother

Fran Konacki , principal of Angela's school

Darla Conners , Green's box office manager

This book is dedicated to my mentors and artistic heroes including Robert Bly, Ursula K. LeGuin, Carol Bergé, Grace Paley, Sam Smiley, Phillip Appleman, Scott Russell Sanders, J. Dennis Rich, Byron Schaffer Jr., and Doug von Koss, as well as the ones I never met but whose work has meant so much: Lawrence Durrell, Jack Kerouac, Anaïs Nin, Eugene O'Neill, Tennessee Williams, Joe Orton, P.G. Wodehouse, Carl Hiaasen, and so many others.

Special thanks to Zoë Engling, Liam Heneghan, Martin Uthe, Bob Fiddler, Jeanne Fredricksen, Ann Keen, Howard Raik, Gail Wilcinski, and Jenny Seidelman for suggestions and assistance concerning this book. Also thanks to Zack Meyer for fight choreography nomenclature and to Robert Falls, Steve Scott, and Adam Belcuore for interviews and a tour of the Goodman Theatre. A deep hat tip and thanks to all the brilliant actors and other theatre professionals in Chicago, especially those who worked with me in the late, great Polarity Ensemble Theatre. And a very special thanks to Gail Wilcinski for being my partner in life.

1

Wednesday, April 7, 2004

"*Che bella! La bambini!*" Angela stood at the window of their room in the *pensione*, looking down at the children playing in the piazza below. "Come here, Dwayne. Look how adorable."

Dwayne left his breakfast cappuccino at the little table and joined his wife for the adorable view at the window. She, he was happy to note, was also adorable. Still in her nightgown with her wavy black hair bed-tousled, she was gorgeous and sexy.

Their *pensione* window overlooked a small piazza with its venerable church at one end, a square of grass at the center with a cobblestone street circling down the hill, and the tables and chairs of a café to one side. Little children, not quite school age, played together on the cobblestone and grass, a puppy frolicking among them, their mothers gossiping and watching from the side. A young man puttered lazily through the square on his Vespa and down the steep hill. All of this was in the old section of the hilltop town of Ragusa, the home of Angela's ancestors. In the distance, over the ancient stone buildings with their terra cotta tile roofs that spiraled down the shore, the Mediterranean glowed to the horizon. Every bit of it was *molto pittoresco*. And he had made it happen. He felt so proud.

"This is gorgeous. I've really got to hand it to you, Dwayne." His wife wrapped her arms around his neck and his heart swelled with pride. Yes, he had done this. Not only had he saved for and arranged a major trip to Sicily, he had scheduled it during her Spring break, fulfilling yet another of his lovely wife's dreams. He felt like he was living in a Fellini movie, vacationing in southern Italy embraced by his voluptuous wife, who had a striking resemblance to a young Claudia

2 ◆ RICHARD ENGLING

Cardinale. They'd just enjoyed a delicious breakfast tray of coffee and pastries the *patrona* of the *pensione* left at their door. Angela kissed him long on the lips and looked back out the window down at the children playing.

"Aren't they pretty?" She sighed with a deep happiness. "This is the perfect time," she realized. "The perfect place. Come on. Let's make one of our own." She pulled the gauzy window curtains closed, took Dwayne by the hand, and led him to the bed.

It took Dwayne a moment to realize what she meant. "You mean make a baby?"

"No more pills, just natural lovemaking between you and me," she promised. "You know you love to make love." She began opening her nightgown, revealing the body Dwayne adored. At the perfect age of twenty-nine years old, Angela was more beautiful and desirable than ever. She gave a warm chuckle. The upturned curl of her upper lip drew him in, so kissable. "Looks like you've got a tent pole in your pajama pants, Dwayne." She shrugged off her nightgown and pulled him into bed, helping him out of his pajamas on the way. Morning light streamed through the gauzy curtains, giving a warm glow to the room.

"I've got a confession," she whispered. "Looking at those little *bambini* and then thinking of making one of our own, I started to get wet." She laughed a little and pressed her body up against him. "That was a first. And I have to say, I like it." She sounded a little out of breath. "I feel super-sexed already."

"Yes," Dwayne agreed, also sounding out of breath. Their flesh pressed together felt so delicious, for the moment he could not form a thought, he could only experience the feeling of his lips against her, their bodies together, his hands on her wonderful curves.

But then, he *did* begin thinking.

Could they afford to care for a baby? Yes, he was the hero of this vacation. He'd wanted to do something special for Angela who worked so hard, so he began secretly saving money bit by bit to bring her here to the land of her ancestors on a vacation she truly deserved. They'd had only a modest honeymoon. Ever since they were married, it was Angela who financed most of their lives. She taught fifth grade in the

Chicago Public Schools while Dwayne struggled to launch a career as an actor and director. He felt embarrassed about the pathetic money he made.

Last year he'd nearly lost the money he'd been secretly saving for this trip. He'd bet on a chance that could have propelled his career to directing at the famous Public Theater in New York City. He could have jumped from directing jobs that barely paid the cost of his carfare, to projects that paid a real living wage. Or maybe even *a lot of money* if he made it to Broadway, which seemed an actual possibility. But it had all gone wrong. He was no closer to a paying career than he'd been a year ago. Fortunately, he hadn't lost the vacation money, as well.

So how would they afford a *bambino*? They barely afforded their monthly car and student loan payments, not to mention rent and electricity and clothing and groceries.

Would Dwayne have to give up the theatre and go work in an insurance office or become a real estate agent? He loved acting and directing. Couldn't they just wait until he was thirty-five maybe? That wasn't so far off. Perhaps by then he could find his way into the ranks of decently-paid theatre artists. He could afford to buy things for the baby and take them all on family vacations. It didn't need to be glorious Italy. A road trip to Yellowstone and camping with Angela and the kid (or kiddies) could be fun. They loved camping. They enjoyed hiking in the woods. They'd even gone camping once with their best friends, although that hadn't worked out so well. He and Angela could each carry a baby or toddler in a backpack. Dwayne would carry the heavier one. He worked out. His body looked great. That was one of his assets as an actor, though it hadn't brought him fame or fortune yet.

"Hey, uh, Dwayne," Angela said. "The tent pole seems to have folded."

Oh God, the shame of it!

"Yeah, um, sorry," Dwayne mumbled. *St. Bridget of Sweden, Patroness of Failures, pray for me.* "I just got distracted."

"Distracted?" She sounded amazed and annoyed.

"I started having all these thoughts." He looked into her

judgmental eye, then looked rapidly away.

Angela sat up abruptly and scooted away from him. "How could you possibly get distracted?" She looked down at her flushed, warm, desirable torso.

"No, sorry, you make an excellent point," Dwayne said. "Here." He patted the bed where she had been so recently lying beside him, but she did not lie back down.

"What is up with you?" Dwayne heard the tang of rising temper in her voice. "I want to hear what could possibly distract you from this golden opportunity to knock me up," she insisted.

So stupid! Moments ago, Dwayne had been happily rubbing bodies with his beloved wife. Angela was beautiful, desirable, wonderful in bed, supportive; she had a career at which she was very good. She had that little line from the center of her ribs down to her navel and below that made her stomach look so super hot. And her smooth roundnesses of…well…she was fantastic in all possible ways. She was very nearly the perfect wife.

But she also had a volatile temper. Her Sicilian ancestry provided her with a fluency of emotions as responsive as a Lamborghini roadster. Dwayne's Irish ancestors, on the other hand, would rather have carried their emotions to the grave than converse about them. Dwayne had inherited much of that.

He sat up on the bed. "I'm sorry, I just started thinking about whether I could hold up my end."

"Clearly, you are not." She gestured to his flaccid member.

He felt his face turn hot red. "I don't mean that. I started to imagine that in nine months I'd need a *family* income. Would nine months be enough to start making money in my field?"

"Your field," she scoffed. "You've never made any money *in your field*. You've made money bartending, but you never stick with it for long."

Dwayne felt the sting of that. "Come on, Angela. You know I'm trying. Bartending is night work. I can't bartend if there's evening performances or rehearsals."

"Trying is not enough, Dwayne." Her voice rose in volume and in pitch. "You've got a college degree. There's a lot of things you could do."

"I know there are. But all the people I've known who moved into career-type jobs end up focused on that. Doing theatre becomes a distant memory."

"So, figure it out. You're thirty-one years old. It's time to get it together. My mother had three kids by the time she was my age."

"She was a fulltime housewife and your father ran a crew pouring concrete. He's still pouring concrete. That's not our life."

She smacked him in the side of the head with a pillow. "There's nothing wrong with my parents' life. Our backyard had the biggest concrete basketball court in the neighborhood. Pull the net across and it was a tennis court. The uncles even played shuffleboard. That concrete was smooth as cream!" Angela got out of the bed and pulled on her blouse.

"Don't go," Dwayne said, reaching out a hand to lure her back to bed, but Angela spoke right over him.

"We had friends over all the time. Sometimes my dad would set up folding tables on the court, and we had huge parties. My mom had a fifteen-gallon pasta pot. One of my uncles made his own wine and brought it in gallon jugs. I had thirty-six cousins, and they all came bearing meatballs and mostaccioli and cannoli. We liked the life my parents made. We lived!" She pulled on her jeans.

"Right, I know. That's a great life." He held out his arms in supplication.

What was wrong with him?

"I used to have faith in you, Dwayne. Yeah, we have debts. But push come to shove, I believed you'd pull it together. You'd be a fun dad, and we would have a good life. I had so much faith, I was ready to get knocked up today, with no doubts or worries about the future, even though you've been pathetic as a breadwinner. But apparently, you don't have faith in yourself. So maybe I shouldn't either."

Dwayne's penis drooped yet more sadly.

"Come on, Angela. Anyone can have a moment of doubt." His heart ached. He could feel it in his chest, aching and humiliated.

"I don't understand you, Dwayne." She pulled back the gauzy curtains from the window sharply and gestured to the scene below.

"You bring me to this beautiful, romantic place. The gorgeous little children are playing in the *piazza* below. The Mediterranean Sea shimmering in the distance. It's so romantic, it's like instant foreplay. This was going to be the best fuck of our lives. We could have been telling our kid about the miraculous morning they were conceived, on the trip for which their daddy secretly saved to take mommy to the land of her ancestors. What could be more perfect? But instead, you start worrying about *your precious career*—and then you can't keep your apparatus working? And let's face it; I'm a pretty good-looking wife, so, what the hell?" She glared at him, then turned and grabbed her bag off the dresser.

Dwayne's penis became so ashamed, it nearly pulled back into his body like a turtle's head going back into its shell.

"Oh, look. Here we are." Angela picked up a book from the collection on the little bedside swap shelf. Travelers were invited to take a book and leave a book. "Just what you need." She threw the book at him and put on her sandals. "I'm taking a walk," she said. "Alone."

She grabbed the only key to the room and stalked out. He followed her into the hall.

"Angela, wait."

She turned abruptly. He was shocked at how angry she looked. "No, Dwayne. You sit down, and you do some reading. I've been totally supportive of you. Now you need to be supportive of me." She lunged down the stairs and out of the *pensione*.

Holy Jesus and the raging Magdalene.

He walked back into the room and closed the door behind him. She wanted him to sit and read until she deigned to return? Her words had stung him so much, he felt a little nauseous.

What had she thrown at him?

He picked up the book off the area rug next to the bed. *Keep Your Eyes on the Prize: The 6 Basic Truisms of Winners.* This is what she wanted him to read? Right now? On their Italian vacation?

Well, no, that's not what she wanted. She wanted him to enthusiastically knock her up. She'd invited him into her most delicious, desirable self, and he'd lost his boner. She had been so beautiful. So aroused. Just thinking about it, his penis began to grow.

You're a little late, my friend.

Ridiculous.

What was wrong with him? It wasn't that he didn't want a child. He just didn't feel ready. It was like, at thirty-one years old, he was still an adolescent. He had a chosen profession, he had training, talent, and expertise in that profession, but he could not seem to make any money.

He'd given some great performances as an actor. He was proud of the productions he'd directed, and he never felt more alive than when he was working on his feet in the rehearsal room with his cast. Working with them to create their characters sometimes helped them transform their very lives! It was exhilarating. And he was good at it. His *Titus Andronicus* was a revelation. If only the frigid polar vortex had not blown down over Chicago twice during the run, they would have sold plenty of tickets. And if Gregor Foxx had showed up like he'd promised, Dwayne might be directing at New York's Public Theater this fall and on his way to a lucrative career. Instead, the only money he made was from temp jobs.

Angela was sick of it. Would she get sick enough to leave him? That would be even worse than having to give up on the career he wanted so much.

Blessed Hildegard of Bingen, patron saint of late bloomers, pray for me.

He picked up the book. Maybe this was part of his destiny. Angela had been propelled into a mighty desire, and, to his shame, he had not been propelled along with her. Might that have been the universe speaking to him?

If he'd just focused on the glory of that most delicious physical sensation, he would have been ecstatically squirting his seed into fertile ground! To live in the moment of that most delicious coitus! His pants snake began to uncoil once again at the notion.

But instead, in the face of all that erotic possibility, he had lost his hard-on. Could that be his destiny taking him by the hand? Was that supposed to happen so that he could discover this book? He picked it up. *Keep Your Eyes on the Prize.* Maybe this manuscript contained the direction he needed. *The 6 Basic Truisms of Winners*. Truisms? Did that subtitle seem a little...lame?

Fifty-seven weeks on the New York Times Best Seller List! the cover exclaimed. He looked at the photo of the author on the back. Madeline Forthright. She talked on TV about how to be a Winner.

He opened the book. The first chapter was called *Scheming to Win*. It introduced the 6 Basic Truisms of Winners: *Winner Boats Rise Together, Get It in Gear, Work Smarter, Visit the Woodshed, No Fears/Big Ears*, and *Winners Are Grinners*.

This got fifty-seven weeks on the New York Times Best Seller list?

He had seen Madeline Forthright on TV several times. He never stayed tuned in, but she was undeniably popular. The first chapter seemed mostly about having a positive attitude toward success.

He would positively prefer to be having sex with his wife right now rather than reading a self-help book. And if they had a baby in nine months? Angela seemed positive they could make it work. Even the most successful artists had times of feast and famine. However, he'd had nothing but famine. So how to achieve the feast?

Madeline Forthright suggested he read biographies of winners whose careers he admired and interview winners in his field to find out how they'd done it.

He could do that. He wanted to be a Winner: a successful theatre artist and a father and an equal partner with Angela.

His two best friends had both lost their wives—through no fault of his own on Aleister's part—but he didn't want to be like either of them. He put the book down on the bed and looked out the window. Angela was nowhere in sight. He was totally ready to have sex with her right now.

She'd taken the only key to the room. If he went out to find her, he'd either have to leave the room unlocked, in which case he'd risk having their luggage stolen, or he'd have to lock the door behind him, which meant he'd be locked out until he could find her.

Was that the worry of a Winner? *Winners are Grinners*! *No Fears/Big Ears*! Although he had no idea what Madeline Forthright meant by either of those things (nor did he have big ears), it did suggest having a cheerful assumption of success.

Yes, he'd take the book home and read it. He would become a Winner, and Angela would be proud of him. They would have a wonderful life and be extravagantly happy, and she would never want to leave him.

He closed the book and put it in his suitcase. He walked out the door, and it locked behind him. If he was locked out of the *pensione*, so be it. He needed to find his lovely wife and put their beautiful vacation and their beautiful life back on track.

2

Monday, May 3, 2004

"Reg, your ten o'clock is here," the woman called toward the man standing on stage looking at large drawings on the table in front of him. He didn't look up. She smiled at Dwayne. "He'll be right with you." She turned and left him at the back of the audience space, a subtle cloud of perfume lingering after her. Sophisticated. The smell of success. That's what this meeting was all about. The success he needed so badly.

But what about him? Did he still smell okay? He ducked his head down sideways, hoping he didn't look like a parrot putting its head under its wing, attempting to detect any untoward aroma that might be emanating from under his arm. However, if he did smell bad, what was he going to do about it now? Run away and wash his pits in the Goodman Theatre Men's Room?

At any rate, he was "Getting It in Gear," per *Keep Your Eyes on the Prize*. Back from vacation, he was about to meet with one of the most successful theatre artists in Chicago. Madeline Forthright really pushed reading biographies, but Dwayne figured it would be way more useful to talk to theatre winners who were working now than to read books about people who'd succeeded elsewhere in some other decade.

"If you'll give me just one moment," the Great Man said from the stage, making a note on one of the oversize drawings on the table in front of him, "then you'll have my undivided attention." He looked from the drawings to the balconies that surrounded the space on three sides and back to the drawings in deep concentration.

If Dwayne's nose did not deceive him, he still smelled okay. He walked toward the stage of the Owen Theatre. This was the Goodman

Theatre's smaller space. The first time he walked in here, he'd felt instant, intense venue envy. He would so love to direct a show here. It was a big, square industrial room that could be reconfigured in a multitude of ways. He looked up into the lighting grid and marveled at the host of lighting positions on the pipes overhead and attached to the balcony fronts all the way around. Some men felt this kind of excitement when looking at a well-appointed sports car. Dwayne felt it looking at an array of new lighting equipment hung on an optimal lighting grid. Even though the new building had only opened four years ago, Dwayne had already seen five shows in here, and each had arrayed the audience and stage in a different way. He would die to direct in here! And here he was with the Big Man, himself. Reginald Camper had been the artistic director of the Goodman for as long as Dwayne had been aware of who was running anything in Chicago theatre. Camper was a genius.

Dwayne had been building toward this meeting ever since his production of *Titus Andronicus* had closed. He'd wrangled a dozen interviews with the top artistic directors in town before he and Angela had gone to Italy. He hadn't managed to land a single directing gig for any of their companies, but he'd continued to build his confidence and fluency in presenting his propositions.

This was the biggest theatre in town, and the biggest interview of all. He was *Keeping His Eyes on the Prize*, following the first truism of winners: *Winner Boats Rise Together*, which meant he needed to reach out and make connections with other winners (and learn from them).

He felt energized that they'd be talking in this room that he loved. The walls and balcony fronts were fronted in warm dark woods and black steel. The comfy armrest-chairs all pointed toward the stage with expectancy. The room spawned great art. Its stage was massively fertile.

He cupped a hand over his mouth and nose, breathed out of his mouth and back in through his nose. Okay. His breath was okay. He felt something in his stomach turn over, and it gave a loud growl. He looked up toward the stage. Had Camper heard that?

Be cool. Just be cool.

"All right!" Camper smiled, came down the steps leading off stage right to the audience level, and sat on the edge of the stage. Dwayne walked up to join him. "I hope you don't mind meeting in here rather than my office."

"I'm delighted," Dwayne said. "I love this theatre." He felt the muscles tighten in his throat. He wanted so much to succeed. He wanted it for Angela as much as he wanted it for himself. And for the talented friends he could bring along. He didn't want to be broke and obscure forever!

"Brad Cunningham told me you wanted to discuss a special program," Camper said.

"Yes!" Dwayne had had a sometimes fraught relationship with Brad over the years, but Brad had come through this time, getting this interview with Camper for him. He was grateful for the opportunity. "Yes. I imagine you are aware of the Emerging Directors Program at the Public Theatre in New York."

"Of course," Camper said. "The Public plucked Brad from obscurity as a young Chicago director."

"I understand Brad is directing here for you this season."

"Yes," Camper agreed.

"I wondered if you considered having an Emerging Directors program at the Goodman like the one that launched Brad at the Public in New York? As the leading professional theatre in Chicago, this is the ideal institution to develop new directing talent from our community."

"I agree," Camper said, looking down at Dwayne as if from a great height. "That's why we started the Michael Maggio Directing Fellowship two years ago."

Michael Maggio Directing Fellowship? *Do your homework, Dwayne!* He felt the arrows of his ignorance entering his body.

"Yes, precisely," Dwayne said, sounding comically uncertain.

Camper laughed. "So maybe you were about to propose a program we already have? I guess we haven't publicized it enough. But, even if it's not a new program, the Goodman would welcome your organization's sponsorship."

Now Dwayne was really confused. "Sponsorship?"

"It's a high-profile opportunity," Camper said.

"I, um…" *What was Camper saying?*

"We'd love to see our program have the stature of the Public's program," Camper said. "That takes more funding. You could earmark your sponsorship for that purpose. I can give you whatever details you need on how the program works, and then I can turn you over to our development people to work out the financials and how your organization's name could be featured."

"I'm sorry," Dwayne said. "I'm not from a funder."

"You're not a funder?" Camper stood up, looking profoundly displeased.

"No." Dwayne felt entirely flat-footed. He'd had some deft verbal footwork planned to take him from introducing the idea of an emerging director's program through promoting himself as the first candidate for said program. When he rehearsed it, he'd been brilliant. Now he couldn't remember a word of it.

"Then what are you?" Camper said. Dwayne felt as though the Great Man were looking down at him from an even greater height.

"I'm a…I'm a director," Dwayne stammered. He clutched at the straws of what he'd intended to say. "The Tribune said my recent production of *Titus Andronicus* was *exciting*, *sexy*, and *kinetic*. The Sun-Times really liked the combination of music and action."

"They did, did they?" Camper said, as though this were a particularly disappointing bit of news.

"Yes," Dwayne said. "I was a candidate for the Public's Emerging Directors program, but our production got caught in that repeating polar vortex in February, otherwise I might have been selected, and so…"

"And so you thought maybe we'd take you after the Public didn't?"

"Well…yes…" Dwayne said lamely.

"We get the sloppy seconds." Camper's mouth looked as though he'd bit into something unspeakably distasteful.

"Well, I don't know that I'd put it like that…"

"I've never heard of you or seen a show you've directed," Camper said. "Well, I'd heard of you from Cunningham, but I thought you were a funder."

"I'm sorry about that," Dwayne said. He wanted to kill Brad. Again. Brad Cunningham had been his most important mentor. But he'd also betrayed and manipulated him, and grabbed his crotch, and sexually harassed him.

"Listen, before you go," Camper said, the offhand dismissal striking a shaft of despair into Dwayne's heart. "You said you loved this space. What would you do in here?"

Dwayne looked up at the empty stage, then turned around and looked at the audience area behind him. Two balconies surrounded the central seating area on three sides with black steel railings all around, separating the balcony seats from the open space. The central entrance doors stood at the back of the auditorium behind the center section of seats. He felt an instant inspiration. He saw it all in a rush.

He took a step toward the back and raised his hands toward the balconies. "See how, even without any decoration, the balconies look like the decks of a great ocean liner?"

"I do see that," Camper said.

"I would do *Titanic*," Dwayne said. "We'd have to get rights and get a stage adaptation written. But I would take out these center seats and turn around the risers so the stage is at the back instead of at the front. The audience would all be facing that way." He pointed toward the back and sprinted to the back of the auditorium. "The ocean would be here," he said, indicating the seats at the back. "The top balcony would be the level for the rich people, where Rose and her crappy fiancé are traveling. The first balcony is where the poor people travel, where Rose dances with Jack. And then down on the floor here is the action in the lifeboats and where Jack saves Rose but sacrifices himself."

"Ha!" Camper said. "I saw almost that exact same thing. But I saw *The Hairy Ape*. Where you see the ocean, I see Yank shoveling coal into the ship's boiler. And the balconies as the ship's decks. I'd like to do a whole O'Neill festival in this room."

"That would be brilliant," Dwayne said.

"Some day," Camper said. He mulled it over for a moment. "So look—invite me to see your next show."

"I would love to do that." Of course, he would love to have Reg

Camper see his next show, but he had no fucking next show. No one had offered him a directing slot.

He needed to *Keep His Eyes on the Prize*! Camper had succeeded like no other director in town. And he *got paid* like no other director in town. Dwayne needed to know his secrets. The Great Man was edging toward the door. Dwayne moved to catch up.

"Listen, I was hoping you could give me some advice. I really need to start earning a living at this, and I don't know where I'm going wrong."

Camper nodded and leaned his head back. "Well, you've got all the Chicago examples. The Steppenwolf people worked for years earning nothing until their reputations took off. David Mamet, the same thing. He started St. Nicholas Theatre with a group of friends until they made their reputations. I built my name at Wisdom Bridge before I got this gig, and I made next to nothing over there. Hardly anyone starts out making any money." He gave a little laugh. "That's kind of the way it is." He shrugged. "Nice to meet you. I look forward to seeing your next show." Camper swept back up onto the stage, retrieved his drawings from the table, and strode off backstage.

Fucking fuck!

Dwayne hadn't delivered a word of the presentation he'd prepared. He'd rehearsed it in front of three people, two of whom had deliberately tried to throw him off his game. Nothing they'd come up with could match Reg Camper telling him he'd already instituted the program Dwayne was proposing.

He was such an idiot!

On the positive side, Camper did ask to see his next show. Dwayne felt pretty sure he'd impressed him with his idea for staging *Titanic*. That had come right off the top of his head, so he'd shown he could think on his feet.

Dwayne walked up the aisle and looked around.

Yes, the two back balconies would be terrific for staging the upper and lower deck of the ocean liner. The side balconies could still be used for audience seating. And all the ground floor risers and seats would be reversed. They could put in some kind of pool so Rose and Jack could actually be in water. It'd need to be a fairly deep pool.

Could they open the floor there?

He felt suddenly overwhelmed by the beauty of the architecture and the theatre technology around him. He bowed his head and dropped to his knees, his hand on the aisle seat. He leaned against it, the gorgeous aisle seat, so comfortable, so well built, so perfect in its portability to be placed wherever the creative team wanted it. This place! So elegant! So ingenious! The lighting instruments overhead, so new, so expensive, so many of them! Enough to do whatever you wanted. Not some crappy collection of beat-to-shit lighting instruments like he usually had to use. And in a space that had actually been built to be a theatre! Imagine! Not a converted storefront or a former bowling alley or a warehouse.

Would he ever direct in the room like this?

He sighed deeply and pulled himself back to his feet.

He had to get a show. He had to get someone to hire him to direct. It had to be a bombshell of a show, and he had to invite Reg Camper to come and see it. He had to build himself into a place where he clearly deserved to direct in this room.

But where would he find a slot? He'd already been to all the bigger theatres. Did he have to call on every tiny theatre in the city that might offer him a hundred bucks to direct? Would he be able to put up something good enough to impress Reginald Camper? Something like his *Titus Andronicus*? If only Camper had seen his *Titus Andronicus*! It had been brilliant.

That was something he had to hang onto. Like Madeline Forthright said in her chapter, *Pop the Corks*, sometimes you don't give yourself credit for being as much of a winner as you are. Sure, *Titus Andronicus* had lost every cent invested in it, but that didn't make it an artistic failure. And he'd been beating himself up about today's meeting, but Camper had promised to see his next show. What better outcome could he have wished?

And yet that moment when Camper said, "So maybe you were about to propose a program we already have?" haunted him. He cringed again hearing Camper's words reverberate in his inner ear.

He gave a heavy sigh and took out his wallet. Seven dollars. He wished he had enough for a nice downtown lunch. There was food back in the refrigerator at home, but that was a long ride away on the Red Line back to Rogers Park, and he was hungry right now.

He walked out into the Owen lobby and down to the super tall main lobby with its bar (closed at the moment) and coat check and box office windows.

"Well, hello!" Tall, handsome, muscular Orlando Gunn descended the wide spiral staircase from the second floor. He danced down the final steps and gave Dwayne a hug. Dwayne had directed him in *Titus Andronicus*. Orlando had played one of the leads, the villainous Aaron. It had taken some work to get Orlando past the realization that Shakespeare had written Aaron as a racist invention. Instead, Orlando could play him as an avenging black man, taking revenge on the racist whites.

"Let me guess," Orlando said. "You are reading for Karl Lindner."

"What's that?" Dwayne said.

"Karl Lindner is the only white man in *A Raisin in the Sun*. Are you here for auditions?"

A tall, pretty actress who looked a dead ringer for a young Halle Berry came down the steps behind Orlando, her lips compressed. She was not happy about something.

"See you, Letitia," Orlando said as she passed. "Nice reading with you."

She stopped and faced him, holding back tears. "I totally went up. Just like that. I had those lines cold."

"It happens. Don't worry. They understand that. You recovered really well."

"Okay," she said, not convinced. She continued on to the revolving doors and out onto Dearborn Street.

"I never audition without the sides in hand," Orlando said quietly, glancing in the direction Letitia had gone. "No matter how thoroughly I have those lines down. Sometime you blank, and it's so embarrassing to have to stop the scene. If the script is in your hand, you can just look. She's good, but she stunk it up today."

"That's too bad," Dwayne said. "No, I didn't know about the auditions."

"Goodman is mounting *A Raisin in the Sun* to tour the high schools. It's all daytime work, so I could be in a nighttime show, as well. And it's nice pay."

"I *should* audition," Dwayne said. They walked toward the main entrance together. Two actors sat on the carpeted floor, facing one another, practicing a scene. "I need to start earning some money. I've been focused on finding a new directing gig."

"Speaking of which," Orlando said excitedly, "I have an idea for the next Psychedelic Dream show. How about we do *Othello* and I play Iago? I loved playing the villain in *Titus Andronicus*. What if I played the villainous Iago, and Othello was white? We turn the races around! Othello would be the only white character and the whole rest of the cast is black? Coco could play Desdemona. Wouldn't that be hot?"

Dwayne not only liked the idea, he'd already discussed doing a reverse-race *Othello* with Bobby, who'd founded the company that became the Psychedelic Dream Theatre. But Psychedelic Dream had lost the twelve thousand dollars invested by Dwayne's two closest friends on *Titus Andronicus*. That had been his first experience with both producing and directing a show, and it had been daunting.

"Bobby had that same idea for *Othello*," Dwayne said. "But I don't know what's going to happen with Psychedelic Dream. Anyway, if we did *Othello* like that, it'd leave most of the ensemble actors without a role."

Orlando put his hand on his chest and took a step backwards in a mockery of extreme shock. "Oh, no! You mean there's a chance that *white actors* might be left out?!?" He shook his head with mock disgust and then came back with an earnest expression. "Okay," he said. "Do you want to direct really cool, innovative shows, like *Othello* with a reverse race cast, or do you want to cater to the whims of the Psychedelic Dream ensemble?"

Dwayne laughed. "Well, when you put it like that…"

"Yes!" Orlando shouted. "All right! We are doing *Othello, the Melanin-Deficient of Venice*!"

"Well, I don't know about *that*," Dwayne said.

"We are doing it!" he said decisively, pointing at Dwayne and rushing toward the door. "Don't try to weasel out of it, Finnegan. I know where you live!" And he swept through the revolving doors out onto Dearborn Street and away.

"Ha! Dwayne Finnegan in the Goodman Theatre!" A familiar voice boomed from behind him. "I see we are coming up in the world." He turned to see the robust figure of Ingrid Baardsen, her straight blonde blunt cut hair bobbing at the surface of her shoulders.

Last year, when he needed a production to show Gregor Foxx of the Public Theatre in New York, he produced *Titus Andronicus* himself, and he'd hired Ingrid to design and build the set. She promptly declared herself managing director of the company, made all sorts of decisions without consulting Dwayne, and finally siphoned off what remained of the money at the end to transform the for-profit company that Dwayne had created into a new federal not-for-profit 501(c)3 corporation with herself as executive director. Dwayne had signed the papers allowing all this to happen in the midst of a chaotic rehearsal, thinking he was signing papers for the purchase of building materials.

Just seeing Ingrid Baardsen triggered his PTSD.

"Are you working here now, too?" she asked.

"Not me," Dwayne said. He felt an involuntary twitch tug at his right eyelid. "You are?"

"Yeah! I'm designing a portable set for this touring version of *A Raisin in the Sun*. We'll be taking it around the high schools. Hey, your wife teaches in the CPS, right? Maybe we'll go to her school."

"Well, she teaches fifth grade, so probably not. But congratulations!" He rubbed at his eyelid as it twitched for the third time. He summoned up as much enthusiasm as he could. "That sounds like a nice gig."

"Thanks, Dwayne! Yeah. It's the best one yet. I'm doing construction at Northlight, too. So that's decently paid. But this gig is design, so I really love it. What are you doing here? Don't you love this place?" She did a quick whirl to take in the full lobby, her heavy black combat boots, the same as what she wore through the winter, tapping lightly on the floor as she turned. She was dressed in blue denim bib overalls with a lightweight plaid shirt underneath. She had a twenty-foot tape measure clipped to her waist and her pockets bulged with a variety of tools. Atop her ice-blonde head perched a paint-spattered brimmed cap with an *SWP COVER THE EARTH* logo on the front. "I love this place. You should see the backstage and technical areas! Hey, you want to get some lunch? I need to talk to you."

Ingrid had apparently had her fill of coffee this morning. She was always a fast talker, but today she was rattling along twice as fast.

"I'd like to get lunch," Dwayne said, "but I've only got seven dollars."

She cocked her head at him. "Who do you think you're talking to, Finnegan? Follow me." She shot up the wide curving stairs to the second floor, her huge canvas shoulder bag bouncing against her side as she climbed. Dwayne caught up to her on the landing.

Ingrid had a lot of connections. Maybe she had a lead on where he could find a directing gig. After all, *Winner Boats Rise Together*. If he could put up a great show before Reg Camper forgot who he was, maybe he could get something going at the Goodman as well.

"I think our timing is good," she said quietly, leading him up a hallway. "When I left the meeting Scott Stevens was still talking to the director, but they should be gone by now. Have you worked with Scott?"

"No."

"I love, love, love him! He's producing *Raisin*. Here, we go this way." She led him through a doorway that was off-limits to audiences and down a hallway past what looked to be rehearsal spaces. "He says to me: *Ingrid*... He's said this to me like three times already: *Ingrid, this is the Goodman Theatre. We have people covering all the areas. You just have to do* your *job. You don't have to do* everything. Can you imagine? *You don't have to* do *everything.* It's like...heaven."

"And that worked?" If he'd been able to get Ingrid Baardsen to stick to her own job and not take over everything around her, that would have been heaven for him. The woman usurped other people's territories like an invading Viking horde.

"Ha! Good one!" She slapped Dwayne on the back, almost knocking him off balance. "In the storefront world, if you don't do everything yourself, it doesn't get done. You and me, we deserve to work in places like this, where they have the money to hire people for everything. Hang on!" She held out a hand to stop him and stuck her head in an open doorway. "All right! They're gone! Come on!"

She led him into an open conference room. At one end, a whiteboard was scrawled with dates and deadlines. Coffee cups and little plates littered the table. Ingrid pulled her oversize drawing pad out of her bag, put it on the table, and opened it to a set design.

"There. Now it looks like we're discussing something. Come on. Help yourself. Lunch!" She gestured to a table at the side of the room with a somewhat-picked-over spread of bagels, cream cheese, jam, berries and cut fruit, some sliced cheeses, and urn of coffee with cream and sugar, and several bottles of water. "If anyone comes, I can tell them you're consulting on the *Raisin* design with me. Dig in!"

Dwayne looked sheepishly toward the doorway to see if anyone was coming, then followed Ingrid's example and filled a plate. He was really hungry after all. She gave a quick look out the door, pulled two one-gallon food storage bags out of her huge shoulder bag, filled one with bagels and cheeses and the other with fruit and put them back in her bag with a few bottles of water. Then she filled a plate for herself and sat down at the table with Dwayne.

"I wanted to fill my bags when the meeting ended, but Scott hung in here talking with the director, and I couldn't just lurk outside the door until they left. But meeting you, I figured they'd be gone by now."

Ingrid did nothing but theatre, most of which was extremely poorly paid. In order to afford her lifestyle, she lived rent-free in her van, did her laundry and took her showers in the backstage areas of various theatres around town, collected free and leftover food wherever it could be found, and attended every art and theatre opening she could for the complimentary spreads of hors d'oeuvres. She knew which grocery stores had the best free samples and when. She knew where to get day-old bread cheap or free. The grocery money she spent went mostly for ramen and apples. She could always heat up a bowl of ramen on the propane stove in her van if she were hungry. And given the amount of bread and cheese products in her diet, she needed those apples to stay regular. Even though she drove him crazy, Dwayne had to admire her. Her van, outfitted with everything she needed to live through the harshest Chicago winter, was her Viking ship conquering the local theatre scene.

"So how did things go with Reg Camper?" She took a big bite of a bagel stacked with slices of cheese and topped with strawberries.

"How did you know I met with Reg Camper?"

"Come on, Dwayne. You know I know everything." He gave her a doubtful look. She laughed. "Okay, I overheard Matilda call his cell to tell him you were here. He asked her to have you meet him in the Owen. So, what were you doing with Camper?"

"I'm trying to get a director's slot."

"Absolutely! You should. What did Camper say?"

"He said he'd come see my next show."

"That's fantastic!" Ingrid slapped him hard on the shoulder. He coughed out a chunk of bagel from his throat. "So, let's get the next Psychedelic Dream production up so you've got something to show him," she said.

"Yeah, I don't know," Dwayne said. "I've been trying to get something going with one of the bigger companies. Something with a more impressive budget."

She blew a raspberry. "*Titus Andronicus* was plenty impressive. That show would have been blockbuster if not for the polar vortex."

"It wasn't just the weather," Dwayne said, barely suppressing a wave of rage. "Gregor Foxx sent Laurie Anderson to see *Titus*, and you turned her away at the door! If she'd seen the show, I might be heading to New York right now!"

"That's on you, Dwayne," she said, clearly unaffected by his anger. "You have to communicate. I was trying to make sure we made some money from the show."

"I communicate!" he shouted. Someone passing in the hallway looked into the door and then hurried away. Dwayne lowered his voice. "I told the box office to let in anyone who said they had a comp. But you swept in and overruled the box office."

"Water under the dam, Dwayne," Ingrid said. "Let's put up a show for Reg Camper and get you working here. We're a great team! You do the actors, I do the tech. I'll make it look fantastic on whatever budget we have. You *know* I can do that." She leaned toward him, and her eyes flared. "We deserve to go places. The Goodman. New York. Los Angeles. And the more high-profile we get, the more interesting stuff we can do whenever we come home to the Psychedelic Dream."

Dwayne felt his blood begin to settle. Ingrid did have good intensions. Even if she were standing on your chest in her combat boots, she'd still be rooting for you.

"I need one of those high-profile gigs *right now*," Dwayne said, in a forcedly quiet voice. "Do you know of anyone looking for a freelance director? Some company that's higher profile than us?"

"I got some ideas," she said. "But, come on, Dwayne, you know we're the only game in town that's going to get you a production while you're still fresh in Camper's mind."

A large man with a crop of curly hair and black glasses passed by the door.

"Scott!" Ingrid called. She jumped out of her chair, stuffed her drawing pad into her oversized shoulder bag, and headed toward the door. "Enjoy your lunch," she said to Dwayne. She slapped a list of theatre companies down on the table in front of him. "Start with these," she said.

Suddenly he was alone in the quiet room. He thought of his wife, Angela, in charge of a class of fifth graders. She was working hard while he was here, sitting down to eat bagels. But he was doing what he needed to do. Every night he read deeper into *Keep Your Eyes on the Prize*. Madeline Forthright's *Six Truisms of Winners* seemed to be based on a bunch of clichés, but there were good ideas. Like: *Get it in Gear*. You had to stop letting your fear of failure get in the way of success. You had to make plans and carry them out. You had to fail and try again. And again. And every time something went right, you needed to *Pop the Corks*. When Dwayne read that chapter, he went to Binny's Beverage Depot for some Cava to have it ready. Maybe he couldn't afford French Champagne, but sparkling Spanish Cava was just as good at a quarter of the price.

The family clock was ticking. They had stopped using any kind of birth control. Ever since Italy, they'd been using nothing at all. Almost a decade ago, when he was twenty-two, he was so convinced he'd never want to have children, he had a vasectomy. Children would only bog him down in his quest for a great career. A few years later he realized that had been a rash decision. He had the procedure reversed before his time on his parents' health insurance expired. The surgeon assured him that his flow would be back to normal. So the pregnancy could happen at any time.

Dwayne had to *Get It in Gear*. He wrapped his lunch in napkins and stuck a bottle of water in his pocket. He headed out the door, down the stairs to the lobby, and out onto Dearborn Street. He turned right on Lake Street and down to the State and Lake elevated station. The metal steps clanged under his feet as he climbed. From the CTA platform he could see the gorgeous old Chicago Theatre on State Street with its iconic red and white marquee proclaiming CHICAGO in big vertical letters. He could see people working inside the second story windows of the vintage office building straight across from the platform. Beneath him people and cars and buses navigated the streets. Everyone all around was *getting it in gear*, like he needed to do, for his own sake and for Angela. The dynamism of city scene, the noise of the cars and horns and sirens buoyed him up.

He loved his wife. He wanted to create a life he loved and to make her happy. Because of his preoccupations, making love had become a form of discipline. Of course, he did have the advantage of being married to an exceptionally desirable woman. And yet the possibility that he would have to give up his dream was daunting. Deflating one might say.

He needed to work hard when he was working and love hard when he was loving.

Camper had promised to see his next show. Ingrid had left him a list of companies that might hire him. He finished his bagel on the platform as the train squealed ear-splittingly around the bend at Wabash and Lake toward him. The doors on the car slid open, and he stepped inside. He'd eat his fruit on the ride home, and as soon as he got back he'd get on the phone.

3

Wednesday, May 5, 2004

*H*oly *Jude, patron of the hopeless and despaired, pray for me.* Dwayne set down his phone, tossed the papers up into the air, and covered his face in his hands.

"Going that well, huh?" Angela said. She stood in the doorway to the kitchen with a large, wet, flat, limp lasagna noodle in her hand. Dwayne was working at the dining room table. She wore an apron her mother had given her at Christmas. It read, "Boss of the Sauce," across her chest and was decorated at the bottom with an Italian flag.

"I've called every theatre company on this list. The ones where I've gotten through were either not interested or suggested I submit a proposal for a production, and they'd consider it for the season after next." He knocked his forehead against the dining room table three times.

"Come in here where I can talk to you."

Dwayne followed her into their little kitchen where she finished putting down a layer of lasagna noodles over a layer of red sauce, mushrooms, onions, and Italian sausage. Her lasagna was truly delicious. Maybe he could make some cash peddling slices on the street.

"If you can't get a production, why don't you try directing commercials?"

"I don't know the first thing about directing commercials."

"How is it different? You work with actors. Instead of the audience you have the camera, and the script is very short."

"That doesn't solve my immediate dilemma," he protested. "I need to show something to Reg Camper. I can't show him a commercial."

She slapped the last noodle down on the row. "A commercial isn't for showing. A commercial is for putting bread on the table. This is a different solution. You direct commercials in the day and direct your little plays at night."

Little plays. He felt the sting of the diminution. "Sure. Great." He threw up his arms. "I'd be delighted to direct commercials. It'd beat the hell out of office temping. But I find it hard to believe that commercial studios are hiring theatre directors."

"Why do you never want to try my advice?" She tossed the empty pasta pot into the sink with a clatter. She slapped the towel that had been slung across her shoulder down onto the kitchen island. "I have faith in you. Where's your *Keep Your Eyes on the Prize?*" Dwayne could hear a touch of irony in her voice. Angela did not have a high opinion of Madeline Forthright. She always changed the channel if the author appeared on a talk show. But she was pleased Dwayne was taking action. "Isn't making money as a director the *Prize?*" she said.

"Yes. Okay. I'll try it. I'll look into it." He turned to the back door to look out toward the alley.

"Good." She took a deep breath and grabbed a tub of ricotta cheese from the refrigerator. "What advice did Reg Camper give you?" she asked more calmly.

"He talked about how the Steppenwolf people worked for years for no money until they built a reputation. Camper himself didn't make much at Wisdom Bridge before he got hired by the Goodman."

"And now he makes what? A half million a year?" She spooned the ricotta into a bowl and mixed it with an egg, some chopped herbs, and salt. "So, you need to show him a good play."

"Right," he agreed.

"And then you get a chance of him hiring you with some of that Goodman Theatre money."

"Yeah. Or put me in the Michael Maggio program."

"Well, I don't understand why you are calling these other companies. You've got your own company."

Dwayne groaned. "We don't have enough money for a production. We lost all Chaz and Aleister's money in the first show. It failed as my Public Theater audition. And some of those people are a real pain in the ass."

She layered the ricotta mix over the noodles. "*Titus Andronicus* was never seen for your audition." She pointed at him with her wooden spoon. "Those actors might be crazy, but you got amazing work out of them. Wouldn't it make more sense to show Reg Camper something with them?" She turned back to the dish, layered more of the red sauce mix over the ricotta and put another layer of noodles over that.

"I suppose now that I know how they work…"

"You go to some other company, maybe you get stuck with actors who are just as crazy but aren't as good. You won't know their weirdnesses in advance. You might spend months on a production that gets you nowhere."

"Everybody in this company wants to call the shots! Ingrid made herself executive director. Orlando wants to do a reverse-race *Othello*." He pulled a crumpled sheet of paper out of a file folder and waved it in the air. "The actors gave me this list of scripts they insist should be our future shows. Picking scripts is supposed to be my job."

Angela sprinkled mozzarella and parmesan over the top of the lasagna and slid it into the hot oven. She shrugged. "If you do plays they want to do, maybe they'll work harder, and you'll impress Camper."

"And to hell with being an actual artistic director?" He stalked around to the other side of the kitchen island.

"What's the *prize*, Dwayne?" she said even louder than he. "To be a *genuine artistic director* at your little company or to mount a show that gets you a foot in the door at the Goodman?"

He stopped and looked around the room. He took a deep breath and let his outrage seep away. "I think you make an excellent point."

She pointed her spoon at him again. "You know what Art Blakey said: *You're either appearing or you're disappearing.*"

"True enough." He smoothed out the crumpled sheet of play titles. "Actually, they selected some scripts I'd like to do," he admitted.

"There you go then!" she said triumphantly. She moved in close to her husband and laid a hand across his forearm. "That lasagna's going to be in the oven for fifty minutes. There's a certain director that

I'd like *to do*." She gave him a seductive smile.

Saint Hypatius of Granga, patron saint of erectile dysfunction, pray for me!

His head was so into his future, so into his career, was he going to be able to keep it up?

She caught the panic flickering through his eyes. "What?"

"It's just." He took a deep breath. "You've been giving me career advice. If we are going to do this, I can't be thinking about my career."

"Are you kidding me, Dwayne?" Her voice rose, and she pulled her hand away. "I just helped you out. You've got an action plan. You should be happy! That advice was so good, *it* should give you a boner!"

"I know, I know! I just need a little transitional time," he felt his face turn hot. He was blushing. He hated that.

"So now you're not going to be able to function again?" She looked at him, one hand on her hip, her eyes flared. "I can't believe this. *Dwayne Finnegan, patron saint of no sex*? Do I have to go out and find a man who can do it?"

4

Monday May 20, 2004

"I'm confused," Aleister said. "Are you saying you and Angela are having fertility problems?" He raised his eyebrows and lifted a snifter of brandy to his lips. Cars drifted by behind him on the other side of the large front windows of Cunneen's Bar on Devon Avenue. They were seated at the big solid wood table on the raised platform in the front window alcove. Spider plants hung around them. Cunneen's was a vintage Chicago bar in Rogers Park. A clock with the face of long-dead Mayor Richard J. Daley hung on the wall behind the bartender.

Dwayne squirmed in his seat. He didn't really want to explain his problem. What the hell was he doing anyway?

Well, he knew what he was doing. He was trying to get free counseling from his best friend who was a rising star among psychiatrists on the North Shore. But he didn't want to reveal his...deficiency.

"It's not a fertility problem, *per se*," Dwayne said. "It's just that when I take the long view of where my career is going, and I think of how in hell I'm going to afford a baby, I just kind of lose my focus..."

"Oh!" Aleister said loudly, suddenly understanding Dwayne's complaint. "You mean you can't keep it up?"

"Please!" Dwayne hissed. He looked around in horror to see if anyone had heard. There were only five other patrons in the tavern. Three were chattering away at a table on the other side of the room, and two were talking conspiratorially at the bar. The barmaid was leaning back against the counter behind her, looking up at the ceiling with her mouth half open like she was deep in a trance. Plus, with the music playing in the background, it wasn't likely anyone had heard.

"Sorry," Aleister said. He cleared his throat. "Yes. That is a…delicate subject. But it's one many men face. Usually *older* men. Still. It's nothing to be ashamed of."

Dwayne looked at his friend's face. Aleister was looking slightly away. Dwayne could imagine his thoughts: *He invites me out for a drink, but he really wants free therapy.*

Dwayne had always come to Aleister for help. Dwayne got kicked out of Pope John XXIII in fifth grade, and Aleister was his first friend at the public school. Aleister helped him get over being *the weird new kid*, and they'd been the best of friends ever since. They'd learned to play tennis together and continued to play through the years. It was Dwayne who introduced Aleister to Lisa, the woman he would marry. And Dwayne had seen Aleister through the incredible sorrow of surviving Lisa's murder. He wrote a beautiful eulogy and asked Dwayne to read it for him at the funeral. It was so sweet and sad; Dwayne could barely keep his composure as he delivered it while Aleister sobbed in the front row.

They'd been through a lot together.

"Do you know what's interfering with your…performance?" Aleister said quietly.

"A lot of people do theatre in their twenties, then they start to have babies, and they get a real job, and that's it."

"You're afraid a new baby will be the end of your theatre career, and then you lose your erection," he said extra quietly.

"Pretty much." Dwayne looked out at the traffic rolling by in front of the bar. A man and a woman walking their dog stopped in front while the dog took a moment to pee on the light post. A dog led such a simple life. It did not tax itself with the forethought of grief.

"How about when your performance is…unimpeded," Aleister said. "What are you thinking about then?"

"I stay in the moment, in the physical sensations, and…I focus on Angela's body."

"Yes, I can imagine." Aleister looked like he was imagining a little too clearly, then caught himself. "No! I don't mean I'm imagining…" he said quickly, then stopped. "I mean…do you ever imagine joy when you think about a baby?"

"Well, I do have this image that comes to mind sometimes."

"That's good. Because I don't think you have a physical problem. You have a fear of pregnancy and its repercussions. Your erectile dysfunction is a psychosomatic response to prevent the pregnancy. If you were eager for a baby, this wouldn't be happening."

"Right," Dwayne said.

"So what is your joyful image?"

"You know our bathroom has that huge old bathtub on feet? I've imagined Angela and me sitting in the bath across from one another in the warm water while a baby is suckling at her breast. Everyone is happy."

"Well, that is…" Aleister stopped there. He looked down at the table. A little silence stretched on.

"Don't get all excited."

"No, no, no," Aleister protested.

"You've been single too long."

Aleister bobbed his head back and forth. "Maybe," he said.

"The bathtub is an image of domestic bliss," Dwayne said.

"Yes," Aleister agreed readily. "Domestic bliss. Have you ever had that image when you were making love?"

"No. It's just occurred to me sometimes. It feels like a happy thought. I'm not thinking about anything else: money, career, nothing."

Aleister smiled in a generous way. "Maybe that's your answer. The next time your career thoughts threaten to derail you and you need something compelling to replace them, bring up that image of the three of you in the tub. Along with the compelling enjoyment of your lovely partner."

"That might work," Dwayne said.

"Unless you just really don't want to have a baby."

Dwayne's body froze for a moment.

"After all," Aleister suggested, "that's what your body seems to be telling you."

"It's not that I don't want a child," Dwayne insisted. "Having a child with Angela would be amazing. I just don't want to have to quit everything and become an insurance adjuster."

"What does Angela say you should do?"

"She thinks I should do another production with Psychedelic Dream and show that to Reg Camper. Or try to get a job directing commercials."

"So, she's not telling you to become an insurance adjuster. If she's being patient with your career, why aren't you?"

"She's patient *right now*. Well, sort of patient. She can have a pretty volatile temper. But what about after we actually have a baby?"

"Angela is already on the motherhood train. I'd say you can either hop on with her or look forward to misery."

"The motherhood train? Is that a psychiatric term?"

"I'm talking to you as a friend. You can't afford me as a psychiatrist."

"You're saying, since she's still supporting my career, I should support her dreams, too."

"Isn't that what successful married people do?"

"They *Keep Their Eyes on the Prize*," Dwayne said wryly.

"Then do it! Do another show with your usual lunatics so you can invite Reginald Camper."

"We don't have the money. Psychedelic Dream lost the twelve thousand dollars you and Chaz invested. And led to his divorce."

Aleister waved him off. The six thousand dollars he lost investing in Dwayne's production of *Titus Andronicus* had been no big hardship. In fact, he'd just spent another six grand on a vintage roll-top writing desk to replace a perfectly good desk that didn't inspire him. "Chaz and I wouldn't have put up that money if we couldn't afford to lose it. And everybody knows having an affair with an actress is not the way to preserve your marriage. If Ingrid says you can do it, she probably has something up her sleeve. So what will you do? Shakespeare again?"

"Wallace wants to play King Lear." Wallace had played the title role in *Titus Andronicus*. After getting past a psychological breakdown in the rehearsal process, he'd been brilliant.

"I'd pay to see that."

"*King Lear* is like Everest. We need to build to that. I was thinking of *Romeo and Juliet* with Orlando and Melinda in the title roles and cast the families racially."

"I like it. If Romeo's family is black and Juliet's white, that punches up the inter-family conflict." Aleister clapped his hand on the table. "Here's my totally non-professional advice: Go direct your play, let Ingrid worry about paying for it, and enjoy knocking up your wife. Let the chips fall where they may!"

"Yeah, but..."

"Forget all that, Dwayne. You can't control the future. Look at me. I had all my ducks in a row. I got through med school. I was building a practice. I had a beautiful wife. We loved each other." Aleister took a deep breath. "And then a junkie shot her down, and suddenly I was alone and heartbroken. So I plunged deeper into my career. I've helped a lot of people, I'm writing these books, and I'm doing okay, but underneath..." He lost his focus for a moment.

"Underneath you're sad," Dwayne said.

"Yes," he agreed. "Underneath I'm sad, and I can't do anything about it. When I date other women, I can't seem to get interested." He looked out the window for a moment at the passing cars, then turned back intently to Dwayne. "The future is going to do what it's going to do. Nobody can control that. Try to enjoy what's in front of you, and let go of the rest."

5

Thursday, May 13, 2004

"Yeah! Yeah! I love it!" Ingrid jumped off the tattered love seat she shared with Joan, pulled a calendar book out of her enormous canvas shoulder bag and slammed it down in front of Dwayne on the wooden cable spool that served as a table in the foyer of the Chicago Repertory Arts Theatre, where they'd produced *Titus Andronicus*. He leaned back swiftly from the impact. "R&J will be great," Ingrid shouted.

It was heartening, if a little frightening, how immediately enthusiastic she was about his script choice.

"Let's schedule the show after that, as well. Get things on the books. And fundraisers. We've got to schedule fundraisers. We are going to be one busy team." Joan looked at Ingrid as though she were a species of bird Joan had never before seen.

Ingrid was like a tornado that could uproot one's life without warning. Joan was a cipher. Dwayne never knew what she was thinking. Angela suspected she was on the autistic spectrum. As a fifth grade public school teacher, Angela had experience with that sort of thing.

"Before you commit me to any events, make sure you confirm it with me first," Dwayne told Ingrid. Setting boundaries. That's what he needed to do with her. Firm and clear boundaries. In her chapter *No Fears/Big Ears*, Madeline Forthright insisted that *Winners* did not fear to make their boundaries known but also listened carefully to understand the wants and needs of their fellow *Winners*, reinforcing the notion that *Winner Boats Rise Together*.

"Yeah, yeah, yeah. Don't worry, Dwayne." She waved her hand dismissively. "I always have access to your calendar. Listen: We did

Titus Andronicus in February. This season we should do two shows. We'll do *Romeo and Juliet* in the fall and another show in the spring. We'll skip the winter to avoid any chance of the polar vortex. Two shows will be enough for our second season as we figure out how to fundraise and get on our feet. And then the following season, we can graduate to three shows."

She was lining up five shows, just like that? Dwayne felt his whole body go hot. "I thought we'd just do *Romeo and Juliet* and see where we are," he said. "And what was that about access to my calendar?"

"That's why *I'm* executive director, Dwayne. I create the big picture. I make the schedule, and you fill it with shows. That's why *you* are artistic director. And I've never worked with a better stage manager than Joan. With our complementary talents, we can create the next great Chicago ensemble company. So let's do it. And if you select another Shakespeare for spring, so much the better. Avoiding royalties to living playwrights would be much appreciated."

Dwayne leaned his head back and looked up at the ceiling. Did they really have the elements for the next great Chicago ensemble company? They did have some fine actors, and he'd helped them improve. Three years ago, all he wanted to do was make great shows, but now he needed to start making a living. To do that, he had to prove himself. If he was going to have a production to show Reg Camper any time soon, it would have to be with these two women in this theatre with his actors. Maybe they *would* become the next great Chicago ensemble company. Why not think five shows into the future? Like Madeline Forthright said, *Winner Boats Rise Together*.

Behind him he could hear the Lincoln Avenue traffic passing on the other side of the plate glass window. The afternoon sun streamed onto his back and onto the rustic table in front of him. They were waiting for Raymond Green who ran the Chicago Repertory Arts Playhouse to talk with them about scheduling. Green was a haphazard facilities operator at best. He'd never provided a rental contract for their last show, but he had given them a favorable rental rate when they promised to be a resident company. The rent was okay, but the light control board had been in horrible shape. Some of the theatre seats were broken. Dwayne received some extreme electrical shocks from exposed wiring. Ingrid described it as being like producing theatre in an abandoned warehouse. That was pretty close to the truth.

The lobby in which they were waiting was no showplace. The ceiling was classic pressed tin, but it had been painted many times and sections were cut away and replaced with drywall willy-nilly. The furniture they sat on had been garbage-picked. The concessions stand was three paint-spattered two-by-tens stretched across a pair of sawhorses. Behind the concessions stand, an ancient refrigerator jerked into life with a loud rattle. The carpeting had horrific stains that suggested a history of vomit. But at least he'd be able to show Reg Camper a production before the Big Man forgot who Dwayne was.

Ingrid shouted to the box office manager who was passing through the lobby. "Hey, Darla, where the hell is Green? He's supposed to be meeting with us right now."

"He's in back by the alley doors."

Ingrid grabbed her canvas shoulder bag and headed toward the ground floor main stage entry. Dwayne and Joan followed her through the theatre space. This 250 seat space was in better shape than the space they performed in on the second floor directly above this, but the upstairs theatre had a much larger stage, which Dwayne had liked for the action of *Titus Andronicus*.

They exited through heavy velvet curtains to a work area by the alley door. Green was kneeling over a vintage lighting control board with a pair of pliers in one hand and a smoking soldiering gun in the other. A gray tee-shirt that had once been white rode up on his hairy back. His belt pushed down low, exposing the top of his butt crack. Around a halo of baldness at the crown of his head, dandruff gathered where the line of hair began. He turned and looked up as they approached.

"Hey!" he said with a big smile. "Look what I got for you!" He gestured to the board, which looked even worse (if that were possible) than the light board they'd used for *Titus*. He flipped a switch on the board and turned up a rheostat. A lighting instrument lying on the floor came on, shown brightly, then the board gave a loud pop and sparks jumped out of its innards, igniting a stack of chintz draperies next to the board. The draperies must have been some highly flammable artificial fabric, because they quickly burst into flames. "Jesus shit!" Green shouted. He hopped up, pulled a mop out of a bucket, and poured soapy water over the draperies, but the water also flowed into the control board. It hissed, then flashed with a loud bang and all the lights around them went out.

As a child, Dwayne had gone on a tour of Mammoth Cave. Once they were deep inside, the guide took a moment to turn out the lights so people could experience what true darkness was like. The backstage was just about that dark, and Dwayne felt a moment's childlike helpless vulnerability. He didn't like it.

"Fucking fuck," Green said. "Okay, don't anybody move. Let me just open the alley door." They could hear him moving toward the door, his feet banging against all the crap he'd left lying around, cursing as he went.

Standing in the dark gave Dwayne a moment to consider his life choices. His father had wanted him to become an architect. He'd been very impressed with Dwayne's early work with Lincoln Logs and Lego bricks. One of his father's high school friends had become an architect. He had an office high in a building in the Loop with a terrific view of the lake and the museum campus and Soldier Field. He imagined Dwayne working in a beautiful office like that, overlooking the city. Dwayne would have a good salary, take the train in to work from his home in the suburbs, and have a nice wife and family. How disappointed his father had been when Dwayne chose to major in Theatre. Especially since Dwayne's mother had been an actress, and that had been so difficult for everyone.

However, if he'd followed his father's dream, he wouldn't be standing here in the dark smelling the burnt innards of a lighting control board, waiting for a man known as the worst theatre venue operator in the city of Chicago to get a door open so they could see again. He might be living in a nice house with his lovely wife (who would not need to teach during the summers), eagerly expecting their first child. He could be building beautiful buildings. Maybe he'd even design performance spaces: gorgeous theatres that would host world-class drama and dance.

But that was not the path he chose.

Even though the office overlooking the lake, and the generous salary, and the wealthy lifestyle seemed more attractive to him now than they had ten years ago, he still did not love the idea of doing architecture.

The door swung open and light from the alley nearly blinded them.

"Don't worry about that board." Green came back in and stood over it, heaving a heavy sigh, then smiled. "I'll get that dried out and working for you."

"Hey, I've got an idea," Ingrid said brightly. She unplugged the board, dragged it out into the alley, and grabbed a large crowbar from inside the door. As she smashed the board beyond repair, Green shouted his dismay.

"There we go," she said happily. She picked up the remains of the board and dropped it into one of three dumpsters along the back wall. "We don't intend to go from one piece-of-shit light board to another piece-of-shit light board," she told him.

"That was Playhouse property! You just destroyed Playhouse property!" Green shouted.

Ingrid held up a hand for silence. "That was an act of self-defense. Any court in the land will accept a plea of self-defense." She pointed at Dwayne. "During our last rental period, your equipment repeatedly shocked my client to within an inch of his life."

"Your client?" Green interrupted. "Suddenly you're a lawyer?"

"I'm role-playing what would be said in court!" Ingrid insisted. "Pay attention: Despite lingering psychological repercussions my client suffered as a result of those events, we have not brought charges against you in deference to the long-term partnership on which we have embarked. In return, we expect you to take all possible actions to prevent the repeat of such events, including, but not limited to, disposing of any equipment that threatens to burst into flames. I have assisted you with that action in this case. You're welcome."

Green looked stunned. He rubbed his palm over the top of his head and a snowfall of dandruff drifted to his shoulders and down the front of his shirt. Joan began a round of slow-clap applause. Dwayne joined in.

Ingrid closed the lid of the dumpster with an air of finality and took a few steps toward Green. "I happen to know you recently purchased this building after years of renting it. If you can afford to buy the building, you can afford to provide us with a control board that was built more recently than Bob Dylan's first album appeared."

Green squinted his eyes. "Where did you hear I bought the building?"

"I hear all. I know all. So now you've got control of the third floor. I understand there's a room up there that's actually large enough to be a rehearsal hall."

Joan perked up at this. "Really? Let's go see." It had given her actual physical pain to rehearse *Titus Andronicus* in a space that was smaller than the stage on which it would be performed.

"I've got a renter up there right now, but his use won't conflict with yours." Green flipped on the circuit breaker that had blown, restoring light. He waved Ingrid in from the alley, locked the alley door, and led them through the theatre and up the stairs.

Approaching the third floor, Joan leaned her head back and sniffed. "I think your building might be on fire," she remarked dispassionately. From a distance they heard moaning.

"What the hell is that?" Green hurried his pace up the remaining stairs, sprinted down the hallway, and disappeared into a room. "What's going on here?" he shouted.

Dwayne, Ingrid, and Joan followed him. In the center of a large rectangular room, two women sat on yoga mats on the floor. One of them was pounding woody vines against a rock with another rock. The other was sorting leaves and brushing any dirt from the leaves' surfaces. Their long, messy hair hung down on every side of their heads, covering their faces. Between them an old cast iron pot sat on a propane camp stove with a mix of vines and leaves and liquid bubbling inside. Rough earthenware mugs sat in front of them with some dark brew inside. A third mug sat alone. The brew had its own pungent aroma, but most of the smoky smell was coming from the end of a bundle of burning herbs in the hand of a man who was slowly circling the room. All three were chanting *OM* as he waved his smoldering bundle around every square foot of the room.

"What the hell is that?" Green said.

The man with the smoking bundle in his hand stopped. He looked at Green, noticing him for the first time. He wore a long, collarless, homespun gown that hung to his ankles, rather like the garment Jesus is pictured wearing, except this gown was tie-dyed in bright colors. The two women were similarly garbed. He smiled brightly. His pupils were wildly dilated.

"What is our chant, you mean?" he queried cheerfully. "We chant, my dear friend, the dial-tone of the universe." He began chanting *OM* with the women once again. "Dial-tone of the universe!" he repeated.

"No!" Green insisted. "What are you burning, there in your hand? And what are you boiling in that pot?"

"Ooooohh," the man said, as though the meaning of Green's query never would have occurred to him. He laughed delightedly and the two women sitting on the mats laughed along with him. The one with the rock gathered a good handful of the pulverized vines and dropped them into the pot. The other woman dropped in a handful of cleaned leaves. The robed man drifted back to the group to grab his mug. All three of them sipped and returned to chanting *OM*, the man rocking his body gently above them.

"Answer my question, please," Green said.

"Ah, ha, ha. Ah," the man said. He held up the long, thin smoking bundle of herbs. "This is Brother Sage. And I am Dan Darwood."

"I know who you are," Green said. "You rented this space from me. What are you doing with *Brother Sage?*"

Darwood placed a hand on his chest, then gestured around the room. "I am smudging the space to cast out negative energies."

"Huh," Joan said.

He drifted sideways in tiny steps around behind the young women and gestured to the steaming pot. "This is Mother Ayahuasca. We drink of our last brewing while we prepare this brewing in an exploratory divination." He gestured to the women on the floor. "Pearl and Armageddon are priestesses. The three of us are engaged in an active divination to explore this space. We seek to discover whether the spirits, energies, and entities in this space are welcoming to our tribe. We cannot join our people with Mother Ayahuasca in a space that will not welcome them. We must divine the space and offer gifts to the spirits of the Pottawatomie, Odawa, Sauk, Ojibwa, Illinois, Kakapo, Miami, Winnebago, Menominee, and all other indigenous human peoples, and the animal peoples, wolf, fox, coyote, squirrel, mouse, bear, rat, possum, buffalo, and all the others who have called this space home over the millennia."

"Okay…" Joan breathed.

"Isn't ayahuasca illegal?" Ingrid said.

The three celebrants began to giggle.

"The Declaration of Independence guarantees the freedom of religious expression," Dan Darwood said. "Mother Ayahuasca is central to the expression of our religious rituals."

"You mean the First Amendment of the Constitution," Joan said. "Freedom of religion. Not the Declaration of Independence."

The man looked at her blankly.

"What the hell is ayahuasca?" Green said.

Dan Darwood ignored him and knelt and slowly lowered his ear to the floor. "Wait! Listen!" Darwood said. The two women followed suit. They seemed to hear the floor telling them something, and then they all three began to moan for a minute and then to laugh and clap their hands.

"It's like South American peyote, or magic mushrooms," Joan told Green. "I stage managed a show about it. It's used for religious rituals by South American native tribes."

"Are you South Americans?" Green asked the three. None of them responded. They continued to hold their ears to the floor in fascinated listening. Green moved closer to Dan Darwood and spoke directly toward his other ear. "Are you all from South America?" he said louder.

Dwayne couldn't imagine how Green thought they might be South American. They looked like white Midwestern suburban hippies.

Darwood looked up with dilated eyes and smiled. "We are Turtle

Island folk. We bend to the wisdom of the indigenous peoples. The spirits in this land on which we live were not born in Bethlehem or on the European continent of the colonizers."

Pearl and Armageddon sat up on the floor and giggled and hugged each other.

Green looked perplexed. "Yeah. Okay." He shook his head. "Sorry to disturb. You've paid for the day." He turned to Ingrid. "You wanted to get the measurements of the room?"

"It's thirty-two foot three inches by forty-eight foot nine inches," Joan said. "It'll do."

Green looked further perplexed. "How do you know that? You didn't measure."

"I looked." She rubbed her eyes, turned, and walked toward the door. "Brother Sage is getting to me."

"Brother Green," Dan Darwood said. "We must have privacy for our rituals. You said that would not be a problem."

"Right. Yeah. Right," Green said. "You told me this was a set up session today. I thought you were setting up chairs and stuff."

"Everything we do is ritual. We strive to walk the path of holiness every moment of our lives." The priestesses increased the volume of their *OM*.

"Yeah. Okay." Green shuffled from one foot to the other. They all followed Joan out of the room and down the stairs, shutting the door behind them. Green looked at Ingrid. "Can I be held responsible if they get arrested for taking drugs?"

"If they start sacrificing animals or human babies, I'd definitely draw the line," she said.

"You really can pick them, Green," Dwayne said. "I liked Brother Darwood's garb."

"But let's be clear," Joan said. "We cannot offer legal advice about your liability for their actions."

As they continued down to the lobby, Green and Ingrid began discussing and then arguing about what performance space they would use for how much rent, what equipment they could expect, and dates they could reserve.

"Whatever space we reserve," Dwayne said, "we can't afford more than a thousand a week."

Ingrid laid a hand on his chest. "This is executive director business," she told him. "Don't you worry your pretty little head."

"Dwayne!" The vibrant sound of Dwayne's wife Angela rang across the lobby. She'd come in the door arm-in-arm with their old friend, Aleister. "I didn't trust you to drag yourself away on time, so I've come to fetch you myself. We are having dinner at John Barleycorn."

"Go! Go!" Ingrid insisted. "Joan and I have this."

Dwayne felt nervous leaving the details to them. However, Madeline Forthright said *All Winner Boats Rise Together*, and *Work Smarter*. And that meant trusting the efforts of fellow *Winners*.

"Joan and Ingrid have this," Angela agreed. "Whatever *this* is. And I'm hungry." She put her arm through her husband's and pulled him out of the building.

It was time for dinner. Sure. Why should he worry?

6

The Same Day

Chaz waited for them, leaning against the brick wall of the John Barleycorn Memorial Pub, a half block up Lincoln Avenue. The trees were coming into full leaf. A soft, warm breeze ruffled their hair. Chaz did not raise his head to greet them.

"It's a beautiful day, and you look like you lost your last friend," Angela observed.

"I think I need a drink before I talk," Chaz said. He led the way into the bar. Inside their eyes had to adjust from the brightness of the early spring evening to the gloom of the pub's scant lighting. The aroma of stale beer soaked into the fiber of the ancient wood floor wafted to their nostrils. It was a voluminous space with high ceilings and large models of vintage sailing ships mounted at the tops of the walls all the way around the room. Slide projectors shot images of gloomy renaissance paintings on the walls in several locations. The sound system played the ominous opening notes of Beethoven's Fifth Symphony, seeming to echo Chaz's mood. As the boys seated themselves at a wooden table, Angela stopped at the bar and asked Barry the bartender to bring them a pitcher of Bass for starters.

"While we are waiting for friend Chaz to imbibe his first beverage, I have news," Aleister announced cheerfully. "Binky said the release date for *The Soul in Grief* will be late September. That's really fast for Random House. They usually take a year from signing, but everyone agreed my book would get a better reception in the fall than the spring."

"Congratulations," Dwayne said.

"I love that your high-powered agent is called Binky." Angela smirked. "Congratulations!"

"Yeah," Chaz agreed, attempting enthusiasm.

"You look like someone shat on your head," Angela told him.

Barry brought them a tray with a large pitcher of deep amber beer and four mugs. They ordered a round of burgers for the boys and a fried shrimp basket for Angela. Aleister filled the mugs from the pitcher as the bartender headed back to the kitchen.

"A whole team of lawyers shat on my head," Chaz replied. "But that's great, Aleister. I think your book is going to do really well." He sighed deeply and leaned back in his chair. "My divorce became final this morning."

"Oh." Angela looked chastened. She was very fond of Chaz's ex-wife Bonnie. Despite Chaz's stupidity, she hated to see their marriage end.

Dwayne reached across the table and squeezed Chaz's wrist. "I'm so sorry."

Three years earlier there would have been six at the table, but Aleister's wife, Lisa, was dead, and now Bonnie had divorced Chaz. She was an attorney at a high-powered family law firm, and her colleagues had crucified Chaz in the divorce. Bonnie's private investigator captured a torrid collection of photos of Chaz and his lover *in flagrante delicto*.

They'd been such a fun circle. Perky, blonde, petite Lisa had been sweet and cheerful and super-smart. Bonnie, with her brilliant red hair and penetrating eyes, was sardonic and comical. Working in divorce, she had a hilariously jaundiced view of the human race.

"I was such an idiot. Why did I risk my marriage? It was so stupid."

"I can't argue with you there," Angela said.

"Bonnie won't accept any communication from me at all, unless it's through a lawyer." He sighed and rubbed his thumb over the back of his opposite hand, as though there were a patch of dirt there. "I thought I was hot shit at the time, having an affair with a woman like Coco. But I'm going to miss Bonnie for the rest of my life."

No one spoke for a while.

"I have no one to blame but myself," Chaz continued. "However, not only is my marriage over, McDonald's has fired me."

"Well, that sucks," Dwayne said. "But you can find another job."

"I've been interviewing, but they always call McDonald's for a reference, and that's the end of it. When Ingrid broke into the meeting with my boss and the Trib reporter, jabbering about how I'd created a toxic workplace, the reporter assumed that was a situation at McDonald's. When a P.R. man makes his company look bad, it pretty much tanks his career."

"So you can't get hired anywhere?" Dwayne asked.

"I called the headhunter that got me the McDonald's job. She'd already talked with my old boss. She just laughed."

"That's horrible," Aleister said.

"And Bonnie took nearly everything I owned."

"At least it makes it easy to move," Angela suggested. All three of the men looked at her disapprovingly. "Too soon?" she asked.

"What are you going to do?" Dwayne said. He never thought he'd see one of his wildly successful friends in worse financial shape than he.

"One of my classmates from Northwestern offered me a job in San Francisco. It pays less than what I was getting at McDonald's, and I don't really want to move, but I'd get a chance to start over."

"If you moved to San Francisco, we would miss you," Dwayne said.

"Yeah," Aleister agreed.

"Sorry to be such a downer when you have great news," Chaz said.

"Never mind. Listen," Aleister said. "I read this interview with Sarah Paretsky. She said one of the reasons her mystery novels have done so well is that she spent the entire advance from her first novel on hiring a public relations person. She said it was the best investment she ever made, so I intend to do the same. You want the job?"

Suddenly the imposing figure of Ingrid loomed over their table, her short straight ice-blonde pageboy flopping across her cheeks as she came to a sudden stop. "Hey, good, you're here," she said to Chaz. "Prompt. On time. I like that."

"Get away from me, you…job-wrecker!" Chaz said.

"Are you still mad about McDonald's?" She cocked her head to one side and smiled.

"Why are you here, Ingrid?" Dwayne said. She really could be annoying.

"I want to offer Chaz some work." She turned back to him. "See? I'm going to make it all good."

"How did you know I'd be here?" Chaz said.

"Oh gosh. Ha! How do I know things? Wow." She leaned on the table. "Listen, I heard McDonald's fired you, and I wondered if you want to do the P.R. for *Romeo and Juliet*. I can get Carl Hofstadter for a grand. He does most of the small and mid-size companies, but frankly, you're a better P.R. man than him."

"How did you hear about McDonald's?" he said, even more amazed.

"You weren't returning my calls, so I phoned for you out there. They told me you were no longer employed."

"Jesus," Chaz said.

"Hey," Angela said. "You could start your own firm. You've got two clients already without trying." She turned to Ingrid. "How much would you pay him?"

"Hofstadter charges a grand, so that's what we'd pay."

"That'd be my retainer?" Chaz said.

"That's the whole shebang," Ingrid said.

Chaz thought it over. "*Romeo and Juliet* is the world's most famous tragedy of love. And *The Soul in Grief* is about living with the tragedy of losing one's love. We could get some synergy between these two products."

"Yeah!" Ingrid said. "You could take our actors to do dramatic dialogues at Aleister's book readings. That'd add juice to his readings and promote our show!"

"I like that," Chaz admitted.

"As long as it doesn't interfere with rehearsals," Dwayne insisted.

"I know people who aren't happy with Hofstadter," Ingrid said. "I'll help you find other theatre clients. I know people at art galleries, too. I can totally make it up to you for screwing the pooch at McDonald's."

"Really?" Chaz looked at her intently. Despite the better weather, he did not want to leave Chicago for San Francisco.

"Sincerely," she said. "You put the Psychedelic Dream Theatre on the map, I'll feed you clients."

"*Winning Boats Rise Together!*" Dwayne cried. He waved his arm at the bartender. "Barry, a round of whiskeys here on me!"

7

Sunday, June 6, 2004

Dwayne walked past the Playhouse down to the Dairy Queen at corner of Webster and Lincoln, feeling jaunty. He was early for the first read-through of *Romeo and Juliet*. He ordered a vanilla soft-serve cone, chocolate dipped. The molten chocolate immediately froze to a hard shell when the cold ice cream was dipped into it. He loved that. His teeth cracked through the thin chocolate shell into the soothing ice cream. He took his cone across the street into Oz Park. A metal sculpture of the Tin Man greeted him at the entry. Further in, an outdoor wedding was in progress, the bride and groom under a trellis of flowers. It was a perfect June day. Even the incessant traffic on Lincoln Avenue sounded cheerful. Perhaps this happy wedding in the park was a good omen for *Romeo and Juliet*. The minister pronounced the couple husband and wife. The guests applauded. The bride and groom turned to one another for their first married kiss, but the bride's train caught on the base of the trellis and it toppled toward the seats, falling so as to hit the bride's mother on the crown of her head. She shrieked in shock and pain, and fell to the ground. The whole party jumped to her aid. Screams and confusion. The trellis snapped at the top as the best man and the father of the bride attempted to set it back upright. Bits of flowers from top of the arch catapulted into the air. The bride and her mother embraced in tears. The groom looked helpless and confused.

Suddenly Dwayne did not feel so confident. Was *this* the omen for *Romeo and Juliet*? He crunched the base of his ice cream cone in his teeth and headed back up Lincoln Avenue toward the theatre, sorely tempted to stop at the Lions Head Pub for a fortifying shot of Jameson. However, that would violate one of the prescriptions of

Madeline Forthright. In her chapter, *Weathering the Hurricanes*, she warned against succumbing to the call of distilled spirits, fermented beverages, and illicit intoxicating drugs. Having fallen into a teenage addiction to Robitussin, she had sympathy for addictive personalities and cautioned winners away from the pitfalls of substance abuse. A little shot of courage, she said, was actually a reinforcement of cowardice.

When he arrived in the third-floor rehearsal room, Joan and the ensemble members were already there. The actors smiled and laughed and talked with one another. Joan stood off to the side, her hand atop a stack of worn paperbacks on a table at the head of the room. A circle of chairs fanned out from the table. "Ready?" she said to Dwayne. He nodded.

"Okay, everyone, let's come to order," Joan said in her spectacularly emotionless voice. The actors turned expectantly toward her. Some of them noticed Dwayne and waved at him. "We'll have a few words from your director and then read through the play. Ingrid, our executive director, picked up these scripts for us. Please take one and find a seat in the circle."

Coco strode up to the table in her yoga pants and skin tight blouse, looking fit and alluring as always. She picked a paperback from the top. She looked at its torn cover and tossed it to the side, followed by another. "Nope. Nah. Nope," she said as she tossed aside another few. She opened one whose pages were not yellowed, dog-eared, or littered with notations. "Marginal," she said, and walked away with it to sit in one of the chairs.

The well-used books were an immediate source of hilarity and outrage as the actors took them and discovered price tags of fifty cents and even, in one case, a dime. In actuality, Ingrid got most of them for no money at all, canvassing members of the Chicago theatre community for copies people were willing to give away.

"Welcome, everyone," Dwayne said as they'd settled into seats. "Very exciting to begin this first new season with all of you as ensemble members." The actors clapped and cheered. "I'm looking forward to building on the artistic relationships we forged in *Titus* and in shows earlier than that for some of us."

"You got that right," Coco said. This would be the fourth show she and Dwayne had worked on together. In each one Coco became yet more magnetic on stage and yet more difficult backstage. The love affair that ended Chaz's marriage was just one manifestation.

"Once again Ry and the band will provide music behind the sword fights and for dancing at the Capulet's party, and Tom will direct the movement." This brought another round of applause from the actors. The music and fight choreography of *Titus Andronicus* had elevated the production to something spectacular, and they'd all loved it. Ry gave a diffident nod while Tom, the exceptionally tall and expressive fight and dance choreographer, got up and took a deep bow.

"I know you are all dying to know your roles." He raised his eyebrows and smiled at them, hoping he looked happy and confident. In truth he felt a little manic and insane. He should have announced the casting in advance, but he and Tom had been debating over it until yesterday. Tom was Dwayne's long-time collaborator and friend. His creative partnership was an essential part of what made *Titus* so extraordinary. "Then we'll read through the script and talk about the production." The actors all hushed into rapt attention. "First off, as well as fight and dance choreographer, Tom will be playing the role of Mercutio."

"You've got to play Mercutio gay," Orlando said. "It's totally supported by the text."

"Oh my God, can you imagine how I'm going to do Queen Mab?" Tom said, referencing the most famous speech in the show not spoken by Romeo or Juliet. He hopped from his seat and performed a lightning pirouette. "Electrifying!" he chanted. The others applauded again.

"Yes!" Dwayne agreed. At least Tom was happy. "In the roles of Romeo and Juliet, Orlando and Melinda." Most of the actors applauded.

Most of them.

"Hey, wait a minute," Coco said. "I thought we'd have Romeo and Juliet played by Orlando and me. After the chemistry between us in *Titus Andronicus* I thought that would be a lock. Melinda walked around like a zombie with her hands chopped off."

"Wait a minute…" Dwayne began.

"That was in the script," Melinda barked. She stood up and stretched her arms in front of her. "My hands were chopped off and my tongue was cut out. *I was playing my role!*" Spit flew out of her mouth as she spoke.

Coco continued to talk straight at Dwayne, right over Melinda, her voice dripping with disgust. "You gonna put a basic white ingénue in the role of Juliet, just like every other absolutely predictable production of *Romeo and Juliet*? Why don't you do something with a little pizzazz and mystique?"

"Don't start that *basic white ingénue* shit with me again!" Melinda shouted.

"Hang on. Hang on!" Dwayne said.

"This casting is racist," Coco complained.

"Okay, stop!" Dwayne insisted. "First, let's have a little respect for one another. Coco, you are out of line. This is an ensemble, and ensemble means we support one another. *Winner Boats Rise Together!* Second, I don't know how you call the casting racist when our Juliet is white and our Romeo is black."

"When Juliet is white in every single production you ever see, that's racist," she said. "Do you ever get to see a black Juliet?"

"Yes, I have seen a black Juliet," Dwayne countered.

"I know I ought to be excited about playing Romeo," Orlando interjected, "but I actually imagined myself playing Tybalt. Since doing *Titus*, I really love playing the troublemaker. Like I told you at the Goodman, I want to play Iago in *Othello*."

"There you go," Coco said. "Let Orlando be Tybalt and make Ry Romeo and Coco Juliet," Coco said. "Black girl, white boy."

Wallace, the elder statesman of the company, cleared his throat loudly. "You do know, Orlando, that Othello is the black role in *Othello*. Not Iago."

Orlando waved him away dismissively.

"If Ry is going to be Romeo, I want to be Juliet," Melinda insisted, ignoring Wallace. She'd had a crush on Ry for some time. Dwayne didn't know if they'd had an affair (or maybe were still having one), but there'd been some serious flirting between the two during

Titus.

"Ry can't be Romeo," Tom declared. "The sword work in this show is going to be killer. He can't wield a sword while playing the guitar."

"Well, I think the show would look way better with Ry and me as Romeo and Juliet," Melinda said. "Maybe we just forget the music this time and have a white Romeo and Juliet."

"All right, hold on..." Dwayne began.

"Now that does sound a little racist," Wallace muttered.

"Tom and I spent a lot of time developing the casting..." Dwayne began.

"And why are we having a gay Romeo?" Melinda complained. "A gay Mercutio works, but a gay Romeo makes no sense."

"Hey!" Orlando said. "I play straight characters all the time. I hardly ever play gay characters. I don't *present* as gay. I'm not like Tom."

"Wait a minute!" Tom complained, looking truly hurt.

"All right, let's..." Dwayne began.

"I didn't mean that as an insult," Orlando said quickly. "I'm talking about how people see us in the world."

"Yeah, okay." Tom relented and stood up. "I'm a proud gay man and everyone knows it and everyone can see it!" He rounded off his comment with a pirouette and got a round of applause.

"Okay, good. Now..." Dwayne said.

Orlando turned suddenly to Dwayne. "So does this mean I'm going to have to kiss Melinda?" He put one hand on his hip and made a grossed-out face.

"Oh my God! See?" Melinda shouted.

"I'm kidding!" Orlando insisted, outrage blossoming on his face. "My God, can't you tell that I'm kidding?"

"So, wait a second," Coco said, suddenly indignant once again. "If you weren't casting me as Juliet, what the hell am I supposed to play?"

"Yes," Dwayne said. He took a deep breath. "Good. Let's continue with the casting. "Coco, you are going to be playing the Nurse." *Nurse* came out of his mouth sounding choked and oddly diminished. He cleared his throat and said it again, more decisively. "The Nurse."

Coco looked shocked and horrified. "Juliet's simpering fucking Nurse? Oh, Jesus Lord! That's an old lady role. You want me to play the Nurse?"

"This is going to be great with your comedic chops," Dwayne said. "You could make a nurse of the kind we've never seen before."

"You want to put *a black woman* in the role of the Nurse?" Coco threw up her arms and rolled her eyes. "*Yes, Massa Capulet. No ma'am, Lady Capulet.* This is totally racist fucking casting!"

"Coco, come on," Dwayne said. "I'm using the members of this ensemble in the most interesting way possible for a specific vision of this show."

"What vision? The vision of Melinda as Juliet?" she demanded. "The vision of me as the Nurse? What justifies this casting?"

Dwayne gave a deep sigh. How to explain his reasoning? "I have seen incredible talent from every member of this ensemble. I have complete faith in the versatility of both you and Melinda as actors. But I also have to consider all our physical instruments: our bodies and our voices, which are the base on which our talents ride. There is an inherent innocence and naïveté in the role of Juliet that is more clearly in the reach of Melinda's instrument and emotional presence than yours. You, Coco, present as more worldly. Innocent Juliet is too afraid to tell her parents that she secretly married Romeo. The audience will more readily believe that coming from Melinda than from you."

Both women looked as though they were not quite sure whether to be complimented or insulted. They both sat back down.

"But for you, Coco, I see a Nurse like none that has been seen before. I think you will be a revelation. And Melinda, I foresee your Juliet will be absolutely heartbreaking. This is a case of *Winners Working Smarter*," he said, invoking one of Madeline Forthright's truisms.

The two women thought it over while the other actors watched them. Dwayne felt his interior tension begin to dissipate.

Then Wallace stood up. "If I might put in a word," he said in his rumbling baritone.

Holy Drogo, Patron Saint of Mutes, inspire the gift of silence in this actor, Dwayne prayed.

"We could avoid all this *sturm und drang* and just move on to a work of considerably greater stature. Might I recommend we do *King Lear* instead? Melinda would make a natural Cordelia and Coco would be an incredible Goneril. Her chemistry with Orlando could be exploited with him in the role of Edmund."

"Yes, but..." Dwayne said.

"I've got an even better idea," Orlando replied. "Thousands of white men have played King Lear, but how many have played Othello?"

"Are you kidding?" Coco said. "Until recently Othellos were all white men in black face."

"Right," Melinda said. "And we can go back to Shakespeare's time when all the women were played by high-voiced young men."

"But wait!" Orlando insisted. "Imagine Othello is the only white man in the show. We know Wallace can play a great general. He did it in *Titus Andronicus.* Now picture him as Othello. Coco, you'd play Desdemona. I'd be Iago. The whole rest of the cast would be black." Orlando looked delighted sharing his brainstorm, but none of the white actors in the room, aside from Wallace, looked at all happy about it. There would be no roles for them.

"Iago?" Tom said to Orlando, mystified. "Sure, Iago is a great role. But my God, don't you want to play Romeo before you age out of it?" And then the whole room broke into wild argument, with each actor calling for *Romeo and Juliet* to be replaced by their favorite play.

It took another half hour for Dwayne to finish the simple task of assigning the actors their roles before they began a read-through of the script. By that time, Dwayne felt like using Romeo's dagger on himself.

8

Friday, June 11, 2004

"This is *money!*" Chaz's eyes gleamed with manic enthusiasm as he led Dwayne and Ingrid into the room. Groups of poker players sat gambling at round tables. Chaz's voice quivered in volume and pitch: "Money that flows like water, streams of money, cascades of money…" He lowered his voice to a conspiratorial whisper. "…and all we have to do is lean in and dip our bucket into the flow." He threw up his hands in a show of triumph. "Now this specific session is set up for a dance troupe, but any federal not-for-profit could do this." Chaz led them into the dance rehearsal space, taking off their shoes first and lining them along the wall by the entrance. "This could make us a pile of money, and there's very little labor involved!"

Dwayne loved that Chaz had taken this initiative. As their P.R. person, finding fundraising opportunities wasn't part of his job. But he began to feel uneasy now that Chaz seemed so extraordinarily exuberant.

Inside the door a man sat at a table with racks of poker chips and two lockboxes at his side. A large iron box with handles sat on the floor next to him. A dour-looking security guard with a gun on his hip stood next to the table, watching the three enter. He nodded at Chaz and then turned back to the action in the room.

The security guard knows Chaz by sight?

Five tables were distributed across the dance rehearsal room. Large area rugs were spread underneath the tables and chairs to protect the sprung wood floor. Sheets hung with gaffer's tape covered the wall mirrors to prevent the players from seeing one another's cards. Five or six men sat at each table, playing poker. They looked extremely serious.

"The house takes a cut off the top of every hand and that goes to the charity, minus a cut for the organizer," Chaz whispered to them, as excited as a nerd who's seen *Star Wars* for the first time. "These guys are playing high stakes poker, so it adds up. I mean, if we do this, we could rake it in!" He rubbed his hands together gleefully. He pointed at the makeshift bar at the end of the room where two of the players went to refresh their drinks while the next hand was being dealt. "Our job would be to provide the space and run the bar. We don't need a license to sell alcohol. We provide the drinks free, but these guys never put less than a ten or twenty in the tip jar per drink, so that covers our liquor expenses. The game is legal because it's being done as a fundraiser for a federal nonprofit. Otherwise, they couldn't find a legal high stakes poker game anywhere near here. So they're generous."

"If the organizers are already doing it with this dance company, why would they need us?" Ingrid said.

"The dance company is a little crazy about their sprung floor. The guys don't like having to walk around in their socks. The wood floor is slippery. One of the guys slipped and hurt his elbow last week. Also, the artistic director acts like this is a traditional fundraiser. She makes a long speech about the company mission, blah, blah, blah. These guys don't want their time wasted, so they're looking for another charity with a 501(C)(3) who will let them play and wear their shoes, not interrupt, and take the money and shut up."

"We could do that," Ingrid said.

Chaz clapped his hands and laughed quasi-manically, frightening Dwayne a little. "I knew it! Ha, ha! You just need to register, show your 501(C)(3), provide the space, and run the bar. The organizer does the rest."

"Our new rehearsal space is not as large as this," Dwayne said. "But it could hold the five tables and the bar area."

"That's all that matters!" Chaz exclaimed, still looking wildly overexcited. "Would the building owner object to poker?"

"He rents to a hippy church that drinks South American LSD," Ingrid said. "This can't be worse than that."

"Perfect," Chaz said. He rubbed his hands together again and looked longingly toward one of the poker tables.

"Hey, Chaz," one of the men at the table called. "You in?"

You in? Everyone here seemed to know Chaz.

"Absolutely!" He turned back to Ingrid and Dwayne. "I just wanted you to see this. If we're agreed, I'll start things rolling. We should be able to host two or three of these over the summer and take in two grand or more a pop." He led them back to the entrance, peeled out five one-hundred-dollar bills from a roll in his pocket, laid them on the table, and picked up a tray of chips. "See you later." He took his chips and headed eagerly back to the bar on his way to one of the tables.

"Jesus," Ingrid breathed. "Did you see that wad?"

"I thought he was hurting for money," Dwayne said. "I don't know how he can afford to gamble like that."

"Chaz never strikes me as someone making good choices," she said. "But for us, this seems too good to pass up."

Ingrid gave Dwayne a ride home in her Viking ship of a van. As they drove north up the magnificence of Lake Shore Drive, the last light of the summer day shimmered on the endless expanse of Lake Michigan off to their right. Traffic whizzed past them at a consistent ten miles per hour or more above the speed limit. Ingrid did not speed. For one thing, she didn't trust the steering linkage in her ancient van. And she absolutely could not afford a speeding ticket.

Her metallic belongings rattled a mad tarantella behind them, oppressing Dwayne's eardrums. She'd outfitted the back of the van with a fold-up cot, a fold-down table, water tank and tiny sink, and lots of storage, inside of which silverware and tools and camp stove and cookware and all the other things she owned rattled with each pothole they hit. Pretty much every bit of the van conversion had been built with salvaged materials from theatrical sets and stage hardware. She'd insulated the walls with Styrofoam salvaged from cheap coolers and packaging. After all, she lived in the van both summer and winter. She had to stay warm.

Stopping in front of Dwayne's Rogers Park apartment, she looked at the odometer. "Okay, that'd come to two dollars and thirty-five cents in gas. You don't mind, do you?" she said.

Dwayne laughed and pulled out three dollars. "Keep the change," he said.

He couldn't stop thinking about Chaz and his manic eagerness to get to the poker table.

"Do you think we should do these poker game fundraisers?" he asked Angela later in the living room of their Rogers Park apartment. He sat down, immediately yelped in pain, and leapt up out of the chair, rubbing his ass.

"What happened to you?"

He leaned over the chair and fingered the edge of a sharp spring that had poked up through the upholstery. "Damn thing bit me."

"We could get rid of half the furniture in this room, and it'd look twice as good." She'd been reading in her favorite easy chair in the large, horseshoe-shaped room. A full array of well-worn furniture lined the walls of the room, most of it rescued from parkways and alleys. Dwayne loved hosting events and having plenty of space for people to sit and talk, even if the furniture was not in the best of repair.

"I can fix that cushion," he said, flipping it so the rogue spring faced down. "But listen, I'm worried about Chaz. He's lost Bonnie, his house, his job. What if he's getting addicted to gambling? I feel a little responsible."

"He brought those losses on himself."

"Sure, but he wouldn't have met Coco except for me. And if we start hosting these poker games, it gives him another excuse to attend when he ought to be breaking away."

"You guys used to have poker nights."

"Sure. But that was fifty cents limit among friends. You wouldn't lose more than forty bucks even on a bad night."

"If he has a gambling problem, deciding not to host these fundraisers will not break him out of it. You should talk it over with him and Aleister."

"Yeah. That makes sense."

"But you know," she said, raising one shapely eyebrow. "I wasn't waiting for you to get home so we could talk about Chaz."

"Oh!" He stood up suddenly. "Okay."

She wanted sex. She wanted a baby. And they'd just been talking business. And business was about his future. He needed to make a transition. He didn't want to be humiliated by his equipment again.

"Just give me a minute." He headed into their shared office, trying to ignore the perplexed look on her face as he left the room. He needed to banish all thoughts of his future and money and career, but he'd been spending all of his time at that. He'd even set up an interview to see if he could get work directing commercials, but thoughts of his career filled him with anxiety. His pecker instantly wilted.

It was like he'd learned from Madeline Forthright's *Keep Your Eyes on the Prize*. The sixth basic truism was: *Winners Are Grinners*. You had to stop and smell the roses. And that included enjoying sex with his wife.

He sat down in the office called up the image of him and Angela lolling naked in the bathtub together, across from one another, and their baby suckling at her breast, all of them naked and wet and warm in the bath water, some candles burning, putting them all in a romantic light. It was beautiful and arousing. And it had all come from the transcendent and delicious act of sliding himself into her. So yummy. It made him long to make love to his wife.

He was ready.

"What are you doing?" she said sharply. He opened his eyes to see her standing at the door, looking cross.

"I was...I was doing a meditation."

"Didn't you know I wanted to make love?" She put a hand on her hip. Her eyebrows pressed down over the intensity of her eyes.

Well, there went that mood.

"That's why I was doing the meditation. I was all ready to join you."

"Why would you need to do a meditation before we make love?" Her voice rose in pitch with every word.

"We were just talking about business. I needed to banish it from my mind."

"We were talking about Chaz." She moved closer. Dwayne could feel the force radiating from her body, and he sat up straighter.

"We were talking about things connected with my theatre

company and that connects with my future as a theatre artist, and I need to not be thinking about that when we make love."

She leaned back against the wall and let out a deep sigh. "I thought you were on board with this now."

"I was. I am. I'm really trying. A second ago I was all ready."

"This makes me really sad," she said. "I don't get why this has to be so difficult. I've been totally supportive of you. We've been living on my salary. Why can't you be supportive of me?"

"I am. I would have been in the bedroom with you, and we would have been making love right now. I just needed a moment to adjust. You know. Of all the people who work in theatre, it's only a tiny fraction that make a living at it. The rest give up at some point. I don't want to be one of those. So it gets in my head. And then it's Wilt City. So I was proactive. I figured out a meditation that would allow me to transition and then we'd be happily making love, and maybe we'd be bouncing a baby in nine months. I *am* being supportive. I even got an interview set up to see if I can direct commercials, like you suggested. But I'm not a robot. I have to deal with my feelings."

"Well," she said reluctantly, "okay. I guess that's fair." She stood back up, away from the wall. "What's this meditation?"

Dwayne smiled. He got up, went to her, and put his arms around her waist. "So you and I are in our great big bathtub, and we've got candles burning. I'm sitting in the warm water at one end and you are at the other, facing each other, and you've got this pretty baby in your arms suckling at your breast. And we are all warm and wet and happy in the tub."

"Aw. That is nice." She put her arms around his neck. Her eyes drifted to the ceiling for a moment. "Yeah. I can see that," she said softly. "I have to admit, Dwayne. That kind of gives me a lady boner. Where did you come up with that?"

"I was talking with Aleister about my problem."

"Wait." She pulled abruptly away from him. "You were talking about our sex life with Aleister?"

"Well, not exactly our *sex life*, but about the problem I had in Italy when we tried to make a baby."

"So: our *sex life*," she insisted.

"Well, I guess when you put it like that…"

"Aleister is not just *your* friend. He's *our friend*. I don't want him having thoughts about our sex life."

"I didn't say anything about you. It was just about me. I was just talking about me."

"If you are talking about not being able to keep it up when you are trying to make love with me, then you are talking about me. Why did you have to bring it up with Aleister?"

"Why wouldn't I bring it up with Aleister? Aleister is a psychiatrist."

"He's not *your* psychiatrist. He's *our friend*."

"You just said ten minutes ago I should talk with Aleister about Chaz's gambling problem."

"That's Chaz's problem. I don't care about his privacy. He's made a spectacle of himself. This is our personal sex life. And I don't want our friends discussing the details."

"Well…" He took a deep breath, stepped forward, and put his hands on her shoulders. "I'm just trying to give you what you want."

"Ugh. You are the worst."

She pushed him away, went into the bedroom, and slammed the door behind her.

9

Monday, June 14, 2004

"This is one of our on-site studios." Eric looked up to make sure the *Recording* light was off, and led Dwayne into the room. It was the last stop on their tour of the Image Imagination offices. This place was so cool! If he got hired to direct commercials, it would certainly be more money than he made as an office temp, and it'd be fascinating. When Angela first suggested it, he had deep doubts, but now he loved the idea. He'd have a decent salary, and he'd be able to continue directing theatre at night.

In the center of the room was a table with a computer on it, a second box that featured a small display screen, and some kind of hand-held scanner. A man and a woman were setting up lights and checking the image on the camera monitor. The whole back wall was green screen. "This is the Data-Surge product?" Eric said to the woman.

"Right," she replied. "We're doing the promotional video this morning. We'll shoot the instructional video this afternoon."

"Ambitious," Eric remarked approvingly. "Come on," he said to Dwayne. He led him back to his office. As he walked behind him, Dwayne noticed the perfect spiral of bright orange hair in Eric's cowlick. Why did they call it red hair when it was so clearly orange? Dwayne took a deep breath and felt his heart flutter. He wasn't used to performing at 7:30 in the morning, and he'd drunk twice his usual coffee before coming. Eric suggested they start their interview with a tour of the facility (which Dwayne loved). Now he'd have to sell himself.

They sat at a small conference table in Eric's office. Dwayne even loved his office. Scripts piled up on a credenza along the wall. Huge poster-size post-its covered in big writing hung on the walls. This was a place where creative work got done. Eric's desk at the far end faced into the room. Behind it, a large window gave a view of the Chicago River flowing toward the Loop. Off to the left, the morning sun was still low in the sky. On the side wall of the office a large whiteboard was decorated with project names, deadline dates, and team leader names in dry-erase marker. Would Dwayne's name ever adorn that board? 'Twas a consummation devoutly to be wished!

"So, you've seen our operation here," Eric said. "We do small scale shoots on site. We rent off-site studio space for larger shoots. And then some of our shoots are at client locations: equipment in action, facilities tours, that sort of thing." Eric smiled a big warm smile on his fully-freckled moon-shaped face. This was the face he offers clients to make them trust his firm's services, Dwayne thought. Eric was the main client contact.

"Interesting," Dwayne said.

"Tell me about your background. What would you bring to Image Imagination?" Eric leaned back in his chair across the conference table from Dwayne. Dwayne leaned back in a similar way. In the chapter, *Winners are Grinners*, Madeline Forthright wrote that it was best to echo the body language of the people you wanted to influence. It made them feel you were like them and could be trusted.

"Probably my greatest skill is working with actors," Dwayne said. "I bring out performances that sometimes surprise even them."

Eric frowned. "That's not actually a big issue here. The on-camera talent we hire doesn't need much coaching. We do mostly B2B work and a bit for the educational market. Clarity. Enthusiasm. Energy. That's what we need from the talent, and they bring that. Have you done documentaries or have all your films been narrative fiction?"

"Actually, most of my work has been live theatre. Classics and contemporary."

"Live theatre?" Eric said the words in much the way he might have said *Juggling watermelons?* "That's something of a...pivot. Where did you go to film school?"

"I didn't go to a film school," Dwayne admitted, his confidence beginning to flag. "I went to Northwestern University."

"Northwestern," Eric said, sounding impressed. "Did you take coursework at the Kellogg Center? Marketing or business?"

"Ah, no. My major was Theatre."

"But surely you studied directing for film."

"Ah...no. Acting. Directing. Dramaturgy. All theatre-focused."

"Just Theatre?" Eric sounded stumped. "No marketing, no business, no film work?"

"Um. No. Not *per se*." Dwayne felt something in his stomach twist, and he sat up straighter. Out the window, he saw his opportunity at Image Imagination begin to founder in the river as it drifted, writhing helplessly toward the Loop.

Eric got up and slid his chair back into the conference table decisively. "Look, Dwayne, I'm not sure who scheduled you for this interview, but I don't see how any of your experience would be relevant to directing for Image Imagination." He sounded profoundly annoyed.

Holy Genesius, patron saint of conversions, help me!

"It's not just directing that I've done," Dwayne said urgently. "It's producing." He stood up and gestured to the whiteboard on the wall. "I understand what it is to muster the efforts of an army of various skills. In my most recent production, I located and rented the performance space. I hired and provided guidance to all the designers and technical people. I hired and led the marketing and P.R. team. I also arranged ticket sales with the box office team. And, of course, I cast the actors, and I directed the play. That's a wide array of skills, and, most importantly, it meant getting the job done. In some of those areas I had no training and little past experience, but I learned on the job. It meant *Getting It in Gear* and *Working Smarter*," he said, throwing in a couple truisms. Eric still looked annoyed, but at least Dwayne had his attention. "It meant *Winner Boats Rise Together*," he continued. "It meant *Visit the Woodshed, No Fears/Big Ears*. It meant *Winners Are Grinners*."

Why the hell couldn't he stop?

Now Eric looked confused. "Whatever," he sighed. He was not grinning. He got up to usher Dwayne out of his office. "I can't use someone who doesn't understand the basics of camera work and lighting…"

"Wait," Dwayne said. "I know all about lighting and angles. In my last show, I was working on a thrust stage. I had audience on three sides of the action. I had to work the blocking so that every audience member was getting an attractive and coherent stage picture from every possible angle. And that meant working with the lighting designer and working on the placement of every actor and all their movement."

"Yeah. Not the same thing." Eric looked at his watch. "Thanks for coming in."

"Would you like to see our next show?" Dwayne asked. "I could provide you tickets, and we could talk more then?"

"My wife likes live theatre. It bores the hell out of me." Eric walked around to the door and held it open for Dwayne. "I like movies."

"Well, if not directing, do you need anyone for general office work?"

"No thanks."

"I mean, there are so many things I can do."

"Nope, we're good," Eric said in a loud and intensely displeased voice.

"An internship?" Dwayne said meekly.

"Thanks. No," he said even louder.

"Okay. Thanks for your time." Dwayne slinked out the door past Eric, feeling the annoyance radiating off him as he passed.

An internship, Dwayne? You asked for an internship? There's no winning or grinning in an internship.

10

Wednesday, June 16, 2004

Ry, his guitar hanging off the front of him like a like a rock-and-roll phallus, stepped on a pedal at his feet. A funereal organ began to play. This would be the first moments of *Romeo and Juliet.* Dwayne's chest fluttered with emotion. Exciting! Next to him, his funky-dressed costume designer, Peaches, took a sharp intake of breath and turned to smile with excitement. Ry stepped forward and put his lips to the microphone and solemnly stated: "Dear loves and lovers, we gather here to tell a story of untimely death. In fair Verona, where we lay our scene, from ancient grudge break to new mutiny, where civil blood makes civil hands unclean. Two star-cross'd lovers take their life and with their death bury their parents' strife." Then he pulled his guitar neck up, the drummer and bass player hooked into a high-energy, funky beat over the top of the organ notes, and Ry stroked out the tune. Dwayne recognized it as soon as the song proper began. It sounded like *Let's Go Crazy* by Prince, slightly altered and with a new set of lyrics. Dwayne had a copy of the words in his hand. Peaches leaned over to read along with him as Ry sang.

> *Capulets and Montagues*
> *They want to fight.*
> *Romeo's in love, but he can't find a wife.*
> *Rosalind hates him.*
> *Like Tybalt hates all.*
> *Benvolio smiles. He's pushed to the wall.*
> *Why can't these people just release their bile?*
> *I don't know, let's go!*

Verona is my city.
And I want the peace.
My ancient kingdom.
Can't get no release.
Put down your swords.
Come sit with me.
Why can't these people just release their bile?
I don't know, let's go!

And Ry broke into a Prince-like solo. After he played a few bars, Tom stood up and raised his hands, calling: "Okay, okay!"

The band wound down.

"That was so cool!" Peaches breathed.

Dwayne nodded agreement and hopped to his feet, truly inspired. "That sounded really fantastic, guys!" He shouted to the band.

What a way to open *Romeo and Juliet*! The music from Ry and the guys had really enhanced *Titus Andronicus*, but this was a whole new level. Now it told part of the story. He loved it.

This redeemed his embarrassment of the early morning. Why would he want to work at a place like Image Imagination making industrial videos for the B2B market (whatever the hell that was)? Yes, he'd loved their facilities, so well-designed for creative work. But he liked Ry's place even more. It was a small storefront on a mostly residential street in the North Center neighborhood. This ground floor had once been a neighborhood tavern. The old bar was still in place, running up one side of the room. Its top was covered in ash trays, empty beer cans, record albums, CDs, and tapes. Ry used the space for rehearsing and recording with his band and other musicians. A beat up set of drums sat permanently at the back of the low stage on which Ry and his bandmates stood, along with some old amplifiers, microphones and recording equipment. The walls hadn't been painted in decades. Instead, local band posters had been tacked up everywhere. All traces of varnish had worn off the wood floor, and some of the tin ceiling tiles hung down at odd angles. The display windows in front had been left unwashed for so long, they provided a modicum of privacy even while allowing some light to seep through. But this was a place where

Ry could ply his art day or night. He lived in the apartment above the former bar. A couple mattresses lay propped against the wall near the front windows in case anyone needed to crash, which was something that happened with regularity, given the uneven nature of Ry's musician friends' incomes.

Dwayne loved it. He loved spaces that were improvised on a shoestring for making art. He liked them better than spaces specifically designed with gobs of money. This was where he felt at home. Like his living room with all its second-hand furniture where he could host big groups of friends and colleagues and never worry about spilled wine or someone jumping up onto the cushions in excitement. This space of Ry's was just like that. It was where you *Visited the Woodshed*, like Madeline Forthright said. Where you practiced and perfected your art and collaborated with your fellow artists. He had a new appreciation for Ry. Ry was *Keeping His Eyes on the Prize*.

The space and the music so inspired Peaches, she was already making costume doodles in her big sketch book.

Tom turned to him. "Ry and I were thinking this song could replace the entirety of Act One, Scene One," he said. He raised his eyebrows, smiled hopefully, and hopped up on the low stage with Ry. "Let me tell you how it works." Ry and his bass player leaned against the back wall. Coco sat on a bar stool over at the bar eating from a Styrofoam cup of ramen. Dwayne wasn't sure why she was there, but he was happy to be surrounded by his creatives.

"Picture this." Tom spread his hands in front of him. Dwayne loved seeing his old friend so excited. "The lights come down. A long moment of silence, then that solemn-sounding organ comes up from a low volume, Ry speaks his voice-over, and they break into the song. *Capulets and Montagues. They want to fight.* The cast begins to move onto the stage. It's a dance. First, we have the combatants. *Romeo's in love, but he can't find a wife. Rosalind hates him.* We get lovesick Romeo and Benvolio entering. A little dumb show of Romeo pining for Rosalind. *Like Tybalt hates all. Benvolio smiles. He's pushed to the wall.* Tybalt enters, aching for a fight. Benvolio tries to mollify him, but Tybalt pushes him away. And into the chorus: *Why can't these people just release their bile? I don't know, let's go!* And then the whole next verse everyone is dancing, with stylized fight, stylized lovesickness. And the next chorus is followed by that solo, and then we break into the serious sword play with the guitar solo in the background. Then the final verses, Ry is singing in the persona of the Prince. He bans fighting between the families on pain of death. We've adapted the Prince's lines to fit the rhythm of the song. And that ends the scene. Taa daa!" He raised his arms and spun around.

"I love it," Dwayne said. "I wonder if there are any other sections of the show we can replace."

"Oh, I think so!" Tom said enthusiastically. "We wanted to run it by you to make sure you liked the idea before we did any more. In *Titus* we used music to punch up the fights. This time we could tell parts of the story."

"I love it," Dwayne repeated. "I have to ask though: Are we going to be able to use this music? That sounded a lot like *Let's Go Crazy*."

"When we did *Titus*, y'all wanted a Jimi Hendrix sound," Ry drawled. "Tom and I looked at this first scene, and the big action is taken by the Prince. We thought: what if *the Prince* was Prince? Or what if I played Prince music and played the role of *the Prince*. *Titus* was all violence and revenge, and Hendrix's slashing guitar was right on. *Romeo and Juliet* is all love and sex and desperation, and to me that's the music of Prince. Funky, sexy, desperate, nearly insane sometimes." He played a few bars of *When Doves Cry* to illustrate.

"Yeah, I like it," Dwayne said. "But what about rights? Would we have to pay royalties?"

Tom put a hand on one hip and cocked his head to one side. "Is Paisley Park really going to pay attention to little old us? Minneapolis is a long way from Chicago."

"I don't know," Dwayne said. "You hear about Disney lawyers descending on all sorts of little productions. The worldwide Olympic committee made Chicago's Improv Olympic change their name. Maybe Prince's people are like that, too."

"I doubt it," Ry said. "I've played covers of hundreds of songs in bars, and we never paid royalties for any of that. If we recorded a CD to sell, then we'd have to, but we've never paid royalties for a live performance. Isn't this the same thing?"

"I don't know," Dwayne said. "If we do a script that's not public domain, we have to pay royalties."

"I changed up the notes," Ry said. "Kept the feel, but made it a new song. Like a tribute to Prince but not Prince exactly."

"I think it's perfect!" Tom said.

"What do you think, Peaches?" Dwayne asked.

Peaches looked up as though startled that anyone remembered she was there. Peaches was deeply introverted, but she dressed like post-punk bird of paradise. She teased up her hair and dyed it in a variety of pastel colors. Her clothes were creative redesigns of fashions she found at resale shops.

"I think it's great," she said, looking around the room shyly. "Do you think it would it be too much to dress the nobles like Prince's Revolution band?" She held up one of her quick drawings, and Dwayne moved in to look closer.

"I really like that," Dwayne said. Tom moved in to see and was nodding his head enthusiastically, and Ry tilted his head diffidently. From Ry, that translated as high enthusiasm.

"I'll work up more sketches, and we can go over them, you and me," Peaches said to Dwayne.

"Great!"

"Hey, if Ry is playing the Prince now, all of a sudden," Coco called from the bar, "how about putting me in as Juliet?"

St. Jude of Lost Causes.

"How about it?" she said.

"Hang on," Dwayne said. He turned back to Tom. "Is that what you want? Ry would play the Prince? Not just provide the music?" Tom and he had cast all the ensemble members, but some roles remained to be filled by outsiders. The Prince had been one of those.

"I love it," Tom said. "The Prince observes everything and calls in judgment. That totally works with Ry on the bandstand. We might create a song for each of the Prince's scenes. But even if not, the Prince can always pronounce from on high."

"Yeah," Dwayne agreed. "I do like that." He was *Getting It in Gear* and *Working Smarter*, he thought, because *Winner Boats Rise Together*.

"Okay, great," Coco said. "Now what about me as Juliet?"

"I don't see how the casting of the Prince affects the casting of Juliet," Dwayne said. "Are you here working on the music with Ry and Tom?"

Coco slid off her bar stool and moved toward Dwayne, reminding him of a jungle cat. In a way it was a shame to use Coco as the Nurse. It was a waste of her incredible animal magnetism. Melinda was a very pretty young woman who would make an excellent Juliet, but Coco was stunning. She was the kind of woman that made men stop when she walked down the street. Her eyes were dazzling and alive. Her lips begged to be kissed. Her dark skin glowed with an inner luminosity. With a body like hers, few men would wonder why Chaz risked his marriage to make love with her.

He suddenly noticed Peaches staring with her mouth open. To say Peaches had a crush on Coco would not do justice. This was a look of open lust. Peaches noticed Dwayne noticing her. Her face turned bright red. She quickly closed her sketchbook, tucked it under her arm, and dashed toward the door. "I've got a...got a...*thing*," she muttered apologetically, exiting to the street.

"That girl's so weird," Coco observed. Two shows ago Coco had brought Peaches to tears with demands over her costuming. She'd put that down to Peaches' weirdness rather than her own high-handed domineering. She took a deep breath and turned to Dwayne. "I stopped over to convince Ry he should play Romeo with me as Juliet, but he and Tom were already sold on him playing the Prince. No matter. You could find some other white boy to play Romeo if you want that interracial thing. Shit. This' Chicago. The streets are crawling with Romeo-ready actors."

"I'm sure that's true," Dwayne said. "But we're operating as an ensemble. And that means some shows you have a lead role, like you did in *Titus*, and other shows you have a supporting role, like the Nurse."

She strode up to the table where he was seated and looked down severely at him. "You seriously think *Melinda* can perform a better Juliet than me?"

He felt the impulse to simply say *Yes*, but he didn't want to insult

Coco. Whether or not they continued to do Psychedelic Dream shows, he wanted to continue working with her. He'd love to direct her as Beatrice in *Much Ado*, Cleopatra in *Antony and Cleopatra*. So many roles in which she would be so good. "You are an amazing actor, and I know it, and you know I know it. But for this ensemble, for this production of *Romeo and Juliet* in this moment in time, Melinda is my choice."

Coco scoffed. "That's your final answer?"

Ry began playing the repeating four note suspense music from *Who Wants to be a Millionaire?*

Dwayne gave him a look with his head cocked sideways. Ry stopped. He turned back to Coco. "That is absolutely my final answer. You don't need to be her buddy, but you do need to stop insulting Melinda."

Coco gave an exasperated sigh. "Huh!" She grabbed her purse and walked to the front door. "Psychedelic Dream Theatre is not the only game in town. Maybe somebody else gonna to make me a better offer." And she walked out.

"That's just *drama*," Tom said, waving a hand after her. "She's not going anywhere."

Dwayne sighed deeply. For every good thing that happened, did there have to be two bad?

11

Saturday, June 19, 2004

"No funds, no shows," Ingrid insisted. "This is on all of *you*." She clapped her hands once in front of the actors in Dwayne's living room. They looked at one another with doubt and resentment. "You don't help raise funds, then we don't *have* funds—and you don't get a crack at your favorite roles. You don't get to suggest titles to your artistic director. You're just one more actor wandering the lonely streets of Chicago like a million other wannabees. You're out auditioning wherever for whoever, and you've got no more advantage than any other actor in the city. You got that?" She flipped her short ice-blonde hair back, standing with her legs firmly spread, hands on hips, like General Patton addressing his troops.

"Jesus..." Coco breathed, rolling her eyes.

Most of the company members were seated in the horseshoe of worn furniture around the periphery of Dwayne's living room. Outside the windows, across the street, a Red Line CTA train rumbled by on the elevated tracks. Ingrid waited for the racket to pass before clapping her hands once and speaking again. "We don't have investors this time. They lost their money on *Titus*, and now we're nonprofit. So it's all up to us."

"If it's a company show," Melinda said, tossing her dark hair back aggressively, "the company should pay for it." Melinda could be a willful fireball or an insecure mess, in turn.

"Excellent point!" Ingrid shouted. "And who is the company?" She looked around intently. "Anyone know? Who is the company?" She looked at them all impatiently for a moment longer, and then shouted: "Everyone in this room!"

The actors looked around at one another as if not sure they believed her.

"Dwayne and I donated our *Titus* stipends to the company. We are the only ones who didn't take their pay. And I found ways to resell some of our properties to put a little money in the bank. But we've got a long way to go before there's enough for a show."

To say he *donated* his stipend from *Titus* was a stretch, Dwayne thought. But close enough. He certainly didn't *collect* it.

"If you're asking us to donate money..." Ry drawled.

Ingrid cut him off. "I'm not. I am saying we all have to work fundraisers and seek out donations. The good news is we are now a federal not-for-profit, so when people donate, they can get a tax write-off. And we can apply for grants."

"Why don't you just do that?" Wallace pushed back his leonine salt-and-pepper hair. "Surely one person writing a grant is a better use of time than *everyone* working on a fundraiser." The other actors nodded and looked approvingly at their elder statesman. In his mid-fifties, Wallace had a couple decades on almost everybody else in the company.

"Until we have a track record of several excellent shows, the funders will ignore us," Ingrid said. "And once we get grants, we'll still need to do all the things: Fundraise, write grants, sell tickets. All the companies have to do *all* the things. Goodman and Steppenwolf have to do *all* the things. That's reality."

Wallace grunted as though not quite convinced.

"Look at the bright side. With no investors making our decisions, we decide our own fate!" Ingrid looked around the room and got a few half-hearted nods.

"So that means as an ensemble, we make the decisions for the company," Melinda asserted.

"Each within their area of expertise," Ingrid agreed conditionally. "It's already happening. Dwayne picked this play from the list you gave him." That received more positive nods. "And Melinda, think what it would be like trying to get the role of Juliet somewhere else. There are dozens of young women in this town who'd be great in that role."

"Yeah," Coco said darkly. Melinda looked at her resentfully.

Chaz got up from a chair at the dining room table where he'd been sitting off to the side of the group. "I got a pledge of support, and I wasn't even looking," he said.

"Really?" Ingrid looked inordinately pleased. "Tell us."

"Wait a second," Melinda said. "Why is he even here? Are we looking for another toxic work environment?"

Half the group looked furtively back at Coco.

It wasn't Chaz and Coco's *affair* that bothered the cast, it was that he featured her photos in promoting *Titus Andronicus* to the exclusion of everyone else. That created a lot of jealousy. Chaz was one of his oldest friends, but Dwayne wasn't going to defend this one. It was Ingrid who'd invited him back to do P.R. on this show. She put her hands on her hips and faced the ensemble fearlessly.

"Look," she said. "Chaz paid his debt on that. He lost both his job and his marriage. But he's an excellent P.R. person, and he knows our company intimately."

"A bit too intimately perhaps," Wallace rumbled. He glanced again at Coco.

"All right, all y'all can just shut the fuck up a minute." Coco had been lounging back on one of the easy chairs, but now she leaned forward into the circle with a terrifying intensity. Ingrid immediately sat down. "Y'all keep talking about this *toxic environment* and *sexual harassment* that Chaz created, but that's just plain bullshit, and all y'all know it. You think I don't have complete independent decision-power over who and when I fuck? I don't apologize to nobody about my sex life, and I'm not going to start now. You think I would fuck somebody just so they'd put my face on a poster? Look at this face." She took a finger and made a manic circle around her visage. "I don't need to fuck anybody to get them to use this face." She looked from one to the next of them and they each looked somewhat embarrassed. "So I don't want to hear no more about a toxic workplace or sexual harassment or any more bullshit about this thing I had with Chaz. I had it when I wanted it, and I stopped it when I didn't. He was already shooting my photos before I decided to take a ride on old Chaz boy. And it was a nice ride for a while. And then it was over. So let's just shut the fuck up about this and move on."

Three times Melinda looked like she was about to object, but she finally pushed back into the couch and stayed silent.

"Okay," Ingrid said at last, uncharacteristically uncertain. "I guess that…

"Hang on," Chaz interrupted. "Yeah, look, I know I was kind of an arrogant asshole, and I made some decisions that looked really bad, and I can totally see how bad they looked." He corrected himself: "How bad they *were*. I'm sorry. I fucked up. Nothing like that will happen again because of me."

"Why should we believe you?" Melinda said.

"I can't say I'll never make any more mistakes," Chaz said, "but I won't make the same ones twice. I promise. And you'll never find another P.R. guy with my abilities for the money Ingrid is paying."

"That last part *sounds* arrogant, but it's true," Ingrid asserted.

"And I want to say, for everything that I did that was offensive, I am sorry." Chaz looked around hopefully, and then sat back down at the dining room table.

There was a long silence. Dwayne waited for the reaction.

"If we've got a choice between a man who has learned from his mistakes and a man who hasn't made his mistakes yet," Wallace said, "I'll take the man who has learned. I'm for letting Chaz back in."

"I agree with that," Joan said, surprising Dwayne. She'd always given Chaz the most dubious of looks. Most of the others nodded along, though some still looked doubtful.

"You said you got some pledge of support?" Ingrid prompted Chaz.

"Unbelievable!" Chaz said. "I was at one of those poker games we set up, and I'd run through my cash. I told the floor manager my luck was turning, and he introduced me to one of the players who makes an occasional loan. This guy asks me what I do for a living. I tell him I'm a P.R. guy and I'm working on this show with Psychedelic Dream Theatre. His ears perk up, and he says, *Wait a minute, is Coco Nesbit in that show?*" Chaz smiled broadly and looked over at Coco. "I say, *Yeah*. Turns out, Coco, he's your Uncle Bull. He not only advances me a personal loan to put me back in the game, he pledges all kinds of support for our silent auction."

"Oh, fuck no!" Coco slammed her hand down on the coffee table. "He said he was *Uncle Bull*?"

"Uh, yeah." Chaz took a step back. "Why? Is that a bad thing?"

"Did you win? Did you pay him back immediately?"

"Well, no…I lost that money, too." Chaz said quietly.

"God damn it! And he called himself *Uncle Bull*?"

"Yes. He was really excited to help out the show. He said he had a guy who could give us a night at a downtown hotel. And a guy who could give us a weekend at his time share in the Bahamas. And a guy who could give plane tickets. That's great stuff for an auction or a raffle."

"He's got a guy, all right," Coco muttered darkly. She shook her head. "And he called himself *Uncle Bull*?"

"Yeah. Uncle Bull. Isn't he actually related to you?"

"Oh, he's related to me all right. What's the vig? You need to pay this off *immediately*."

"Well, I can't *immediately*," Chaz said. "I mean, I've got to…"

"I've got news for you." Coco got up and talked intently right into his face. "Next time he's talking about *he's got a guy for this, he's got a guy for that*, *you* are one of those guys. As in: *I got a guy who can do free P.R. for you.* What's the vig?"

"What's the what?"

"You don't even know what's the vig?" Coco shook her head in disbelief.

"What's a vig?" Melinda said.

"It's like the interest," Wallace said. "The vigorish. The amount in addition to the loan that has to be paid back. If Chaz is dealing with a loan shark, it can get pretty steep."

"I'm in trouble?" Chaz said. "I figured since he was your uncle, and he was so eager to help the production, he was a good guy."

"He's not my uncle! Shit!"

"If he's not your uncle, who is he?" Chaz said.

"Never mind. I'll try to talk to him." She got up and headed for the door. "You have to pay back this loan and the vig as fast as you can. Until that happens, he owns you. And sometimes afterwards, too."

And she was gone.

12

Saturday, July 10, 2004

"So his whore's uncle is a loan shark, and now he's going to be breaking Chaz's legs? Ha! I love it!" Bonnie leaned back and laughed heartily, her red curls shaking in vengeful merriment.

Dwayne looked out the window at the tourist boats sailing by on the Chicago River, his stomach turning over. Angela had prompted him to tell Chaz's story at dinner, but now he was regretting it. Bonnie's venom against her ex-husband was hard to take, even if Chaz did deserve it.

Bonnie had invited them out to dinner on her dime, treating at the Smith and Wollensky steak house downtown on the riverfront. Bonnie (and Chaz) had eaten many times at Dwayne and Angela's place, but Bonnie didn't like to cook. She wanted to return the favor, but the menu made Dwayne uncomfortable. The price of a steak was hugely out of his range. Bonnie encouraged them to order whatever they wanted, recommending the most expensive steak on the menu.

"You're just spending money my team extracted from Chaz." She laughed darkly and took a long sip of wine, then emptied the bottle of Barolo into her glass and waved to the waiter to bring another.

She'd made reservations in advance and laid a good tip on the maître d' to secure a table by the windows overlooking the river. The view was gorgeous. They could see the edge of the Marina towers next door to the south of them, with the iconic corn cob shapes rising to the sky. Across the river stood an array of Chicago's finest architecture. And on Dwayne's plate was the finest steak he'd ever tasted.

But the conversation was less than appetizing.

Dwayne had actually hoped that the subject of Chaz would come up. He thought that over time and with gentle reminders of the good things about Chaz, Bonnie might come to forgive him. Maybe there might be a reconciliation. But with every sentence out of Bonnie's mouth, it became clear St. Jude himself could not change her mind about Chaz.

"He thought he was going to be okay after I took all our marital assets," Bonnie scoffed. "He had that fancy six-figure job at McDonald's. God, how I laughed when he got fired. And now he's doing P.R. for your nickel and dime outfit!" Bonnie looked at Dwayne. She covered her mouth and shook her head, but could not stop laughing.

Rude.

Angela was laughing along, but at least she shot Dwayne a *Sorry!* look.

Bonnie took a deep breath to pull herself together, drained her wine glass and held it up for the waiter returning with the next bottle of Barolo. Dwayne was amazed the first bottle went so fast.

"Keep an eye on us," Bonnie told the waiter. "There's a good chance we're going to need a third one of those." She looked out at the river. For a moment her face softened, and then she looked sad. "Sometimes, I don't even feel like myself anymore," she said quietly. She missed life before the betrayal. Then she shook her head and forced a smile. "But wine helps!"

Dwayne had only had one glass, so clearly the girls were pouring it down with a vengeance. Bonnie's orange-tint complexion glowed, making her armies of freckles stand out. She pushed her curly red hair back with both hands, then pointed at Dwayne.

"Say, you brought both Chaz's femme fatales into his life. Ms. Tits-And-Ass that he could not resist and the blonde storm trooper who blew his McDonald's job for him. You're a real pal, Dwayne!" She gave a muffled snort and sliced a piece off her dry-aged bone-in rib eye. It dripped bloody juice as she raised it to her mouth.

"Chaz told you about that?" Dwayne said.

"Angela told me Ingrid made a Trib reporter think McDonald's was a toxic workplace. Ha!"

"You can't blame Dwayne for Chaz's…whatever." Angela waved

her hands vaguely. Dwayne recognized that his wife was feeling the effects of the red pretty hard, too. Clearly, he was the designated driver tonight.

"Well, what about Dwayne's decisions?" Bonnie said archly. "Is he keeping *his* dick in his pants? *Oh, Dwayne, I'll do...anything if you cast me in your show....*"

A middle-aged man at the next table looked over, enjoying Bonnie's performance.

"He knows what my Uncle Guido would do," Angela slurred darkly.

"Well, why would he stray anyway?" Bonnie said, mollifying. "After all, he has you at home, Ms. Voluptuous Claudia Cardinale Clone."

"Isn't Claudia Cardinale, like, in her eighties?" Angela protested.

"Not *now*," Bonnie said. "Do you get the classic movies channel? I watched *Once Upon a Time in the West*? Claudia Cardinale back then. She was so hot. Like you."

"Well..." Angela looked suddenly drunkenly shy.

"I mean it," Bonnie said. "You are so gorgeous. I'd lick your muffin myself if I went that way." She laughed and laughed, and then added: "Hell, why not anyway? I could take a little vacation from straightness." She snorted a laugh and took another gulp of wine. "You wouldn't even be cheating on Dwayne since neither of us is a lesbian. Ha! Right?"

"You are a riot." Angela smiled and stretched luxuriously and winked at Dwayne, then poured herself another glass of Barolo.

"Am I right, Dwayne?" Bonnie said, leaning crookedly toward him. "You couldn't hold that against us." She winked at Angela. "Or maybe he should *hold it against us.*"

"Oh, stop!" Angela said, laughing to the point of spilling her wine. The wife of the man at the next table slapped his arm and pointed at his plate. He was enjoying the girls a little too much.

"Yeah, I'm not so sure about that," Dwayne said. This line of talk made him even more uncomfortable than having his old friend Chaz raked over the coals.

Bonnie laughed and poked Angela. "He's not so sure about that."

"I think he's got a point," Angela said, but she couldn't stop laughing, which did nothing to make him feel any more comfortable.

"Maybe he'd feel differently if we let him watch," Bonnie said giggling to herself.

"Maybe then he could keep it up," Angela slurred. Dwayne felt a shock of horror run up his spine. Did she really say that? He looked at the man at the next table. Had he heard that? He felt a strong urge to leave the restaurant and take a walk down along the river.

Or maybe to throw these women in.

"Well, I'm not letting him watch," Bonnie said, clearly not having heard Angela.

Thank God for that.

"So that's out."

"Well, I don't understand Chaz, either," Angela said. "I mean really. Look at you. You are so pretty. And you have that amazing hair!"

Now the both of them seemed tremendously drunk.

"I do have nice hair." Bonnie said, speaking mainly to herself. She refreshed her glass. "And my BFP is very low," she said airily.

"BFP?" Angela said, suddenly amazed. "Are you pregnant?"

"Pregnant?" Bonnie shoved back in her seat and sloshed some of her wine onto her lap. She didn't notice.

"BFP," Angela said. "Big Fucking Positive. Like on a pregnancy test."

"Ha! That's crazy." Bonnie chuckled to herself, leaning back into the table. "No, I am not *pregnant*. BFP. Body Fat Percentage. My Body Fat Percentage is very low." She took a sip of wine. "I mean really." She flipped her hair back. Her teeth were beginning to take on a purple tint. She shook her head and refocused. "But old Chaz. He couldn't resist Ms. Bubble-Tits." She breathed a sigh and her face took on a look of amazement as she remembered: "Her skin was so creamy dark. She was...stunning." She laughed weirdly. "If I didn't hate her, maybe I'd do her, too, on my vacation from straightness." She raised her glass to Angela. "But I'd do you first," she promised. She looked around for the waiter and pointed at the bottle of Barolo, which was somehow again already nearly empty.

Dwayne looked at Angela. She was looking up at the ceiling in a world of her own. Bonnie didn't seem to notice she'd lost her audience. She sighed. "Sometimes I wish I didn't have freckles on every inch of my body," she said.

This was nuts.

Bonnie may have been bent on revenge for Chaz's infidelity, but she didn't look like she was doing any better emotionally than he.

"Hey, how about some dessert?" Dwayne startled them both with the volume of his suggestion. "I noticed they have tiramisu."

"Tirami-shoe," Bonnie said. "I love tirami-shoe."

"And coffee?" Dwayne asked hopefully. "Espresso? American?"

"Oh…" Bonnie seemed to think about it, but then her mind drifted. She turned to Angela. "Say, did you ever want to be an actress?"

"Not really."

"Dwayne could probably give you a part."

Angela scoffed. "None of Dwayne's people make any money." This was true, but Dwayne felt the sting of it anyway, like he'd been personally insulted.

"Why *don't* you make any money?" Bonnie asked Dwayne pointedly. "All your friends make money. *I* make money. *Big* money. Aleister, too. Chaz used to." She snorted. "But not you. Why is that, Dwayne?" She turned suddenly to Angela and whispered. "I didn't want to say anything, but I saw a cockroach in your apartment last time." She turned back to Dwayne. "Here you are married to Ms. Authentic Gorgeous Claudia Cardinale, and you keep her in a cockroach palace. I mean, she's Ms. Super-Pretty Magic-Torso Claudia Cardinale. Really. What's up with you?"

Angela looked ever so slightly more sober and leaned in toward Bonnie. "You leave Dwayne out of it," she said quietly.

"Hey…" Bonnie started, but Angela raised a finger to her, and she fell silent.

"Excuse me. I just need to…." Dwayne headed to the men's room. The two women might not remember the conversation tomorrow, but they'd both said things that stung him. At least Angela had shut Bonnie up on this last one.

He felt pressure slowly release from his body as he walked away from the table.

He stepped into the washroom and discovered the urinals topped full of ice cubes. He never understood why these upscale places filled their urinals with ice, but he did enjoy pissing into it, melting some of the cubes with his hot urine.

All his friends were going mad. They'd all had such wonderful marriages, but look at them now.

Chaz and Bonnie had been lively and wild. If there was an opportunity for skinny dipping, they were the first ones with their clothes off and into the water. You never knew what they were going to say or do. Bonnie had always had a sharp tongue, but she'd never been so mean. Cockroach palace! What vintage apartment building didn't have a few bugs? They had a big formal dining room and a huge living room where he could host parties and meetings. They had a second bedroom for their office. They got to see the El train go by. It was a great apartment.

This was the most expensive dinner he'd ever had. Even though Bonnie was treating, he would rather have picked up a burger at a drive-thru window and eaten in peace. He washed his hands and dried them with a warmed terry cloth towel and tossed it into a hamper, and stepped out of the elegant Men's Room. The river and the city glowed outside. He was tempted again to slip out of the restaurant and go for a walk.

What did Madeline Forthright have to say about moments like this? She had a short chapter called *Keep the Home Fires Burning*, in which she wrote about the importance of time for your partner and children, if you had them. She acknowledged that some of the most seemingly successful people completely ignored their families, being married to their work. But was that real success? Yes, they might be CEOs of Fortune 500 companies with seven-figure salaries, but was their success fully rounded? Were they happy?

Dwayne was doing his best to keep his partner happy, to have their *Winner Boats Rise Together*. But he couldn't say he was either successful or happy at the moment. Had Angela really said: *Maybe then he could keep it up*? She would reveal his penile problem so casually?

Nobody had seemed to have heard. But still...

To give her credit, she'd also told Bonnie: *You leave Dwayne out of it*. That was a nice moment.

Well, the ladies were having their drunken night. It seemed to fluctuate between rude hilarity and mourning. It was like an Irish wake, and the corpse in the coffin was Chaz and Bonnie's marriage.

As he arrived back at the table, Bonnie was standing looking over Angela's shoulder at something on her phone. "Oh my God, he *is* gorgeous."

"The kids love him. He's got them all writing poetry."

"He's one of those poets in the schools?" She leaned forward and swiped to the next photo. "Oh my God! Look at that sexy bubble-butt!"

She was so loud. People from three tables around looked over. The women seemed totally unaware. Angela laughed. "He is good looking," she allowed.

Bonnie took the phone out of Angela's hand, sat back at the plate, and continued swiping.

"So, are we getting dessert?" Dwayne said, practically whispering, hoping the ladies would get the hint to quiet down.

"Your kids are cute, too, but I'm telling you. This poet in the schools?" She hummed low in her throat and raised her eyebrows, still swiping through the photos.

"How many pictures of this guy do you have?" Dwayne said, beginning to feel disturbed.

"Lots," Angela said loudly. "We have to document these *Artists in the Schools* all the time."

"Whoa!" Bonnie had swiped to a photo she particularly liked. "This man is so sexy, I'd lick Alfredo sauce from his butt crack!"

Purple liquid shot out of Angela's nose in reaction, and she raised the tablecloth to her face trying to catch it, knocking over two glasses. "Oh, Jesus! Not fair." She grabbed a napkin to wipe her face clean, and dabbed down her blouse to see if it had wine on it, laughing too much to really care. "You can't say things like that when I've got something in my mouth."

"This man could put something in *my* mouth."

"Stop!" Angela insisted, laughing harder.

The mouths of some of the nearby patrons were hanging open.

"Please," Dwayne breathed. The waiter swooped in with a towel, looking at the women doubtfully. "May I be of any assistance?" he said, a hint of sternness in his voice.

"Everything's fine," Bonnie said, startling Dwayne with how suddenly sober and commanding she sounded. "We'd like a round of tiramisu and coffees, please."

"Very good, madam." He finished mopping the spilled wine and went away.

"Well, that was embarrassing," Angela whispered.

"Oh, baloney," Bonnie said, once again sounding drunk. "We're spending plenty, and we're here to have fun." She grabbed Angela's phone again. "There's no way this *Mr. Poet Man* doesn't have a crush on you," Bonnie said.

"You are too much." Angela was enjoying this much more than Dwayne was.

"Well, if you don't want him, turn him over to me." Bonnie settled back in her chair. "My husband had his hot black woman. Maybe it's time I have my hot black man."

"Chaz is not your husband anymore, remember?" Angela said.

"Oh yeah." Bonnie stared dead forward for a moment, looking every bit as drunk as she was and suddenly deeply unhappy, too.

13

Sunday, August 15, 2004

"Good God!" Wallace groaned. Ry looked at him disaffectedly as he set down his guitar, having finished singing and playing the opening song for *Romeo and Juliet*. Wallace stood up, making rumbling sounds in his throat, raised his head, and pushed back his salt-and-pepper hair with both hands. He turned to Dwayne in front of the whole rest of the cast. "You can't be telling me this song replaces *all* the dialogue in the first scene right up to my line as Lord Capulet?" He raised his eyebrows in a look of vast incredulity. Ry had added Shakespeare's opening chorus to his variation on Prince's *Let's Go Crazy* along with some additional lines of his own. "It's a travesty!" Wallace exclaimed.

August had come, and this was the first full read-through of *Romeo and Juliet*. Peaches' drawings of the costume designs were hung on the wall. She'd taken the cast through her ideas for the show in her painfully shy way, but the actors loved the designs she and Dwayne had agreed upon. The prospect of being dressed like band members of *Prince and the Revolution* excited them.

Dwayne had added the final additional cast members and the full group was seated around the long tables with their scripts—all except the actor playing Lord Montague. He'd dropped out to take a role at the Lyric Opera for their opening show of the Fall season. Dwayne resented actors who dropped out, but who could blame him? The Lyric paid well while Dwayne paid crap, and Montague wasn't much of a part.

"All those lines…gone?" Wallace sounded like Macduff learning that Macbeth had slaughtered his children.

"That's right." Dwayne had suspected Wallace would be a

Shakespeare traditionalist. "In *Titus Andronicus* we used instrumental music to heighten the action. This time, we'll also use a few songs to advance the story."

Wallace threw up his hands. "Why not just do *West Side Story*, for the love of God?"

"Oh, Jesus H. Christ!" Tom said, standing up to his full six foot six. He put his hands firmly on his hips. "I, for one, love what Ry has done. This is an incredibly dynamic way to start the show, and he should be applauded!" Tom began clapping. He looked around and the rest of the cast (except Wallace) joined in with him, Peaches clapped particularly heartily.

"Thank all y'all," Ry said. He turned off his amp and sat down at the table with the group.

"We are not remotely close turning the show into a musical," Dwayne said. "We are replacing some text that I might have cut anyway and making the show more dynamic."

"Well, I don't like it," Wallace countered. "There are funny lines you've cut here. The puns on *coals* and *choler*, and *press the women to the wall…*"

"Yes, there's nothing funnier than a rape joke," Joan, the stage manager, said dryly.

"That was a rape joke?" Melinda asked.

"There you go," Dwayne said. "Nobody even understands those jokes because those words don't mean the same things anymore."

"I understand them," Wallace said, slapping a hand to his chest. "And true Shakespeare lovers understand them. We think they're hilarious."

"Very few people know Shakespeare's vocabulary well enough to get those jokes," Dwayne insisted. "And the ones who do have heard those jokes already. Could you hold your objections to the end and read your first line?"

Wallace gave a sorrowful laugh. "I hope you don't intend to add any *tap dancing* when we do *King Lear*."

"And Joan, please read Montague for us. I still need to find a replacement," Dwayne said.

"Daddy!" Coco shouted, looking toward the door. "Never mind,

Joan. He's here." Coco got up to greet a tall, handsome man standing in the doorway. She kissed him on the cheek and turned to the cast. "Everyone, this is my father, Rockwell Nesbit the Third. He'll be taking over the role of Lord Montague." Coco came back to the table and whispered in Dwayne's ear. "Sorry. I didn't know he'd be coming today. This'll save Chaz from broken legs, and he's a natural actor. You'll see."

"The fuck?" Dwayne whispered back. This was the first he'd ever heard of Rockwell Nesbit III.

"If you embarrass my Pops now, you can kiss Chaz's ass goodbye," she whispered deeply, her eyes squinted with intensity. "We'll talk later."

"Everything good?" Rockwell Nesbit III glared at the confab between his daughter and Dwayne with suspicious intensity. Dwayne felt a little shiver, as though there were something fatally threatening in those two words.

"Dwayne didn't realize you were coming already today," Coco said swiftly. "You can look on my script with me. Joan'll have a new script for you next time." She pointed at Joan. "She's our stage manager."

Joan nodded extremely slowly. She didn't like surprises.

"Good." His voice sounded silvery smooth as he approached the group. A professional voice. Dwayne had seen him somewhere. Was Coco's dad a professional actor?

"Why don't you introduce yourself?" Dwayne suggested.

"My pleasure," he said as he moved to the head of the table. "As Coco said, I'm Rockwell Nesbit the Third, proud father of a talented and beautiful daughter." He blew a kiss to her. "Y'all can call me Rocky." He winked at them and stepped up onto the little platform from which Ry had played his guitar.

He certainly knew how to take the stage. Every eye was on him. Dwayne wasn't surprised that he was a remarkably handsome man, being father to Coco. But he was surprised at how naturally and dynamically he moved in front of the group. He was mesmerizing. Rocky spread his arms. "I am a lifelong Chicagoan. My grandfather was a Pullman porter, the best job a black man could find in the day, serving the white man. My father turned away from that life and sought his living with our own people. He started with a grocery store but supplemented his income as a *craft distiller*. That's what you'd call it now. Back then they called him a bootlegger." He winked and laughed. "He made a quality whiskey, and he found revolutionary ways to expedite the process. Rather than age it in oak casks for years, he stirred roasted oak sawdust into the whiskey, aged it a couple months, and then filtered it through charcoal. The surface area of oak sawdust in contact with the whiskey was radically multiplied. He made an exceptional product in a fraction of the time, and the charcoal filtering made it smooth. He made a lot of money. That paid for elocution lessons and law school for me." He gave Coco a challenging look. Coco looked oddly uncomfortable.

What was that about?

"And that set me on course to build a successful personal injuries firm."

That was where Dwayne had seen him! He'd seen him hundreds of times in some of the most annoying commercials on late night television. With the musical theme from the movie *Rocky* in the background, he stood and declaimed: *You got a fight on your hands? Call Rocky! Injured? Sick? We put the insurance companies on the ropes and get you the money you deserve!*

Rockwell Nesbit III, Personal Injuries Law. That was him.

He sat down, and they began reading through the play.

Lord Montague only had a few scenes. If Dwayne could get Chaz out of trouble, he certainly wanted to do that. Rocky actually looked like he could be the father of Orlando. That was a nice touch. Lord Montague and Romeo Montague. As they read through the script, Dwayne was impressed with how well Rocky handled the language. It seemed like it might turn out okay.

Afterwards when everyone was breaking up to go home or get together for a post-rehearsal drink, Dwayne overheard Coco talking with her dad.

"What's up with Uncle Bull?" she whispered intensely, backing him up to a wall.

"He likes poker," Rocky said off-handedly.

"He shouldn't be playing poker or anything else." Coco sounded oddly annoyed.

"He's fine."

"Why aren't you taking your pills?"

"If I want nagging, I can go home to your mother."

She sighed deeply and softened her voice. "You know I've always wanted to act with you. This could be fun. But you have to take care of yourself. We can't have Uncle Bull spoiling things."

"Don't you worry about Uncle Bull, little girl. Neither of us would be living the lives we've got if it hadn't been for Uncle Bull."

Coco closed her eyes in anguish.

What the hell was that about?

14

Friday, August 20, 2004

"The first hurdle in promoting *The Soul in Grief* is that nobody knows who you are," Chaz said, tapping his finger on the battered coffee table in front of the shabby sofa on which he sat in Dwayne's living room. He wiped the sweat from his forehead as an El train rumbled by on the tracks outside the windows. It sounded extra loud because the windows were open for any cool evening air that might drift over from the lake, two blocks away.

"Maybe that's the first hurdle," Aleister said doubtfully. "Or maybe *you* are the first hurdle." He leaned back in the overstuffed chair next to the sofa with an expression that Dwayne imagined he used with his patients: Ready to listen without judgment. He even looked like the heat didn't affect him. How did he do that?

Chaz pushed back away on the sofa. "How am I a hurdle? I'm not a hurdle." He mopped more sweat from his forehead.

"Aren't you?" Aleister kept that neutral expression. He sat very still. Dwayne felt tempted to say something to release the tension, but stopped himself.

"You're talking about the loan, right? That's what you're talking about?" Chaz gave a feeble laugh. "I can deal with that. I want to talk about your book promotion."

"Okay," Aleister said.

Immediately the tension in Chaz's body dissipated. "Good," he said.

He's playing him like a fish on a line.

Chaz pulled an Advance Reader Copy of Aleister's book from his attaché case. These ARCs were printed copies of *The Soul in Grief* bound in a plain paper cover with just the title and author on the front and promotional copy on the back. Random House sent Advance Reader Copies out to reviewers and bookstores in advance of the book's September release date. He flipped it open to a page marked with a Post-It and leaned over to Aleister. "In this section you write about how love can be overwhelming. Imagine reading this to your audience and then Orlando and Melinda do the balcony scene. The world's most famous overwhelming love." He flipped to another Post-It marked page. "And then you could read this part about unbearable grief, and the actors do the scene where Juliet wakes to find Romeo dead and takes her own life. And you finish with something transformational from the concluding chapters. Maybe this." He handed the open ARC to Aleister. A passage was highlighted in yellow. "Not only do those readings reinforce one another, they make the event more compelling and entertaining. And we follow that with Q&A and book signing."

"That sounds really good," Aleister admitted. "I had my doubts about bringing in the actors."

Dwayne was looking over a copy of Chaz's proposed event schedule. "You've got my two lead actors tied up on an awful lot of rehearsal nights."

"You can work around them," Chaz said.

"Work around them?" Dwayne said in amazement. "There are almost no scenes without either Romeo or Juliet in it."

Chaz snatched the paper away from him. "Don't worry about this. This is a best-case scenario schedule. We won't find places to present on all those dates, I'm sure."

"Worst case scenario, as far as I'm concerned." He pulled out a handkerchief and mopped his brow. He wished he could afford an air conditioner for this room. They should have met at Aleister's. He had central air.

Chaz took a quick breath and turned back to Aleister. "What has Random House said about a national tour?"

"My editor said they can't afford it, but Binky says if we can make the book pop in Chicago, she'll pressure them to loosen up some money."

Chaz clapped his hands. "There you go! What we've got planned is going sell gobs of books and piles of *Romeo and Juliet* tickets!" He smiled broadly at his two friends. Dwayne saw the gears shifting in Chaz's head. "And speaking of loosening up money, I had some thoughts about resolving my loan." He laughed to himself and shook his head, clearly seeking a path into what he wanted to say. "See, this P.R. plan is really going to make the trees shake. I mean, you've got a tremendous book. In your events, we'll have performances from three amazingly beautiful human beings. I mean, Aleister, you know you are a handsome man. Your face beams intelligence."

Aleister cleared his throat and looked at his friend tartly. Chaz was trying to build a case, but he sounded like he was babbling.

"Yes." Chaz waved his hands as though to brush that away and laughed again. His face was flushed red and sweaty. "All that aside, this is going to be *money*. This book is going to *sell*. And I absolutely predict that what we are doing is going to prompt Random House to approve your national tour."

"And?" Aleister said, as though he didn't know what was coming next.

"And I knew I'd find an open bottle of wine here," came a lyrically feminine voice. Angela emerged from the study, the second bedroom she and Dwayne used as an office where she had been lounging since dinner, reading a book. She headed toward the bottle of wine on the coffee table.

Dwayne noticed his friends' eyes.

It being a hot August night and their apartment having only one little window air conditioner in the main bedroom, Angela was dressed in shorts and a loose white linen blouse that was tied below her breasts. Her long curly black hair was pulled back, but some strands stuck to her face that was flushed slightly with the heat. She was trying to stay cool, but she looked extra hot.

"Hey, Angela," Chaz said in greeting, getting out of his seat as she poured herself a glass from the wine they'd been sharing. They'd arrived after dinner and hadn't seen her yet.

"Angela," Aleister greeted.

"Sit down, sit down. It's too hot for all that," she said. She took a sip. "Hey, not bad. I'm guessing Aleister brought this bottle."

Aleister chuckled and Chaz watched intently as she walked back to the study and closed the door.

Had Chaz always ogled his wife like this? Or was it just since Coco dumped him and Bonnie divorced him?

"You were saying?" Aleister prompted.

"Yes!" Chaz said. "I see us creating a lot of buzz for your book." Chaz mopped more sweat from his brow. "So I was hoping…wondering if I could get something of an advance. Or call it a loan. However you prefer to structure it, to get Uncle Bull off my back so I can really focus on *The Soul in Grief* and *Romeo and Juliet*. One can sell the other. We can pass out show handbills at the readings, and we can sell your books at the show. And run an ad for the book in the show program. See?"

"You want me to pay off your gambling debt." Aleister looked as unflappable as James Bond. How was he able to look so cool?

"Well, a structured loan, a professional advance…"

"To pay off your gambling debt."

Dwayne was impressed again how nonjudgmental his friend looked. Did they teach that in psychiatry school?

"Well. Yes," Chaz admitted. "He's threatening to break my legs. Just last night at the game…"

"Ah." Aleister said. "You were gambling again." Chaz looked truly horrified at what he'd revealed.

"I just thought if I had a good night…"

"Do you think I'd give heroin to a junkie?" Aleister asked.

Chaz got off the couch and walked around behind it. "Why would you compare me to a junkie?"

"When you are deeply, dangerously, in debt, and you continue gambling, that's addiction."

"So…you're just going to let him break my legs?" Chaz backed up further until he bumped into the coat tree by the door.

"You need to pull yourself out of this. I can help you find the resources."

"If by resources you mean money, that's what I need! I need money! What about you, Dwayne? Are you going to let Uncle Bull break my legs?"

"You know I don't have the money," Dwayne said. "But I've been reading *Keep Your Eyes on the Prize*. Madeline Forthright says you need to *Work Smarter*, and that means focusing on what you can actually control."

"Are you insane?" Chaz rushed toward them, his face yet redder, sweat dripping off his chin. "I don't need a fucking self-help book. I need money!"

"Ironic you'd call it that," Aleister said coolly, "since my book is also self-help."

"No!" Chaz sat abruptly on the end couch. "Your book is great! But if I don't pay this loan..."

"Listen to Aleister," Dwayne said. "Anyway, it's Coco's Uncle Bull. Is he really going to break your legs, or is he just trying to scare you?"

"Coco said he would! And I believe her!" He wiped sweat off his forehead with his hand and wiped it on his pants. "Are you really not going to give me any money?" he said to Aleister.

"I need to see you break this addiction."

"But I need the money now! He's after me now. If you could even give me part of the money..."

"...you could use it to bankroll a quick winning streak?"

Chaz looked guilty and confused.

"There's a right way to do this..." Aleister said.

"Yeah," Chaz yelled, throwing up his arms. "With broken bones, lying in the hospital." He shot from the couch and stormed out of the apartment, sweat splashing from his face.

15

Saturday, August 21, 2004

"**D**o you think he might really break Chaz's legs?" Angela's eyebrows scrunched together in worry. She sat across from Dwayne in a red naugahyde booth along the wall at Gino's North. Their pizza sat on a metal stand raised above the surface of the table, and glass dispensers of grated cheese, Italian herbs, and dried red pepper flakes sat below it.

Dwayne shrugged uncertainly. "His brother and niece are in our show, so maybe not? But maybe it's a good thing that Chaz thinks he will. He's probably not going to break his addiction until he hits bottom."

"You sound like Aleister." Angela picked up the piece from her plate. Crispy squares of bacon and slices of mushroom and black olives showed their edges from beneath a blanket of bubbly browned mozzarella on a crunchy thin crust. The aroma was delicious. She took a large bite.

Dwayne looked at his pizza and set it back down on his plate. "Still, I can't help but feel a little guilty."

"Don't be dopey, Dwayne," Angela said, chewing her pizza all the while. "You didn't tell him to gamble or to have sex with Coco or to borrow money from a loan shark."

Dwayne let out an ironic laugh. "The funny thing is, Aleister intended to give him the money, but Chaz stormed out first. He wanted Chaz to fully commit to recovery. Otherwise, the money would just enable more gambling."

"Chaz always had an addictive personality. He drinks the most at parties. He talks about his epic hangovers, but never a word about cutting back."

"I always thought of that as part of his exuberance, but you might be right." Dwayne leaned back and stared at the tall statue in front of the big mirrors behind the bar. She was some kind of naked Greek muse in a provocative posture atop the pedestal in front of the gleaming liquor bottles along the wall. She looked like she never felt guilty.

But he didn't come here to talk about Chaz, or his theatre company, or his career. He'd invited his wife out to enjoy pizza and *Keep the Home Fires Burning*, as Madeline Forthright said. There was no *winning* without a happy family life. This time was to be about them. About their relationship. About enjoying time together.

"What if we went for a Sunday morning swim tomorrow?" Dwayne suggested. "We could stop for coffee and pastry and then walk down to the beach. Our rehearsal isn't until seven, so I'm free most of the day."

Angela gave a momentary smile, then looked up.

"Hey, Angela." A young good-looking man stood at their table, staring at Dwayne's wife. He was not tall, maybe 5'8" at best, but extremely buff. He wore tight shorts and a tight tee shirt that showed off his muscle definition. His dark skin glowed like it had been oiled, and the air suddenly smelled of aftershave. Dwayne instantly recalled a drunken Bonnie saying: *He's so sexy, I'd lick Alfredo sauce from his butt crack.*

"Hey, Jayden." Angela perked up immediately. "What a surprise to see you here."

"Yeah. A dude I used to run with lives up here now. We're meeting for pizza. It's supposed to be good."

"It is," Angela said brightly. "This is one of our favorite places. Really old school." They looked back at the long serpentine bar, the custom woodwork, and the dramatically lit curved ceiling. Jayden stared at the naked statue in the niche behind the bar.

"I think she's called Snowflake," Angela said.

"Yeah," he said. "She's something." He turned back to Angela. Dwayne could see it in his eyes: *But she's not as sexy as you.*

"Oh!" she said suddenly, as though she'd forgotten he was there. "This is my husband, Dwayne. Dwayne, this is Jayden. He's one of the Poets in the Schools. He's been working with my kids recently."

So he *was* Bonnie's butt-crack guy.

"Husband, huh?" Jayden looked severely disappointed. "Nice to meet you."

"Hi." Dwayne' voice likewise lacked in enthusiasm.

They exchanged an awkward fist bump.

"Yeah, okay, good to see you," he told Angela. He walked abruptly to the front and out the door. A moment later Dwayne could see him standing in front of the window, out on the sidewalk, presumably waiting.

"Was it something I said?" Dwayne asked wryly.

"I think he has a little crush on me," Angela admitted.

"You think?"

"Usually, he chatters on with me like he's got nowhere else to go."

"There's *some place* he'd like to go."

Angela found that inordinately funny. She held up a hand while she was laughing and pulled out her phone. She could not stop laughing. "When Jayden saw I was taking photos of him working as a Poet in the Schools, he volunteered more photos. Look what he sent me." She held up a photo on her phone for Dwayne to see.

"The fuck?"

The screen on Angela's phone showed Jayden with his shirt off, lifting a barbell, wearing extremely tight workout shorts. The lighting clearly showed off the outline of his lower equipment.

"Good God. That's practically a dick pic. What did you say to him?"

"Nothing," Angela scoffed. "What am I going to say? It's harmless." She was still holding up the phone.

"Doesn't look that harmless to me." From the outline in his shorts, Dwayne suspected the poet had a nicer-looking dick than his. "If you were to show that to your principal, *Mr. Poet Man* would be out of there."

This struck Angela as even more hilarious. "Dwayne, you're jealous!" She was enjoying this way too much.

"For the love of God, turn that off," he told her, waving the phone away.

"Okay, okay." She put her phone away. "Anyway, you are right," she admitted. "It's totally inappropriate. But so what? I'm not going to rat him out to Fran. We have a hard enough time keeping our artists programs going as it is. We were supposed to have a performance from some visiting Shakespeare company from England, but they cancelled on us."

"Really?" Dwayne said.

"Yeah. They were supposed to perform a short version of *The Merchant of Venice* in October. I was going to have the kids read it and have lessons tied in."

"Well, now," Dwayne said with a flush of grandiosity, "what if you had *Romeo and Juliet* instead?"

"Really?" She looked very pleased. "Your guys would do it at our school?"

"I think I could make that happen." Dwayne actually had no idea whether he could make that happen, but he loved the excited look on his wife's face. He knew how to *Keep His Eyes on the Prize*. "Just give me the contact info for whoever runs the program at your school, and I'll see if we can work it out."

"Dwayne, that would be so cool. Talk to Fran; she's in charge. I'd much rather do *Romeo and Juliet* with fifth graders than *The Merchant of Venice*. Do you think you could come and talk to my kids in advance of the assembly?"

"Absolutely."

"Oh, Dwayne, that would be great." She was beaming at him. He loved it.

Maybe he didn't have the intense muscle definition of *Mr. Poet Man*, but he was the one taking this sexy teacher home tonight.

16

Sunday, August 22, 2004

"Your rehearsal is scheduled to start at seven p.m. It's only six thirty-five." Green stood in the lobby of the Chicago Repertory Arts Playhouse with his hands on his hips in a posture of defiance. Dwayne had just walked in from what had been a lovely day with his wife. They lived two blocks from Hartigan Beach, just north of Loyola University. After breakfast at a coffee shop, they'd enjoyed swimming and lounging on the sand. Then they'd walked back to the apartment and made love in the afternoon. He was keeping the home fires burning. But now apparently there was conflict. His stage manager, Joan, rolled her eyes at the ceiling. Green was wearing some kind of striped button-down shirt. Where had Dwayne seen that shirt before? Yes! On the cover of a sixties folk record that his aunt liked. The Kingston Trio. Green was wearing the Kingston Trio striped shirt and a pair of baggy shorts and cheap rubber flip flops. He hadn't shaved, and his hair looked unwashed, as well.

"We have the space from six thirty when I arrive for set up until eleven," Joan said. "That's our contract. Rehearsal is scheduled to start at seven, which means everyone is there, ready to go. You've got to get those people out of there now."

"There are people in our rehearsal space?" Dwayne felt instantly annoyed. He needed every minute of rehearsal time.

"The parishioners of the Indigenous Connection Church are lying on the floor and drooling on themselves," Joan said, curiously emotionless. "When I informed them that their rental time was up, some of them giggled and others didn't seem to hear me at all. They are Green's tenants, so he needs to get them out."

"Raymond?" Dwayne said to him. He seldom used Green's first name. It did seem to focus his attention.

"Look," Green said. "I can't interfere with the exercise of religious freedom. It's in the Constitution."

"The Constitution does not guarantee anyone's right to practice their faith in a space we paid for," Dwayne insisted. "We need to usher them out before our actors start arriving."

Green grumbled and rubbed the top of his head with the palm of his hand, releasing a sprinkle of dandruff to the shoulders of his Kingston Trio shirt. Parts of the shirt were so worn, they were nearly transparent, giving a gauzy view onto flesh that Dwayne would have preferred never to see. The three climbed the two flights of stairs to the rehearsal room. As they approached, the percussive music of Rusted Root floated down the hall to them.

Dwayne plunged into the room first. As Joan had said, a number of the church members were lying on the floor, some of them on yoga mats, some on sleeping bags. They came prepared for reclining. Everyone there looked like a throwback to the hippie era. Long hair on the men. Lots of tie-dye. The room smelled like it had been anointed in patchouli.

Two pony-tailed men shuffled around like drunken bears at one end of the room. Dwayne realized they were performing some kind of inebriated dance to the music, which was turned up as loud as the boom box would allow.

Joan stood at the door looking up at the ceiling. Clearly this situation was not in her wheelhouse. Green stood next to her, rubbing his palm on the dome of his skull. Joan glanced at the dust floating down and took a step away.

Dwayne walked over to the boom box and turned the volume all the way down. Instantly groans emerged from the throats of the worshipers. One woman began to softly weep. A man who'd been lying face down on the floor got up. It was Dan Darwood. He wore his colorful Christ-like tie-dyed homespun gown. He looked around the room. "Pearl? Armageddon?" Two women Dwayne recognized from the first time he'd met this self-styled minister got up from their yoga mats and joined him. His priestesses.

Dwayne led the three of them, as urgently as he could, over to Joan and Green by the door. "You have to get your people out," he told them.

"I sense we may have gone over time," Dan Darwood replied in a dreamy voice.

"Our actors will be arriving now," Joan said.

"You have to leave," Green said.

Pearl and Armageddon began to moan miserably.

"No, no," Dan Darwood admonished them. "Dial tone."

They sat on the floor right where they were and began to chant *Om.*

"We are all with Mother Ayahuasca now," Dan Darwood said.

"How's that?" Green said

"Mother was very strong today. Much stronger than we expected. We never know how strongly she will call us."

"Sounds like you need some dosage control," Dwayne said. "But we need this room. You all have to go."

Dan Darwood lowered his voice. "You see my dilemma. I can't take my people outside. Some of them might wander onto Lincoln Avenue and get run over."

"Good point," Joan said, surprising them all. "Lucky for you, it's Monday night and all the theatres are dark. I'll unlock the upstairs mainstage, and you can lead your people in there."

"If it's dark, they aren't going to like that," Darwood said.

Joan sighed. "*Dark* means there's no show. As in: the stage lights aren't on for a performance. So it's *dark.* I'll turn on the work lights. And then there will be light."

"Oh! Theatre talk!" Darwood looked as though he'd reached a new stage of enlightenment.

"They didn't pay for the theatre," Green objected.

"You work out your rentals as you see fit," Joan told him. "But these people are leaving this room. Unless you want to lead them somewhere else, I am taking them to the theatre." Joan walked over and picked up the boom box. "Follow me, children! Bring your belongings! Mother Ayahuasca is taking you to a beautiful theatre." She turned the volume back up and walked slowly backwards toward the door.

"That's right," Dan Darwood agreed. "Follow Mother Ayahuasca."

The woman who had wept when the music went off began weeping again. She pointed at Joan. "Mother Ayahuasca!"

They gathered themselves and followed Joan down the stairs to the sounds of thunderous percussion.

"There is nothing a good stage manager cannot do," Dwayne said. He felt an immense sense of relief as the parishioners straggled out of his rehearsal room.

"They're going to have to pay extra to be in the theatre," Green grumbled.

"If you go right now, Dan Darwood will probably sign anything."

Green seemed to like that idea and hurried out of the room just as the actors were beginning to file in. Dwayne arranged the room for rehearsal. Joan must have come in earlier. The set was already taped out on the floor.

Wallace walked in, chuckling in his low baritone. "Coming up the stairs I thought I was passing through the Woodstock Nation."

"You recognize anyone?" Ry asked, carrying his guitar case and a messenger bag.

"I am old," Wallace said, "but I am not quite old enough to have been at Woodstock."

"Too bad," Ry said. "Some of those bands were the shit."

"Well, the weather was shit," Wallace allowed. "But the bands were good."

Ry squinted his eyes, shook his head, and moved on. He dropped his messenger bag next to a chair by the wall as more actors walked in. Dwayne pulled the table to where he and Joan would sit. Tom swept into the room and began helping prepare the acting space.

"Ry!" Melinda came trotting like a pony into the room and put her arms around the guitarist's neck.

"Here we go," Coco said lightly, following behind.

Melinda pulled away abruptly and faced her. "What?" she said sharply.

"Nothing. I'm just wondering how long before he dumps you and you come crying about the end of your *showmance*."

"Did I complain when you were fucking one of the show's investors?" Melinda said.

"Did you complain?" Coco's laugh rose an octave. "You stood on a desk shouting: *No hostile workplace*."

"That wasn't about you *fucking* Chaz. That was about Chaz giving you all the publicity in return."

Rockwell Nesbit III had come into the room. "What's all this?"

"Sour grapes," Coco told him.

"Right," Melinda scoffed. "And now the actor playing my nurse, my greatest support, is the person who most undercuts me on stage."

Dwayne and Tom finished moving the chairs and sat down at the table to go over their notes before rehearsal started.

"Maybe *you* should play the Nurse, and I'll play Juliet," Coco suggested. She laughed and did a little dance.

"What are they saying?" Tom whispered.

"Hey, that's right," Rocky said. "How come you're not playing Juliet?"

"Director's choice," Coco said.

He looked Melinda up and down. "Seems like kind of a dumb choice."

"Oh, now…" Tom breathed.

"Hey!" Melinda objected.

"Okay, actors!" Dwayne stood up to intervene. "Mutual respect. This is an ensemble."

"You told me you wanted to act with me," Rocky said to Coco. "We don't have a single scene together. I'm playing Romeo's dad, but you work in Juliet's household."

"But we're in the same cast. Maybe next show we'll have scenes together. Melinda is a good choice for Juliet."

Dwayne liked that response. Maybe Coco was coming around.

"I don't think so. We need to fix this," Rocky replied. He came back to Dwayne. "Coco should play Juliet, and I should play Juliet's dad." He looked exceedingly grim.

"Pops, leave it alone," Coco said quietly.

Rocky looked Dwayne in the eye with a challenging, even murderous look.

"I'm not changing the casting, Rocky." Dwayne was a good actor. He wasn't showing it, but underneath he felt a shiver of fear. Was Rocky as violent as his brother Bull? "But I appreciate your suggestion."

Time to redirect the energy. *Get It in Gear*, as Madeline Forthright said. Action begets action and negates negativity. He turned to the rest of the company.

"Okay, everyone," he called out. "Let's get ready to rehearse."

17

Tuesday, August 24, 2004

"I don't think I've heard of your company, Dwight," Fran Konacki said. "Psychedelic Dream Theatre is an unusual name. What country are you from?"

Dwayne took the phone receiver away from his face and looked into it. She was calling him Dwight? She wanted to know what country were they from? Did she forget he'd just told her he was married to Angela, one of her teachers?

"We're a Chicago-based company," he said, deciding to correct just one misapprehension at a time. "All local talent."

"Oh." Fran Konacki sounded disappointed. She was Angela's principal. She was in charge of the Shakespeare assembly. "The company that canceled on us was from London. They were coming do a show at Chicago Shakespeare Theatre. We were very excited."

"Yes, Angela told me about that. The good news is, as a local company, we are not going to cancel on you."

"No, I suppose not." Was that a hint of regret in her voice? "But I have to make sure this is going to be a quality presentation. What is your web address? I could look over your materials there."

Web address. Yes. Ingrid had purchased a web address. If the principal brought it up on her browser right now, it would say *Web Site Under Construction*. Not exactly a confidence booster.

"I can do better than that," Dwayne said cheerily. "Let me send you a packet of our press materials. The reviews of our shows have been stellar. Both the *Tribune* and the *Sun-Times* love us. And all the little papers, too. What date had you set for the London company?"

"Wednesday, October twentieth at one p.m. Would that work for you?"

That was in the fourth week of the run.

"That'd be perfect," Dwayne said. "What sort of payment was the London company receiving?"

"Payment?" Fran Konacki said. For a school principal, she seemed vague on a lot of things.

"Yes," Dwayne said. "A stipend to be paid to the company for the performance?"

"Oh!" Why did she sound so surprised? "They weren't getting any payment, Dwight. They were providing the performance free."

"Really?" Dwayne said. This was disappointing. Much more disappointing than being called Dwight. "Do you happen to know how they were paying the actors for the performance?"

"They had a couple grants lined up. I had to fill out paperwork for their granting organizations in advance, and then we were going to provide some follow-up documentation."

"I see." Dwayne tried his best to sound upbeat. The point of this whole thing was to make Angela happy. But how was he going to pay his actors? They weren't likely to want to do it for free.

"So," Principal Konacki carried on, "the assembly is set for seventy-five minutes. That means the play should be fifty-five to sixty minutes to allow for a little introduction and question-and-answer afterwards. How does that sound?"

Sixty minutes. That would mean a lot of cutting. Maybe that was good news. He could do just scenes with Romeo and Juliet. Well—no—not if he wanted to give a version of the whole story. But Romeo, Juliet, Friar Lawrence and the Nurse. He could tell the story with the four of them.

"Are you still there?" Fran Konacki said.

"Yes, absolutely. Sorry, I was just thinking how to present the story in sixty minutes. We could absolutely do that."

"Okay," Fran Konacki said, sounding slightly bored. "Send me your packet, and if it all checks out, I'll send you a contract."

"Great!" Dwayne said. They hung up the phones. Yes, of course, he'd have to sign a contract in order to provide an afternoon of free entertainment for school children. That, probably, would just be the beginning of the hoops through which he'd have to jump. But he was doing this for Angela. She'd been so excited when he suggested it. He was determined to make it happen.

✦ ✦ ✦

"It takes money to make money." Chaz gave a smile that was only halfway to confident. His mouth trembled at one corner as he leaned back against the brick wall of the Biograph Theater. "My father always said that. Takes money to make money." Dwayne had gone from his phone call to this outdoor meeting.

"What do you intend to do with the money?" Ingrid asked him. At Chaz's request, she and Dwayne were meeting with him before the Tuesday rehearsal to discuss the Fall Fundraiser. He'd insisted on meeting in the alley next to the Biograph rather than at the Chicago Repertory Arts Playhouse. It was only a block and a half from the Playhouse, so they'd gone along with his request.

"I'm not even a company member," Chaz said. "But I've already rounded up more items for the silent auction than anyone. And it's not cheap shit, either. I got a night at the Four Seasons Chicago. A weekend in the Bahamas. Plane tickets. Those are going to bring in a lot of money for the company. I had to expend my own resources to bring in those things. I want to bring in more, but I need funds, like an expense account, so I can keep it up." Three little beads of sweat appeared in the top right corner of Chaz's forehead.

"As I understand it," Ingrid said. "You got all these things from the man who extended you a juice loan."

"Well…" Now three more little beads of sweat appeared in the top *left* corner of Chaz's forehead.

"Why are we meeting in this alley?" Dwayne said.

Chaz looked out toward Lincoln Avenue. "Because Bull wouldn't be looking for me here. I'm afraid he might be watching the Playhouse."

Dwayne laughed.

"What's funny?" Chaz said.

"You do realize this is the alley in which John Dillinger was shot to death, don't you?"

Chaz turned pale. "Is that true?"

"Oh my God." Dwayne laughed some more. "I thought every Chicagoan knew that."

"It's not funny!" Chaz insisted.

"Let's get back on topic," Ingrid said. "So the *personal resources* you expended is money you lost at poker, right?"

"When you've got a heavy hitter who can donate big ticket items, you've got to wine and dine them," Chaz stammered. "Everybody does that. The Goodman does that. Steppenwolf."

"I don't think Reginald Camper or anyone from Steppenwolf lost a bundle gambling and then got stuff donated by the gangster who advanced them a juice loan," Ingrid said. "Or ended up hiding from them in the Biograph Theater alley."

"That is putting a very dark twist on how I procured some really excellent resources for the Psychedelic Dream Theatre silent auction," Chaz protested. "You know, I was in the room when this company got its name. Half the money that launched this company's first show was mine. I didn't get a penny of six thousand dollars back. Your characterization is really not fair at all. If you want me to continue supporting the company in this way—in a way that *no one else is doing*, I might add—I'm going to need some expense money. It's as simple as that." He raised his voice to be heard over a police siren going by on Lincoln Avenue. They retreated deeper into the alley.

"Is this to pay back your loan, Chaz?" Dwayne said quietly.

"Well." Chaz's eyes darted to the right and left. He took a deep breath. He brought his arms down and rested his hands on the knees. "I do need to clear the decks financially so I can provide the best service possible."

"So: yes," Ingrid insisted.

"Yes," he agreed.

Dwayne could smell the liquor on his breath. It was only six p.m. "Look. The company doesn't have the resources to pay off your loan. We just don't." He didn't imagine they had the resources to pay the actors for a school assembly either, but there was no point in discussing that before Fran Konacki sent him a contract.

"And even if we did…" Ingrid said sharply.

Dwayne held up his hand to stop her. "Go back to Aleister. Talk to him about your gambling problem. Get it under control. He'll help you deal with the finances."

"I don't need to sit in a circle pulling my dick with a bunch of addicts," Chaz said. "I need to get Uncle Bull off my back before he starts breaking my legs." He grabbed Dwayne's shoulders abruptly. "He leaves me phone messages every day. I can't sleep at night!"

"Didn't Coco and Rocky talk to him?" Dwayne said.

"If they did, it didn't do any good. Last night he said he wants all the tickets for opening night of *Romeo and Juliet* so his associates can see it. And he wants a case of Dom Pérignon and pretty actresses to refill their glasses during the show."

Ingrid laughed.

"Oh sure. Laugh!" Chaz shouted. "Everything is so God damned funny to you two. It's not your legs he's going to break!" He stormed down to the entrance of the alley, looked both ways down Lincoln Avenue, and disappeared north.

18

Later the Same Day

When they arrived back at the Playhouse, Aleister followed them into the lobby with a carton of Advance Reader Copies. "Hey ho!" He rested the carton on the back of the loveseat. "Has Chaz showed up yet?"

"We just saw him, but not here," Ingrid said. "I'll be on my way," she told Dwayne. She swooped out the door.

"He told me to meet him here," Aleister said. "I got a carton of ARCs from Random House. He wanted to mail them out to reviewers."

"He asked us to meet him in the alley next to the Biograph theatre. He wanted the theatre company to pay his gambling debts."

"The alley next to the Biograph?" Aleister said. "Isn't that where Dillinger was shot?"

"Ironically, that's where he felt safer. He's worried Uncle Bull would find him here."

"Then why would he tell *me* to meet him here?" Aleister set the carton on the love seat cushion.

"He probably forgot. He's really beside himself. He thinks Bull is going to break his legs."

"You think he will?"

Dwayne shrugged.

"I'll talk to him," Aleister promised. "Can I leave these with you for when he returns?"

"I doubt he's coming here, but I can put them in our props locker for the next time we see him."

Aleister followed Dwayne to the rehearsal room, carrying the carton up the stairs. When they got to the third floor, the hallway reeked of burnt herbs. Dan Darwood was waiting in front of the rehearsal room door, holding a smoldering smudge stick.

"Whatever you've been doing in this room," Darwood told Dwayne angrily. "It's got to stop."

"How's that?" Dwayne smiled. He was more concerned about the haze of smoke floating in his rehearsal room than Darwood's apparent outrage.

"We had to smudge this space after whatever you were doing last night. This can't happen again."

"I'll agree with that," Dwayne said. "Smoke is bad for my actors' throats." He snatched the burning sage bundle from Darwood's hand, pulled cut flowers from a vase, and plunged the smoldering stick into the water.

"Hey!" Darwood shouted.

"Aleister, would you mind opening the windows, please?" Dwayne asked. Aleister set his carton on the director's table and began opening them. The sound of traffic from Lincoln Avenue wafted in.

"You had no right to do that," Darwood said. "We had to purify the space by burning sage and crushed cedar. With the vibes you left behind, we could not practice our worship."

"Vibes?" Dwayne said.

"Armageddon is very sensitive to vibes. Pearl, too. You and your people thoroughly polluted our space. We can't spend every session burning sage and cedar. We might as well disband."

"Disband, don't disband, is entirely up to you. But you cannot burn your herbs in here before our rehearsals," Dwayne said. "Actors' voices are their instrument, and all this smoke is damaging to their vocal cords. When your activities interfere with our activities, it's a violation of your rental agreement."

"Your vibes are interfering with us. That's the violation."

"Don't be a goof," Dwayne said. "We didn't leave any vibes."

"No one argued? No one showed ill-will?"

Dwayne immediately thought of Coco and Melinda—and then of the look Rocky had given him last night. But none of that could leave a *vibes residue*. That was nonsense.

"Even if they didn't, I found a copy of *Romeo and Juliet*. Look at this." He opened the script. "*O, then, I see Queen Mab hath been with you. She is the fairies' midwife. She gallops by night through lovers' brains; sometime she driveth o'er a soldier's neck, and then dreams he of cutting foreign throats.* No wonder this room is corrupted. You invoke possessing spirits!"

Aleister rejoined them after opening the windows. "What's happening?"

"They call themselves a church," Dwayne answered. "They come here to drink ayahuasca."

Aleister laughed. "Oh my God. I have a couple clients I need to keep away from you."

"And who are you?" Darwood said in a tone of high outrage.

"Aleister is a psychiatrist," Dwayne said.

"Quack profession," Darwood observed. "True healing comes from the earth. Not from Big Pharma."

Aleister looked at him in that nonjudgmental way that brought forth the deepest confessions from his clients.

Darwood took a step back. "What?" He looked as though Aleister was trying to probe his thoughts.

Melinda and a few of the other actors entered. "Aleister!" she said. She laid a hand on his arm. "So nice to see you." She was still grateful for the pro bono therapy he'd provided her during *Titus Andronicus*. The show had triggered lingering anguish from a date-rape in college. Aleister helped her through it.

"How are you?" He looked at her with deep affection.

"I am taking this up with Raymond Green," Darwood blurted. "This has got to end."

"I certainly hope so," Dwayne muttered as Darwood exited.

At the director's table, Melinda and Wallace were looking over the Advanced Reader Copies of Aleister's book. Others began performing stretches in the area taped out for the set. Wallace held up the book as Dwayne approached. "This is the answer, old man!"

"You're going to read Aleister's book?"

"No, no, no!" he scoffed, then realized how insulting he'd sounded and put a hand up. "I mean, yes! It sounds fascinating." He turned back to Dwayne. "But, no, I mean the answer to *my* dilemma.

I should write a book."

"A self-help book?" Dwayne asked.

"What do I know about helping people?" Wallace retorted. "No! A story of my life in the theatre."

"A memoir," Aleister suggested.

"Exactly!" Wallace said. "See? He knows." He turned back to Aleister. "Say, do you think you could introduce me to your agent? I think I could write faster if I had a book contract. You know, writing to the deadline!"

"I haven't actually met her yet in person," Aleister said. "But you could certainly write to her."

"Yes! I could write about the psychology of acting. That would be a fascinating wrinkle. Maybe you could write the introduction to the book! How many psychiatrists, I wonder, have also been theatre producers?"

"Well..." Aleister demurred. As theatre producers go, he had been extremely hands off.

"Don't sell yourself short, man! I heard what you did for Melinda."

"What?" Melinda looked alarmed. "Who told you what?"

"All right. There I go. My big mouth," Wallace said. "I didn't actually *hear* anything. I just saw you crying, and I saw Aleister talking to you, and later you were much better, so I just thought maybe he'd given you some therapy..."

"If you write a book, don't go talking about me!" she said. "Because you don't know anything."

"There I go. Put my foot in it." His eyes suddenly brightened. He turned to Aleister. "But maybe that's how you write a good book. Speculate on paper." He nodded to himself and walked away without waiting for Aleister to agree or disagree. He lowered himself laboriously to the floor in the corner to page through Aleister's book.

Later, as they worked through the first scenes of the play, Wallace annoyed the hell out of everyone by stopping the action occasionally to run off stage and jot down an idea for his memoir. Every time he dashed off stage, Rocky gave Dwayne a look that he could only interpret as murderous.

Dwayne didn't believe in vibes residues, but if anyone could leave them, it would be Rocky.

19

Monday, August 30, 2004

A few days later they were working on one of the early Nurse/Juliet scenes. Coco delivered the line: *Thou wast the prettiest babe that e'er I nursed*, then she turned to the audience and rolled her eyes.

"Okay, let's stop there for a moment," Dwayne said. It wasn't like Coco to let a personal grievance affect her performance. No matter how wild she could be offstage, she was a dedicated performer. But what was she doing?

This production needed to open the door to the Goodman Theatre. He hadn't yet invited Reg Camper to see the show because he didn't feel secure about it. He needed it to be great. He needed to turn a corner toward a real career before one of his frequent assignations with his lovely wife turned them from a duo to a trio. With a baby he'd absolutely need to bring in real income. He couldn't do that directing shoestring storefront theatre like this.

"Yes, let's stop. Thank you!" Melinda said. "She is undercutting me every chance she gets."

"Okay, hang on." Dwayne got up and walked around the director's table to the two actresses on stage. "The Nurse is Juliet's only confidant, but you are playing her like she resents Juliet."

"Yeah," Coco said simply.

Dwayne waited, but she didn't say anything more. "So, that doesn't seem supported in the text," he said.

"Yeah," Melinda said belligerently. Dwayne raised a hand for her to wait.

"Sure it is," Coco said. "Just because you haven't seen anyone play it in the past doesn't mean it's not there."

"Tell me," Dwayne requested.

"I run errands and everything and help Juliet get married to Romeo. I'm the only one in the play, outside of Romeo, Juliet, and Friar Lawrence who knows they are married. They are married in the eyes of God, which was a very big deal. Juliet goes to confession all the time. They *believe* in heaven and hell. And what happens when her parents tell Juliet she has to marry County Paris? Do I conspire to spirit her away rather than condemn her soul to an eternal fiery hell for marrying twice? No. I say: *I think it best you married with the County. O, he's a lovely gentleman, blah, blah, blah...* Juliet asks me: *Speakest thou from thy heart?* And I say: *And from my soul too.* Everyone thinks the Nurse loves Juliet, but she doesn't. Juliet can *go to hell.* You hear how Lord and Lady Capulet talk to me. I'm nothing but a servant. I've *always* resented this spoiled rich girl. She's going to hell? Great! Let that bitch burn in eternal fire!"

"Wow," Dwayne said. "I've never thought of it that way."

"How am I supposed to play Juliet, trusting you, if you are always sneering at me?" Melinda demanded.

Coco scoffed. "Your family treats you like shit. You're desperate for affection from wherever you can get it. Besides, Juliet is not that bright. You don't make a single smart choice."

"I'm in love!" Melinda said.

"*As all is mortal in nature,*" Coco said, "*so is all nature in love mortal in folly.*"

"Yes, love is folly, but Juliet is not stupid!"

"No? Who are more *mortal in folly* than you and Romeo? You kill yourselves out of ignorance."

"Well, Romeo does," Melinda pouted.

"Right," Dwayne said, "and Juliet does out of despair." He turned to Coco and gave a short laugh of amazement. "I got to hand it to you, I see how the text supports your interpretation, though I have to admit, it really blows me away. And your interpretation gives Melinda a real challenge in how to react."

"Well, that's her job." Coco nodded at Melinda. "Is she desperate because she really has no one else to trust? Is she in denial? I'm giving her something interesting to play against. She should thank me."

"Oh right," Melinda said.

"Look," Coco said to Dwayne. "You put me in a servant role to a white family. This is 2004. You couldn't possibly expect me to give you Hattie McDaniel."

"Who's Hattie McDaniel?" Melinda said.

Coco snorted derisively. "The very first black actor…oh, never mind."

"She won an Academy Award for playing Mammy in *Gone with the Wind*," Dwayne said.

"You ain't getting no Mammy in this production. So deal with it," Coco said.

"I don't want one," Dwayne said. "Now that I understand it, you are offering a really interesting interpretation."

"Damn right," Coco said.

He turned to Melinda. "Now that you understand what she's doing, what do you think?"

Melinda's eyebrows rose. "It's totally the opposite of what I was expecting." She turned to Coco, still with a challenging look in her eye. "I thought the way you were acting was about me personally."

"Naw," Coco said. "I might give you some shit sometimes, but when we're on stage, the play's the thing. You and me are *ensemble*."

"Really?" Melinda said.

"This is *our* company, right?" Coco said.

Melinda nodded hesitantly.

"You're damn right it is. We don't have to be best friends for me to want your work and my work to be the very best. That's the way I am. I assumed that's the way you are, too."

Melinda looked surprised. "I am like that, too. Yeah."

"All right then." Coco reached out a hand, and they shook. And then they surprised everyone around by taking the handshake to a hug. They both laughed.

"Okay," Dwayne said. "We're going to show this relationship in a way it's never been seen before!" He was pleased to see his two actors look at each other with new respect.

But as they moved on to work the first of the scenes between Juliet and Romeo, Dwayne had a bigger problem. Orlando showed absolutely no chemistry with Melinda. It couldn't be because Orlando was gay. Hundreds of gay male actors had played men in love with women. Rock Hudson made his whole career at that.

At the end of the rehearsal, Melinda was hanging on Ry's shoulder, but Ry was not showing the look of love, either. Would she be spurned both onstage and off?

On the other side of the room, Orlando and Tom were whispering and giggling and touching one another's arms. When had that started?

And when were his lead actors going to start showing some chemistry? That would be the day he picked up the phone to call Reg Camper.

O, what fools these mortals be!

20

Saturday, September 4, 2004

"I'd like to show you something," Angela said with a wink, her voice floating in a gentle, musical lilt. She led Dwayne into the bedroom and he sat on the edge of the bed. She opened her robe and Dwayne could see and sense her eagerness in the tilt of her breasts and the wafting of her pheromones. Instant arousal. He opened his pants to allow himself room where he suddenly had none. "That's what I wanted to see," she breathed.

And then a knock came at the door.

"Ignore that," Dwayne said. He flipped onto the bed, pulled her on top of him, and pressed his mouth to her glorious lips.

The knocking got louder.

"Please!" came a desperate voice from out in the hallway. Angela rolled to the side of him and took Dwayne's face in both hands, kissing and kissing.

The knocking came yet louder.

"Please. Please. I need your help."

Now they recognized the voice. "Fucking Chaz," Angela said. She stopped and lay still next to Dwayne. The knocking continued. They thought they heard weeping.

"He's never going away," Angela lamented.

"Fuck," Dwayne said.

"Unfuck, I think is the word. Go get rid of him."

"Jesus," Dwayne breathed. He tucked himself back into his pants, but the shape was obscenely obvious. He was supposed to go to the door like that?

He went into the kitchen, put on his *Master of the Flames* apron to disguise his protrusion, and opened the front door, where Chaz had continued to knock.

Chaz's left eye pulsed with a red and purple swelling on the cheekbone. A deep scratch above the eyebrow crusted at the edges with dried blood. He clutched his left index finger with his right hand. His cheeks were wet with tears and marked with dust from tears that had dried.

"What happened to you?" Dwayne opened the door wide to let him in.

"Uncle Bull. Do you have any ice?"

"Don't be long," Angela called from inside the bedroom door.

"I'm sorry," Chaz said. "It sounds like I'm interrupting." He looked at Dwayne's apron. Cooking at nine p.m.?

"Good guess," Dwayne said.

"Oh!" He noticed the shape beneath Dwayne's apron. "I'd turn around and go, but I don't know where to hide. I'm afraid he might kill me."

"Let's get you some ice on your face, and you can tell me about it. Swiftly." They went into the kitchen and Dwayne started loading ice cubes into a plastic bag.

"My face hurts, but I really need the ice for my finger." He opened his right hand to reveal his left. The index finger was massively swollen and purple. It showed strange parallel scratch lines.

"*Saint Stanislaus Kostka,*" Dwayne said.

"Two thugs held me down while Bull broke my index finger with a pair of pliers."

"You're kidding." He gave Chaz the bag of ice. He looked again at his hand. "Well, no, I guess you're not." Chaz sat down at the dining room table and wrapped the ice bag around his finger, wincing with every movement.

"He plans to break a bigger bone every day until I pay him. He wants double of what I borrowed for the inconvenience of having to break my bones. And that will go up every day. He acted like I was really putting him out!"

Dwayne shrugged. "Those henchmen probably don't come cheap."

"Really? You're going to joke?" He clenched his eyes and bent over his broken finger on the table. "Fuck, fuck, fuck!" He slowly sat back up. "Do you have a tongue depressor and tape? Once this gets numb, I'm going to need you to pull my finger to make sure the bone is set and then tape it down to keep it immobile."

"You're not going to fart when I pull your finger, are you?"

"What the hell, Dwayne!"

"I'm sorry. I joke when I'm nervous. I've never done this."

Chaz moaned and sweat ran down his face. He looked very pale. "What do you have for a splint?" He sounded out of breath. "You need to help me set the bone."

Dwayne's eyebrows went up. Then he shook his head. "You need to go to a doctor."

"Do you think I'd be letting some lunatic break my finger if I had the money to go to a doctor?" He looked at Dwayne in the most pathetic way. "I had great health insurance with McDonald's until Ingrid got me fired. Now I've got nothing."

"We don't have any tongue depressors."

"What do you have?" He picked up the edge of the table cloth and used it to wipe the sweat on his forehead.

"We've got those frozen fruit bars."

"We can't tape my hand to something frozen. It'll melt!" Chaz shook his head disgustedly.

"I mean the popsicle stick inside."

"Oh! I think we'd need two of those sticks. They're smaller than tongue depressors."

"I'll eat one, and you can eat the other."

"Just push the frozen stuff off with a knife into the sink."

"Those fruit bars are expensive."

"For the love of God, Dwayne." Chaz shook his head. He looked like he might faint.

"Pardon my rudeness, but why is he still here?" Angela stood in the dining room archway. She'd gotten dressed in sweat pants and a robe. Then she noticed Chaz's face. "Good God. What happened to you?"

"Uncle Bull." He lowered his head and breathed like he could hardly speak.

"They broke his index finger with a pair of pliers," Dwayne said.

Angela shook her head. "I love you, Chaz, but you really are the prize winner for winding up in the shit."

"I can't argue with you there." He rearranged the ice around his finger, wincing with every move. Condensation was soaking the table cloth beneath it.

"He expects me to set the bone for him and tape it with popsicle sticks!"

"Oh, yeah. We can do that," Angela said.

Dwayne's head snapped to his wife's direction. "We can?"

"Sure. Uncle Guido and Uncle Paulo were always getting into some kind of jam. I watched my grandmother set broken bones a number of times. There's not much to it."

"Every time I hear another one of these stories," Dwayne said, "it makes your family reunions less inviting."

"Don't be silly. They love you. However, if you ever mess around on me, you won't come through the divorce as easily as Chaz."

"That was easy?" Chaz said.

"It'd be like Bonnie and Uncle Bull combined. And they won't start with something little, like a finger," Angela said while getting two frozen fruit bars out of the freezer. "Who wants the other one?"

"He doesn't want to wait for us to eat them," Dwayne said.

Angela scoffed. "His finger isn't going anywhere." She unwrapped one and started eating it.

"I can't believe this," Chaz moaned.

"I do enjoy these," Dwayne said, unwrapping and eating his.

Angela fixed Chaz with a severe look. "Dwayne says you're still gambling. YOU ARE NEVER GOING TO WIN BACK WHAT YOU OWE!" Angela shouted. "Have you never read a biography of Dostoyevsky?"

"No."

"Read one. Learn something. You've still got a chance to straighten yourself out." She licked the remains of the fruit bar and rinsed off the popsicle stick at the sink. Then she went to the bathroom and came back with first aid tape and grabbed a whiskey bottle from the hutch. She rinsed Dwayne's popsicle stick and poured

Chaz three fingers of cheap bourbon. "Down the hatch."

Chaz gulped down the whiskey and took a deep, wheezy breath. "Jesus," he complained.

"Good." Angela positioned his arm resting on the dining room table with the butt of his hand on the edge and his palm and fingers hanging over. She pushed back his shirt sleeve. "Hold his wrist exactly right there and do not let it move for any reason," she told Dwayne.

"I'm not really comfortable with this," Dwayne said.

"No one requires you to be comfortable," she said.

"Okay." He held it down tightly to the table.

"Hey, that hurts," Chaz said.

"Ignore him," Angela said. "That shows you've got the right amount of pressure. Keep it." She took the end of his finger and pulled, increasing the tension as he began to scream. Dwayne looked frightened, but Angela seemed entirely composed. She pulled a little more, and they all heard a subtle click. Chaz screamed yet louder, then settled into whimpering.

"Okay, good," Angela said. "Good thing we did that. Your bones were not lined up." She aligned the popsicle sticks under his finger and up his palm and taped them into place, and then taped the whole thing to the finger next to it. "That'll do for now," she said. "A tongue depressor would have offered more stability."

"Fuck," Chaz wheezed.

"Okay, good." Angela stood up. "We'll see you soon."

"I can't leave. I was hoping to sleep on your couch."

"Why?" she said.

"Uncle Bull said he'd break a new bone every day."

"He already broke the bone of the day," Angela said. "You're good until tomorrow."

"Tomorrow starts in the morning. I don't want to wake up and find him next to my bed with the pliers!"

"Jesus, Chaz," Dwayne said.

"Listen." He grabbed Dwayne's wrist with his good hand. "He said if you to let Coco play Juliet, I only have to pay back the original loan by the end of the run."

"Coco play Juliet?" Dwayne looked like he'd stepped in shit.

"That's what he said."

"This is beyond me," Angela said. "I'm going to bed." She looked sternly at Dwayne. "Don't be long." She stalked off to the bedroom.

"Can you recast Juliet?" Chaz said.

"No. It's too late for that. Besides, my ensemble would lose its collective mind."

"Yeah. But… Look, can I at least sleep on your couch tonight? I won't make a peep."

"All right," Dwayne said reluctantly. He brought out some spare blankets and set him up in the living room. In the bedroom he found the vintage skeleton key in his dresser and locked the door behind him.

"Is he still out there?" Angela whispered when Dwayne turned toward her. She sat on the bed with her knees up, her eyes glaring toward the unseen living room.

"He's terrified of Bull."

She clutched her curly black hair in both fists and shook it. "I don't want him listening! This is my time, Dwayne. I'm due to drop an egg!"

Dwayne raised a finger, went to the clock radio on the dresser, and turned on the classical station. An orchestra swirled into the opening strains of Bolero. This would not only provide them sonic privacy from Chaz, it would help Dwayne ease into the mood. "Perfect," he said. He turned up the volume, stripped off his apron and clothing, and approached his wife.

"Oh, my clever boy." She giggled as he climbed into the bed with her.

21

Sunday, September 5, 2004

D wayne rushed into rehearsal the next night looking for Coco. Did she know what Uncle Bull demanded of Chaz? When he arrived, however, the parishioners of the Indigenous Connection Church were not only still in the space and extremely high, they were talking in tongues and handling live snakes. Apparently, Dan Darwood took a radically ecumenical approach to ritual. Coco walked in shortly after Dwayne arrived.

"Aw, hell no," she said. "I ain't going to be anywhere there's snakes." And she promptly turned tail and headed back to the stairs. Dwayne pursued her but first he had to get around some gawking actors at the doorway, and then Ingrid blocked his path.

"Say, Dwayne," she said. "I saw Rockwell Nesbit…"

"Excuse me," he said. He darted around the Viking princess and shot down the stairs.

How could Coco have moved so fast? He ran down the two flights of stairs and out into the street. She was nowhere. He came back in, searched the lobby, and even asked one of the other actresses to check the ladies room. No sign of her.

Had Coco put her uncle onto Chaz to get the role of Juliet? Was she still after the lead role? If she'd known Bull was going to break his finger, that was pretty ruthless. After all, Chaz'd been her lover not so long ago. He thought she'd embraced playing the Nurse. She was certainly giving the role an original interpretation. In fact, he kind of loved where she was taking it. It made so much sense, and it was something he never would have imagined. He adored that about directing. You start with a conception for a show, but then all the other creatives bring in their ideas, and the conception expands in ways you'd never predict.

Dwayne stopped on the landing where the stairs turned to the final flight before reaching the third floor, and he was overwhelmed with the realization: He loved theatre. A weird sensation of well-being washed over him. He was directing *Romeo and Juliet*, and he loved it. Why would he feel so good about that right now? A loan shark planned to break a new bone in the body of one of his dearest friends every day. A band of drugged lunatics were handling snakes in his rehearsal space. He didn't know if maybe Coco was deliberately undermining the production to get her way—and no doubt she was skipping this rehearsal. In this context, it was weird to feel so good.

But finding his way through all the chaos: that took every bit of his ingenuity! What else could he be doing that would call on so many parts of his brain? So much thinking-on-the-feet. It was exhilarating.

Stoned hippies and snakes in his workplace! Ha!

He sprinted up the stairs back to the rehearsal room.

On the floor outside, Tom and Orlando sat leaning into each other, smiling and talking, their foreheads nearly touching. Tom looked up. "You know what they've got in there this time?"

"Yep," Dwayne said. He walked into the rehearsal space where Joan was attempting to corral the snakes that slithered all over the floor. Suddenly Dwayne saw it: Dan Darwood was not just using the guise of a church to allow his friends to get high together. He was actually attempting to create a religious experience. It looked weird and chaotic, but Dwayne realized it was totally sincere. (He also knew enough about native fauna to recognize the snakes on the floor were harmless Midwestern garter snakes).

Dwayne knew about ritual. He had grown up with it as an altar boy. He would get up at five a.m. for weeks at a time to go serve at the daily early morning mass. He loved ritual. That's what he loved about theatre. He loved spending weeks crafting the ritual of the play until it was ready to welcome the audience and create the shared experience with them, triggering emotion and thought and catharsis. It was a holy practice and one worthy of passion—a passion that might even bring in mobsters to force the recasting of a show. He didn't want to allow that to happen, but he loved the passion that prompted it.

He began scooping up snakes with Joan and putting them in the snake carrier. He chuckled to himself. These were holy snakes. He looked one in the face. Those little dark eyes. The tongue slipping out at him. He slipped it gently into the carrier.

He felt himself in the presence of Saint Ignatius of Loyola, patron of vocations, founder of the Jesuit order. Theatre was Dwayne's spiritual practice. It was a rigorous discipline, and he rose to the occasion with all the spiritual fortitude of the most dedicated Jesuit.

Dwayne grabbed the last of the squirming reptiles and put it in the carrier. "Now what?" he asked Joan.

"I'm moving all these hippies and their snakes into the upstairs mainstage," she said, taking a lock out of her stage manager kit and locking the snake carrier. She'd give Darwood the key after he sobered up. "Green can sort them out from there."

"Excellent!"

Ingrid was rounding up parishioners like a border collie rounds up a flock of sheep. She herded them toward the door to follow Joan downstairs to the theatre. "Heeyaa!" she cried. The inebriated parishioners looked back at her in fear and alarm as they moved toward the door, like flock animals look at a herd dog.

Dan Darwood approached Dwayne, his pupils alarmingly dilated. He leaned toward Dwayne in a way that Dwayne feared he might fall on him. "I finished reading it! *Romeo and Juliet* is an idolatry of sex and suicide. Romeo loves Rosaline and cannot get over, and then suddenly he loves Juliet, and then they kill themselves. And with this energy you befoul the air of my temple!"

"Then go somewhere else," Dwayne suggested.

"We have consecrated this space," Dan Darwood said. "We are two days into a novena."

"A novena!" Dwayne felt amazed. "You blend a Catholic novena with Pentecostal snake handling and South American ayahuasca drinking? I have to say, I am impressed."

Dan Darwood looked confused. He'd never received any appreciation from anyone outside of his cult. "Thank you," he said uncertainly.

"But I can't call off rehearsals for seven days while you finish your novena."

"You'd better catch up with your flock, parson," Ingrid said, coming back from herding them downstairs into the theatre. "If they let those snakes out down there, they'll crawl under the theatre seats, and you'll never find them again."

Dan Darwood looked alarmed and rushed out of the room.

"Thanks, Ingrid," Dwayne said. "Listen, we have an opportunity to do a special assembly in one of the Chicago Public Schools."

Fran Konacki had liked the packet of reviews Dwayne had sent her and had sent him a contract to be signed for the short performance on October 20. He was holding on to it until he could figure out the details. "The only thing is, they aren't offering any money," he said. "We'd be replacing a company from London that was going to do *Merchant of Venice*. They were getting grant money for it, but they cancelled their Chicago tour."

"Can we get their grant?" Ingrid said.

"No. I made some calls."

"That assembly would be a good thing for us," Ingrid said. "Education programs are a big plus for winning grants. But we don't have the cash to pay the actors for a daytime performance."

"I'd just need Romeo, Juliet, Friar Lawrence and the Nurse." He really wanted to make this work and be the hero for Angela.

"Honestly, Dwayne, we might end up in the red as it is. And then what? You and Joan and I are on the hook for the company's debts." She waited to see if he had anything to say about that.

He didn't.

She headed down the stairs and away.

His extraordinary good mood subsided slightly for a moment—but then he remembered he had a rehearsal ahead of him—and that would be fun!

22

Tuesday, September 7, 2004

Joan looked at her watch in disgust. "Seven fifty-five. They're always here by now."

"What's up?" Dwayne looked up from his notes for the night's rehearsal.

"Neither Orlando nor Melinda are here." She picked up her cell and punched in a number.

That gave Dwayne a jolt of alarm. They were both usually twenty minutes early to do physical and vocal warm-ups.

"Who is this?" Joan said. "Chaz? Why are you answering Melinda's phone?" She looked straight forward, squinted, then closed her eyes. "They are both supposed to be here, right now. You get them here immediately." She looked at Dwayne, actually looked him straight in the eye, an event that truly shocked Dwayne. Had she ever looked him straight in the eye before?

"No. No." She looked straight forward again. "No. NO." She held out her phone in front of her. "He hung up on me," she said to it.

"What's going on?"

"Chaz has got Melinda and Orlando at an event for Aleister's book launch. They are doing a scene from the show, and then Aleister will do a reading and talk. Chaz said he'd bring them back as soon as they finish their scene."

"Fuck. Where are they?"

"The Book Cellar. Lincoln Square."

"At least they're not out in the suburbs somewhere."

But what to do without Romeo and Juliet? His pulse began racing. He scanned the spreadsheet with the actor/scene breakdown.

There was really almost nothing without one or the other of them in it.

"He said they'll be here by seven forty-five at the latest."

Dwayne called Tom over. "We aren't going to have Orlando and Melinda for forty-five minutes. Could you do the top of Act Three? Are you ready to choreograph the sword fight?"

Tom moaned. "That's supposed to be on Thursday."

"I know. I'm sorry, but we are missing our leads, and we can't afford to waste this rehearsal time."

"You're killing me, Dwayne. Romeo is in that. His interference gets me stabbed," he said, identifying himself with his role as Mercutio.

"I know. I'm sorry. I'll stand in for Romeo."

Tom groaned again and closed his eyes. He took a deep breath and settled himself. "Okay. It's not like I haven't pictured that fight a thousand times in my mind."

Joan announced the schedule change amid complaints from those who had been called to rehearse at seven but now would not be needed until seven forty-five. Many of them went out into the hall to work on memorization. Coco, who had groaned the loudest, stayed in the room to watch the fight choreography. She picked up one of the rehearsal swords and brandished it. "When are you going to give me a role where I can fight with a sword?" she asked Dwayne. "I got all this training, but I never get the role."

"We'll see what we can do," Dwayne said. He still hadn't had a chance to question her about Uncle Bull.

"Yeah, right. I ought to quit this company and go join *Babes with Blades*."

"You know we love you here," Dwayne said. He helped Tom prepare the stage for the scene.

Dwayne blocked the opening of the scene until it came to the sword fight with Mercutio and Tybalt, then Tom took over and Dwayne stood in for Romeo. Since Tom was also playing Mercutio, he was able to work through the moves with his opponent faster than usual. The climax of the fight came when Romeo pushed between the fighters, trying to get them to stop. He had just secretly married Juliet and now Tybalt, unknown to anyone, was now his cousin by marriage. With Romeo blocking Mercutio's view, Tybalt was able to fatally stab Mercutio from under Romeo's arm.

"All right, all right, all right," came a booming voice. "Stop the action." Rocky stood in the doorway, imposing as always but also looking slightly unsteady on his feet. He wasn't scheduled for rehearsal. "I want to know about the casting change."

"What's that?" Dwayne said.

"I'm talking about my daughter Coco!" he said. "When are you putting her in as Juliet?"

"Pops, what are you talking about?" Coco said.

She looked absolutely startled. So, she hadn't been conspiring with her uncle. That was good.

"You told Melinda that you should be playing Juliet," he said. "We need to make things right."

Dwayne walked up to Rocky and Coco. He could smell whiskey on his breath.

"Pops, this is an ensemble. It's not my turn to play the lead. I had a lead last time. I'll have a lead next time."

Dwayne was heartened to hear her say it. As unreasonable as she could sometimes be, she really did get it.

"No, no, no, no, no, no, no," Rocky said. "You are obviously the better actress. And more beautiful. Any Romeo falls a lot faster for you than for that skinny white girl." He gave a loud guffaw. Dwayne was glad Melinda was not back yet. "No damn contest." He turned to Dwayne. "What's it going to be Finnegan?"

"We aren't changing anything, Rocky."

"No, no, no, no, no, no, no. It don't mean a thing if it ain't got that swing. And this *ain't got that swing.* I've done two hundred fifty-some television commercials, and I am ready for the role."

Anyone in Chicagoland who had ever turned on late night television on virtually any local broadcast channel had seen Rocky's television commercials. He'd become so successful, he didn't even practice law anymore. He had other lawyers to do that. Some of them were even good at litigating. But his company's reputation was such that most defendants settled before the case ever came to court, and the money kept rolling in. So much money that Rocky kept his daughter on a generous allowance. She had a nice apartment and a car and paid her bills without needing a day job like most actors.

"So the best idea is to put Coco in as Juliet..." Here he leaned forward toward Dwayne for emphasis, but had to catch himself off-balance. "Put Coco in as Juliet...and me as ROMEO!" he said grandly.

"Oh, Pops, for the love of God!" Coco said.

"What?" Rocky looked shocked at her objection.

"You are I are NOT going to play Romeo and Juliet."

"Why the hell not? You wanted to act together. We don't even have a scene together now."

"No. No. No." Coco stood with her hands on her hips.

"You think I can't do Romeo?" He chuckled to himself. "You know, after I'd been doing the commercials for...I don't know how many years...I met the director of one of the *Rocky* movies. *Rocky Five*? I forget which one. You know how we used the *Rocky* theme in the commercials? *We fight for you!*" He laughed to himself. "He told me I was just as good an actor as Sylvester Stallone! *Sylvester Stallone!*"

"Pops, it's just gross! I'm your daughter."

"This is acting! You think people will not be impressed?"

"People will..." She couldn't even complete the sentence. "*I* would be totally grossed out. No. No way. You are not playing Romeo with me as Juliet. That is never, never, *ever* going to happen!"

Rocky looked like some internal pressure was building inside him. Everyone in the room could see it.

"Well, then," he said in a quiet tone that sent shivers up and down Dwayne's spine. "You can keep playing the Nurse. You can play the fucking Nurse for the rest of your miserable life!"

Just as he turned, Chaz came into the room with Melinda and Orlando. When he saw Rocky, his eyes widened, and he immediately shrunk back against the wall.

"You!" Rocky shouted on seeing him. Then he made a loud, growling, disgusted sound in his throat, waved at Chaz dismissively, and stormed out of the room.

"Pops!" Coco shouted. She ran out after him.

"Oh my God," Chaz said. "Did he come here looking for me?"

"For you?" Dwayne said. "No. He wanted to play Romeo and Coco to play Juliet. Obviously, she didn't want to play lovers with her dad."

"Her dad?" Chaz said. "That wasn't her dad. That was Uncle Bull."

"That was her dad. Rocky," Dwayne said. "He's been playing Lord Montague."

"No, no! Nobody forgets the face of the man who broke their finger with a pair of pliers." Chaz held up his bandaged hand. "I can tell you without a shadow of a doubt that that was Uncle Bull!"

23

Wednesday, September 8, 2004

The next morning Dwayne was awakened by knocking. He got out of bed and was greeted at the door by a messenger handing him a cease-and-desist letter from the law firm of Baker, Drumwell & Connors.

Apparently Baker, Drumwell & Connors was taking exception to the practice of the Psychedelic Dream Theatre polluting the consecrated worship space of Dan Darwood's Indigenous Connection Church. This pollution had advanced to such an egregious degree that the lawful practice of the religious rites of the Indigenous Connection Church had become impossible. Not only had the lawful practice of its religious rites become impossible, severe emotional and psychic harm had been inflicted upon the practitioners. Should the Psychedelic Dream Theatre choose to immediately and permanently vacate the consecrated worship space of the Indigenous Connection Church, no further action would be taken. However, should the Psychedelic Dream Theatre choose to continue its activities in said space, Baker, Drumwell & Connors would begin immediate action in a suit for damages including lost rental payments, emotional and psychic harm, inconvenience, and costs. No communication with Baker, Drumwell & Connors was invited. Only the immediate removal of the Psychedelic Dream Theatre properties and persons from the worship space would be acceptable.

"St. Yves, patron of lawyers, pray for me," he said.

"What's that?"

Dwayne screamed, startled by the sudden male voice behind him. He'd forgotten that Chaz had slept on his couch again, hiding out from Uncle Bull. He handed him the cease-and-desist letter.

"You scream like a little girl," Chaz said. He sat down on the couch and read it over, chuckling.

Dwayne went into the kitchen and came back with two mugs of black coffee. Angela had already been up and left for school. She always left the remains of a pot behind for him. He handed one of the mugs to Chaz.

"They couldn't really sue us over this, could they?" Dwayne asked.

"Having been married to a hotshot lawyer until recently, I can tell you that people will sue over any little thing that comes into their heads. That doesn't mean they can win. However, if you don't hire a lawyer to defend you against even the most frivolous of suits, you could find yourself in hot water. Even a baseless nuisance suit can end up being expensive."

Dwayne's cell rang. It was Ingrid. A messenger came knocking on the door of her van to deliver her a cease-and-desist letter, as well. They decided to meet at the theatre to discuss. Dwayne promised to bring along a thermos of coffee and a couple bagels.

As he exited the CTA station at Fullerton to walk down to the Chicago Repertory Arts Playhouse, Dwayne saw a familiar young woman in a homespun gown that would have looked biblical had not been tie-dyed. Messy dark hair obscured much of her face. "Pearl?" he said.

"Who are you?" she responded, pushing some of the hair behind her ears.

"Dwayne Finnegan. I direct the theatre company that uses the same rehearsal room as your church."

"Oh, right," she said. "Sorry. I don't always remember people I meet around the times of our...rituals."

This did not surprise Dwayne. "Did you know that Dan Darwood is threatening to sue us?"

She giggled a little. "Yeah. He does that. He's funny."

"You mean it's just a joke?" Dwayne asked.

"Oh no." She straightened up and looked him in the face. "No. He's very serious about all that. I mean, I just find it cute how serious he is. It makes me laugh sometimes. You know how that is." Her gaze wandered off to the underside of the train viaduct above them. "Some people are so serious about some things, and you really have to wonder. What's up? Why so serious? I mean. Why?"

Dwayne wondered what Pearl might be serious about.

"Mr. Darwood said you and Armageddon had detected *bad vibes* that we put in the space," Dwayne said.

Pearl began giggling once more. "*Mr.* Darwood." She giggled some more.

"No one calls him Mister, I suppose," Dwayne said.

"Not him. Not Danny. You've never met *Mister Darwood.* That's something else." Pearl pointed at him meaningfully. Dwayne was beginning to suspect this conversation was not going to get him anywhere.

"Right. Danny said it. But I was wondering why you and Armageddon thought our vibes were interfering with your rituals."

"Danny said *I* said that?"

"He said you and Armageddon were very sensitive to these *vibes.*"

"Oh. Oh," Pearl said, stretching out the vowels as she came to understand. "Yeah. It's just..." She leaned in toward him. "Don't tell anyone this, but Armageddon *scares* me. I just kind of agree with whatever she says, because it seems to go better that way."

"Ah," Dwayne said. "I looked up this law firm. Baker, Drumwell & Connors. It's a huge firm. I was surprised they represent your church. They specialize in corporate law."

"Oh, yeah," Pearl said. "That's because of *Mister.* Danny's dad. He'll do anything for Danny. You know, most churches ask for money from their people. Money in the collection plate, or everyone pools all their money, or whatever. Nobody in our church pays anything. Danny even covers personal expenses for Army and me, because *Mister* will do anything for him."

"Huh," Dwayne said. "So it's his father's law firm?"

"I don't know," Pearl said. "But *Mister* is where the money comes from." And without another word her head turned and then she turned and then she drifted west on Fullerton Avenue.

Dwayne entered the Playhouse to find Ingrid already there. She and Dwayne attempted to call Baker, Drumwell & Connors to discuss the cease-and-desist letter. However, the letter had been signed *Baker, Drumwell & Connors* rather than the name of any individual at the firm, so the receptionist was not able to put them through to anyone helpful. They also found out there was no one with the name of Darwood at the firm, so the famous *Mister* was not employed there.

In any case, they did not intend to cease or desist.

24

Later the Same Day

Chaz had scheduled a book launch event before the rehearsal that night. Chaz and Aleister walked over after the event with Melinda and Orlando to say hello. When Rocky saw them, he shouted: "You!"

"Bull!" Chaz said. "Listen, we are going to work something out…"

"That's not Bull," Dwayne said. "That's Rocky."

"If that's Rocky then they look *exactly* alike," Chaz said.

"Oh, so you're one of those racist assholes who think all black people look alike?" Rocky grabbed Chaz by the throat and began shaking him as Chaz screamed. And then everyone was screaming and trying, completely ineffectually, to get him off Chaz.

Coco arrived at that moment and ran up and grabbed his arm.

"Pops! Pops! What the hell are you doing? Let him go!"

"I'm not your Pops!" he said, giving her barely a glance and continuing to throttle Chaz.

Coco backed off for a moment, her face registering shock and panic, then realization, acceptance, and determination. She grabbed his shoulder firmly again. "Uncle Bull," she said firmly. "You have to let him go. You don't want to fuck this up."

He looked at her in surprise. "Fuck this up? This fuckup took my money." He let go of Chaz who fell to the floor and scurried away. The big man straightened up to address Coco directly while Chaz coughed and choked and tried to get back his breath on the other side of the room. "He didn't pay his debt. He didn't pay the vig. He didn't deliver anything when I give him an alternative."

While Bull wasn't looking, Dwayne pulled Chaz away and

pushed him out of the room.

"You need to relax, Uncle Bull," Coco told him intently. "Bad things can happen."

He looked deeply confused.

"I know you love me, Uncle Bull," Coco said calmly. "You know I love you. Can you sit down for me?"

"You don't have to get all emotional," he muttered, sitting down. "I'm just doing business."

"You moved on from that business," Coco reminded him. "Now you get all the money you need from the law firm."

"I do?"

"Yeah," Coco reminded him. "It brings in so much money, it pays my rent and expenses. It covers Mommy. It covers Pops. It takes care of us all."

"Yeah…" That seemed vaguely familiar to him.

Coco moved over to Aleister and leaned in to him. "Can you help get my dad back to himself?" she said quietly. "Sometimes he forgets to take his meds. He drops into this old identity."

"Does he have other alternate personalities?" Aleister asked.

Coco looked startled. "No. Just Uncle Bull. And Pops. I mean, himself."

"I'll do what I can," Aleister said. Dwayne was amazed how calm he looked. Dwayne's heart was racing. The rest of the cast had moved away to the far corner of the room.

"You like to be called Bull?" Aleister asked him.

"Who the hell are you?" Bull stood up tall and threatening.

"I'm George Aleister, a psychiatrist. Coco asked me to help you come to a calm place. Would that be okay?"

He looked confused and then suddenly panicked. "I'm just trying to get what's right." He looked around for Chaz. "I can't let people cheat. News gets around."

"Absolutely," Aleister agreed. "Why don't we get to a calm place, and then we can figure out how to deal with that. I know where that guy lives."

"Oh." That sounded helpful. "Okay."

"Just have a seat in this chair," Aleister suggested. He made a quick gesture to Tom who brought over the most comfortable chair in the room. Bull settled into it. Aleister took a folding chair and sat across from Bull. Coco put her hands on her uncle's shoulders. "This is good, Uncle Bull," she said. He smiled up at her, still looking a bit confused.

Ingrid stood to the side, looking like she wanted to take charge of something, but she didn't know what to do.

"Okay," Aleister said gently, "now just close your eyes." He was gratified to see Bull follow his instruction. "Imagine your eyes are floating in water in your eye sockets. Just floating gently relaxed." He waited to see Bull relax into this first suggestion. Then he had him relax different parts of his body, one by one, until he looked fully physically relaxed throughout his body.

Across the room, Melinda went to say something to Ry, but Dwayne stopped them. Wallace leaned over to whisper in Coco's ear: "Great stuff for my memoir…" but she flicked a sharp knuckle to his forehead. He looked shocked and pained, and closed his mouth.

"Now I want you to see a stairway going down before you. With every step downward you are descending deeper into your most essential self. Your true self. Your calm and centered self. Go ahead at your own speed, step by step, and tell me when you reach the bottom at that very calm and centered space."

Aleister waited, looking very calm himself. Bull looked like he was on some journey to the center of his mind. After a time, he said: "I'm there."

"Without opening your eyes, look around," Aleister said. "Where are you?"

"It's my bedroom when I was a little boy," he said, his voice sounding far away.

"And who are you?" Aleister said.

"I'm Rocky. Rockwell Nesbit the Third."

The people in the room stirred with excitement. They looked like they wanted to burst into applause. Dwayne held up both hands to keep them quiet.

"I want you to hold onto to who you are, Rocky," Aleister said. "And when you are ready, walk back up those stairs, and tell me when you reach the top."

Aleister brought him gently back to the reality of the room, and when he was fully aware of himself and his surroundings, he was still firmly in his identity of Rockwell Nesbit III. Coco gave her father a huge hug. "You've got to stay on your meds, Pops," she whispered. "Uncle Bull could ruin everything. He could get you disbarred."

"One more thing I want to help you with," Aleister said. He signaled Dwayne to bring Chaz back into the room. "This guy owes you money." Chaz looked like he wanted to run back out of the room. "He went through a horrible divorce. He got in over his head gambling. He owes you money, but he's got none."

"He borrowed money from Bull and didn't pay?" Rocky said.

"That's right, Pops," Coco said.

"Not acceptable," Rocky said.

"No," Aleister agreed. "However, I understand you run a large law firm. This guy is a top public relations man. He's worked for McDonald's Corporate. He's handling the launch of my new book, just out from Random House. He's a two-hundred-dollar-an-hour man," he said. "I suggest you have him work off his debt. The return on investment for your firm will be worth way more than the cash he borrowed."

"Huh," Rocky said. "We get plenty of business from late night advertising, but I'd be curious what P.R. could do."

"Why don't you two talk tomorrow?" said Aleister. "Meanwhile, Chaz and I will go have dinner and leave you all to your rehearsal."

Aleister got a generous round of applause as he and Chaz and Ingrid left. Rocky stood looking bewildered for a moment, then walked over to Joan on his way out of the room. "I'm going home to lie down," he said. She nodded approvingly.

25

Yet Later the Same Day

Angela met Dwayne at the door when he arrived home. "Lock the door," she said. "Bolt it. Double lock it. The signs are clear. I'm ovulating today. I don't want Chaz in here messing up my vibes."

Suddenly everyone was worried about *vibes*.

"Don't worry. He's staying with Aleister tonight." Dwayne dumped his shoulder bag with his script on one of the couches. "It looks like the Uncle Bull thing might be resolved."

"Thank God. I've seen more than enough of Chaz for a while."

"It's quite a story…"

Angela gave him a huge, but slightly impatient, smile. "Great. But I don't need to hear it right now. Come with me, sir." She led him into the bedroom.

"I know I'm not Bonnie's favorite person right now, but you've stayed good friends. Do you think she'd do a favor for the theatre company if you asked her?"

"What?" Angela looked at him with hands on hips and eyebrows lifted.

"Yeah. You know that goofy church might want to sue us. They can't win, but we need to have a lawyer to make it go away, and we can't afford one. I know it's not the kind of law she does, but maybe she knows someone who does pro bono."

"Why are you talking about this now?" She looked at him impatiently.

"It's just on my mind."

"Just…get your clothes off and get into bed. This is why you have an executive director." She began discarding her clothing.

Dwayne began unbuttoning his shirt.

"Well, Ingrid is your woman if you need to find day-old bread. She's not so hot at finding pro bono lawyers."

"Dwayne, for the love of God." She discarded her underpants and climbed under the sheet. A CTA train rolled by, filling the room with its racket through the open window. A breeze lifted the closed drapes slightly.

"No. Right." He finished undressing and climbed in on the other side of the bed. "It's just...well, if the company gets sued, the court can come after our assets."

"What the fuck, Dwayne."

"Yeah. Yeah. Sorry."

He scooted over to her and awkwardly put his arms around her. She reached a hand down. "What's the matter with Mr. Pecker?"

"Hey. We just got in here," Dwayne said.

"This is my ovulation day," Angela said. "My cervical fluid looked like raw egg white, I had a slight decrease in basal temperature, my breasts felt tender, and I'm feeling an increased sex drive."

"Okay..." Dwayne said uncertainly.

"Come on, Dwayne! This is serious. "I get home from school, and I'm taking all these measurements. You think that's what I like to do? Like suddenly my body is some kind of chemistry set? And then today I might have the winning ticket, but I have to wait until almost eleven o'clock for you to get home when I like to be in bed at nine o'clock because I get up so damned early. But I have to wait because I need your sperm. And you come in talking nonsense about your theatre company."

He sat up on the bed. "Hey, Angela. I'm sorry you had to wait, but I don't know why you're so worried. We haven't been trying all that long."

Suddenly Angela looked ashamed. "That's not entirely true," she said.

"What do you mean?"

She pulled her pillow up against the headboard of the bed and leaned back against it. She pulled the sheet up to cover her breasts. "I mean I stopped taking the pill a year ago."

"You did?" Dwayne turned, cross-legged on the bed to face her.

"I thought I'd stop taking the pill, and I'd get knocked up just in the normal course of making love, and I'd present it to you as a wonderful surprise. Hurrah." She waved her fingers in the air in a limp pretense of celebration. "But a year went by with no baby, and I started to think that we'd have to take extra measures. So, I brought it up when we were on vacation in Italy. I had no idea you were going to be weird about it. And now here we are, and we still aren't pregnant, and now I'm ovulating today, but what are we doing? Are we having fun making a baby? No. We're sitting here talking."

They sat in silence for a while.

"You went off the pill and didn't tell me?" Dwayne said. He felt betrayed.

"I thought it would be like a fun surprise. That you'd be happy. I never imagined you'd be all weird about it."

"I'm being weird?" He shook his head. He took a deep breath. He got out of the bed and stood by the door. "This is something huge, Angela. Having a baby is not like having a surprise birthday party. It's...like buying a house. You wouldn't do that without talking to me. Actually, it's bigger than that, really. It's really big."

"What? Now you're going to be mad? You're going to get mad and not be able to get it up?"

"Jesus, Angela. That's a really shitty thing to say." He pulled on his robe. "I'm going to need a minute." He walked into the dining room and poured himself a stiff brandy.

26

Thursday, September 9, 2004

All right. This is a problem. At the end of the next night's rehearsal Dwayne was reading out from his notes. "Romeo, Juliet, act one, scene five." He looked up to make sure he had Orlando and Melinda's attention. *How do we solve this?* "That first moment when your eyes meet: I want to see a bigger reaction. Maybe even take a step back as this vision hits your eye. It needs something. This is the most famous love-at-first-sight in all of literature. The audience must feel it. And Ry, can we have something musically to underscore that moment? Something from your guitar?" Ry nodded and made a note.

"Yeah, good point," Wallace said. "Melinda, you've got a long way to come here. I don't believe you are in love with Romeo at all." Several of the actors looked at Wallace in confusion. "It almost looks like you are standoffish towards him because he's black," Wallace continued, "and that's really not going to work."

Melinda looked at Wallace in amazement and hurt. "Are you saying I look racist?"

"Hey, hang on a minute here," Dwayne said sharply. "Wallace, what are you doing?"

"I'm giving notes," he said, looking innocent. Orlando blew air through his lips.

"No, no, no," Dwayne said. "If you have any suggestions about the show, you tell *me*. You don't start giving notes to other actors. You know that." A few of the actors nodded along with this.

"I know it's not usually the thing," Wallace admitted. "But I'm not getting anywhere with writing my memoir, so I thought I'd try my hand at directing. I just wanted to test my acumen at giving notes."

"This is not your show to direct," Dwayne said. He hated to reprimand Wallace in front of everyone, but he needed the rest of the cast to feel secure.

"Yes, well…" Wallace looked up at the ceiling. "You know how it is." He looked around at his castmates with a pitiful expression. "You get to my age and you start to think: what is my impact on the culture? Time is running out. I thought maybe a memoir, but I'm no writer. So maybe I'd direct? It was just something…you know…." He looked intensely at Melinda. "But, say, did you find the note useful?"

Melinda was looking at him with a deer-in-the-headlights expression.

"Wallace, no," Dwayne insisted. "These actors are your ensemble mates. If someone *asks* for advice, so be it. But to start giving notes when they aren't requested undermines the trust. Okay?" This was something Dwayne always believed, but it was also, he suddenly realized, one of Madeline Forthright's six basic truisms of winners: *Don't work harder, work smarter, work united.* Everyone needed to be able to trust one another to win together.

Which seemed to him what Angela had violated by going off the pill and not telling him. She was trying to get a Win for herself without making sure it was also a Win for him.

"Right, right, right," Wallace said. He launched into a story about how an older actor had helped him find his way when he was in his twenties. Dwayne didn't cut him off. He didn't want him to feel ashamed. Just like *he* didn't want to feel ashamed with Angela. Sure, she made most of the money, but he worked hard, too. It's not like he'd tricked her into thinking he was a well-paid architect before they got married. She knew what she was getting into.

Why would she have kept it from him? That was not *working smarter* or *working harder*. It certainly wasn't making his dick any harder.

He had a sudden memory of watching one of the old *Thin Man* movies with Angela. Somewhere near the end Nora reveals she is pregnant, and Nick is surprised and extremely pleased. At that moment in the film Angela said, *Aww*, and snuggled up to him on the couch. That was the moment she was hoping for, wasn't it? He was supposed to be like Nick, surprised and happy that they were having baby. Instead, when she announced she wanted to make a baby in romantic Italy, he hadn't been able to get it up.

That's not what would have happened if she'd been married to Nick Charles.

Wallace finished his tale and sat back down.

"And by the way, I am not racist," Melinda insisted. "I personally think Orlando is incredibly good-looking. It's just that Orlando is so *gay.*"

"Wait a minute!" Orlando said loudly. "I have played the *straight* love interest in several shows. I do not *read* to the audience as gay." The other actors perked up further and a few of them started giggling.

"Okay, thank you, everyone," Dwayne said, looking to contain the situation. "Melinda and Orlando, let's talk just the three of us at the end of notes, okay?"

Why did this *have to get extra complicated?*

And then Dan Darwood, Armageddon, and Pearl burst into the room and began chanting some pseudo-indigenous mumbo jumbo. Pearl sang in a gratingly high pitch tone, Armageddon covered the alto, and Dan Darwood did something very low pitch, like Inuit throat-singing, all the while playing a wooden beater on a large rawhide frame drum. They swirled around the room, dancing. Pearl and Armageddon each had an abalone shell in one hand with some kind of burning resin in it, and the wing tip of a large bird in the other, waving smoke in all directions around the room and at the actors. Some of the actors shouted complaints and moved away when the priestesses came near them.

"Hold on, hold on," Dwayne shouted. He tried to block Darwood from coming any farther into the room.

Suddenly the room filled with an ear-splitting blast and when it stopped there was silence. Everyone looked at the source of the sound. Joan stood atop a table, with an aerosol horn in her hand.

"We will brook no interference in our rehearsals," she said quietly, looking directly at Darwood, Armageddon, and Pearl in turn. Dwayne was impressed. He knew it took her an effort to look any other human in the eye.

"That's it," Dwayne said to the three. "Out." He looked at his watch. There were only ten minutes left of their scheduled rehearsal. There was no way to get back to sensible communication in that time. "Okay, everyone, I'm going to email the rest of my notes to you individually. And unless Joan has something, you are all released. But Melinda and Orlando, please hang in a minute." He looked expectantly at Joan.

"Dismissed," she affirmed. They all began clearing out.

Dwayne moved Orlando and Melinda to a far corner of the space. "I'm not seeing the deep and instant attraction between the two of you. I'm not seeing Romeo and Juliet emerge. Somehow you need to find that chemistry. I recommend we schedule an additional meeting for the three of us to work."

Orlando took a deep breath and looked over at the windows. Melinda shook her head and laid a hand on Dwayne's forearm. "I know we aren't there yet." She put her other hand on Orlando's arm. "I really want to make this work. I know Orlando does, too. I'd like to try a session with just the two of us first. Break through whatever's holding us back." She looked at Orlando. "Does that sound all right with you?"

"Yeah. Yeah!" he said. "We'll figure it out, Dwayne. Absolutely."

"Great. And if you need help, that's what I'm here for. I'll make myself available whenever it works for you." He glanced over at Darwood and company. "I need to talk with you about a possible school performance, too. We can discuss that later." They nodded.

Then he moved on to Dan Darwood as his leads gathered their things and left.

"What the hell are you doing?"

"I was doing you a favor," Darwood said, looking extremely put out. "I saw you had not yet ceased-and-desisted from polluting our worship space. We came to purify your group to end the pollution of our vibes. Then we could both inhabit this space without interfering with one another." He swung his right arm out to gesture to the room in disgust. "But rather than let us remedy this situation, you insulted us, and that woman assaulted our eardrums. Those damages will be added to what we demand in court. Good day to you, sir!" Darwood turned sharply and strode out of the room, followed by his priestesses, Pearl bringing up the rear and looking back somewhat apologetically.

"What a bunch of lunatics," Joan said to no one in particular. Did she mean Darwood and company, or did she include Dwayne and the cast, as well?

27

Tuesday, September 14, 2004

The next day, Dwayne couldn't get Nick and Nora out of his thoughts. Nick Charles: he was what men were supposed to be. Mature men, ready to step up to the real business of life. (But maybe with fewer martinis.) He felt disappointed in himself. Why couldn't he embrace Angela's desire and go wholeheartedly toward making this baby? He'd been doing his best to not think about his career when they were making love, but that didn't seem good enough.

Finding out she'd been secretly trying to get pregnant for a year felt like a betrayal, but what if she truly believed he would have been surprised and delighted? He didn't feel betrayed when she'd thrown him a surprise birthday party. If she'd expected him to be equally surprised and delighted by a pregnancy, that wouldn't be a betrayal from her point of view.

There was the rub. Had she withheld the information so he'd get a delightful surprise? Or had she withheld it because she feared he would resist?

That was the question.

When she got home from school, he received no enlightenment. She barely talked to him. Even as they ate dinner, she uttered only monosyllables. Last night he'd come home after rehearsal and attempted to make love with her, but she'd refused. They'd already missed their chance, according to her. You had the days leading up to ovulation and the day of. After that, you had to wait another month.

He pleaded with her. Was she totally sure about that? Couldn't the egg be waiting around for an extra day?

She'd have none of it. On a hot night in August, he'd gotten the cold shoulder. He hated when she was mad at him.

"Angela Monica Guiseppelli Finnegan?" Dwayne sang to her, attempting to bring some life to the dinner table. Soon he'd have to leave for the theatre. He didn't want to go like this.

"Don't call me Finnegan," she said dourly.

"Angela Monica," he crooned to her. "Next month is another month."

"Is it though, Dwayne?" She put her fork back noisily on the table, a fragment of mashed potato flying off the surface. "What if something is wrong with me? Or with you? What if you are shooting blanks? What if I have bad eggs? I don't know why I'm not pregnant already. In six months I'm going to be thirty years old. My mother had three kids by the time she was thirty. You hit thirty, your fertility starts to shrivel up like an old prune."

"That doesn't happen until you are forty."

"So now you're an expert, Doctor Finnegan?" she said in high outrage. "You've been reading up? Doing the research?"

"Well…no." Dwayne felt his mashed potatoes and sautéed chicken go rolling unpleasantly in his stomach.

"No. You haven't." She picked up her dinner plate and took it into the second bedroom to the table they shared as a desk. She slammed the door behind her.

That hadn't gone very well.

Dwayne jumped at a sharp knock at the door. He opened it to discover Chaz, which did nothing to lift his spirits.

"Hey, I've got really good news." Chaz looked inappropriately cheerful.

"Do you have your car?" Dwayne said.

"Sure."

"You can drive me to the theatre and tell me on the way." He wanted nothing so much as to get out of that apartment.

"Okay."

Dwayne pointed at one of the sofas in the living room, and Chaz sat down to wait, looking perplexed at Dwayne's obviously sour mood, while Dwayne put the dinner leftovers in the refrigerator and the dishes in the sink.

He tapped cautiously on the second bedroom door.

"What?" Her voice sounded curt.

"I need to grab my bag with my script."

"Come in." Her voice had a frosty bite to it. She did not look at him when he came in. He grabbed his shoulder bag from next to the table and made sure it had everything he needed.

"Chaz is here. He's going to give me a ride to the theatre."

"He's not sleeping here tonight." She still didn't look at him.

"No."

She said nothing more.

"All right then. I'll see you later," he said.

"Maybe." She still didn't look at him.

"I left the dishes in the sink. I'll wash them later."

"If they're in my way in the morning, you'll find them in the trash."

"Okay." He waited a moment. She still didn't look at him. He gave up and left.

"Things not okay?" Chaz asked as they walked down the stairs.

"No." He couldn't bring himself to say more until they were in the car. Then he let Chaz know what was happening as they drove south on Broadway.

"Obviously, I'm not an expert on marriage, but I would suggest, whatever you do, just because she's not sleeping with you right now, don't think you can sleep with someone else."

Dwayne glared at Chaz like he was completely stupid. "Do you think I'm completely stupid?"

"You mean like me?" Chaz looked momentarily miserable. He still missed Bonnie horribly.

Dwayne shook his head. "Even if I thought that was okay, one of her Sicilian uncles would kill me. Or worse."

"Maybe having a divorce attorney wife was the lesser of evils," Chaz said. "But you and Angela are great. You'll work it out."

His phone rang. He attempted to answer it, but a loud buzz came out of its speaker. He hung it up. "Ingrid did something to my phone to record the book launch event with Melinda and Orlando. It's been acting weird ever since then."

"Letting Ingrid play with your phone might not have been a great decision."

"She wanted to create some kind of podcast, which I thought was a good idea. But, hey, I have some actually good news." He pulled around a corner on Sheridan Road onto the entrance to Lake Shore Drive and accelerated around the curve to send them south toward the center of the city. It was a beautiful evening and the air conditioning in Chaz's car blew cool air into their faces. A stiff breeze stirred up white caps on the lake to their left and the skyline lay ahead, lights just starting to come on in the skyscraper windows. It was all beautiful, but Dwayne could feel no joy.

"I spent some time dogging the people at Baker, Drumwell & Connors," Chaz said. "Nobody there wrote that cease-and-desist letter. Baker, Drumwell & Connors represents Darwood Energy, which mines coal and drills for oil and gas. The Darwoods are old, old money. I found one junior lawyer who spilled the beans for me. I got him drunk on some single malt scotch at Delilah's. It turns out Dan Darwood is an embarrassment to the family. They give him an allowance to stay out of their hair. Baker, Drumwell & Connors has dealt with his legal problems in the past. Hush money traded hands. Apparently there's *lots* of money. Darwood Energy never went public, so all that cash is in family hands."

"Huh," Dwayne said.

"Being the good P.R. man that I am, I contacted the P.R. firm that handles Darwood Energy. I told them I was working on a story about how the scion of Darwood Energy was persecuting a not-for-profit theatre company and impersonating the company's law firm to intimidate them. Would the family like to make a comment? It turns out the Darwoods don't like publicity. They don't want the world to know about Danny and his weird cult. They wanted the story to go away. I told them publicity from the story would help ticket sales. Burying the story would be a financial loss for a struggling not-for-profit theatre company. Well, happily for us all, the Darwood family also administers the Darwood Foundation, which had never yet given to an arts nonprofit. They've focused on cancer and lung disease so as to give back toward the problems their products create. But now they are giving a generous donation to the Psychedelic Dream Theatre. Rather than cease-and-desist, we are getting release-and-assist."

"Wow," Dwayne said. "Not a great pun, but very good news." He took a deep breath. His chest still felt just as heavy. He could not feel the enthusiasm this news deserved.

"Yeah," Chaz said. "So don't cheer too loudly. It's not like I didn't work my ass off for your benefit."

"No, it's just..."

"I know." Chaz lay his hand on his friend's forearm. "It's hard to feel happy when Angela has kicked you out of bed."

28

Later the Same Day

Dwayne walked into the rehearsal room and sat down next to Joan at the director's table. He still had the problem of two lead actors with no chemistry—an absolute disaster for the world's greatest love story. He was surprised to see Chaz run in, out of breath, right after he'd dropped Dwayne off at the curb.

"Sorry, I forgot I need to clear some dates with you. I'm setting up some more readings for Aleister's book launch, and I'd like to use Orlando and Melinda." Chaz looked at Joan. "You have the schedule, right?"

"Of course I have the schedule," she said, looking into blank air in front of her.

"Good," Chaz said. "It's this coming Thursday in Evanston and the following Thursday in Winnetka, both at seven o'clock."

"Absolutely not," Dwayne said.

"They aren't available," Joan agreed.

"You didn't even look at the schedule," Chaz complained.

"I can see the schedule in my head," Joan said. "I know where Evanston is. I know where Winnetka is."

Chaz turned to Dwayne. "We're raising a lot of interest for the show. Giving out fliers. We're selling more *Romeo and Juliet* tickets than books. The people love those two."

"They are pretty." Joan's monotone made her statement sound like an insult.

"Pretty?" Chaz said. "They're *magnetic*."

Joan raised her eyebrows and got up to move props and furniture into place.

Chaz turned back to Dwayne and lowered his voice. "Melinda's beauty sells tickets. You know that! Even her breasts move with an expectancy which makes one long to cup them in one's hands."

"For the love of God." Dwayne looked around to see if anyone had overheard. "Could you please remember that Aleister helped her deal with the trauma of rape during our last show," he whispered. "It really doesn't do to objectify her."

"No. Sorry. Absolutely." He closed his eyes and took a deep breath. "Ever since Coco dumped me and Bonnie divorced me, I've been a little…." He looked weirdly lost and backed away. "I'm such a fucking idiot," he said to himself. He looked back at Dwayne and forced himself back to the topic. "I'm just saying it's good for the show and good for Aleister's book to have the actors appear at these events."

"It's not going to be good for the show if I don't have these actors ready for opening," Dwayne said.

"How am I supposed to promote this show if you won't let me use the actors?" Chaz threw his arms up in the air. "It's not like I have an advertising budget."

"What about that new Darwood money? Go talk it over with Ingrid." Dwayne waved his hand dismissively, and Chaz exited the room grumbling.

As he walked out, Orlando and Melinda walked in, her arm through his, talking in low tones and smiling and giving the occasional shared laugh. They settled down together, sitting on the floor with their backs to the wall in a far corner, off by themselves. If Dwayne didn't known Orlando was gay, he would've assumed they'd become lovers. He got up to move some furniture into place.

Tom stormed into the room and headed straight for Dwayne.

"This is your idea of how to direct a play?" he said in a barely contained whisper. "If you can't *direct* the actors to give a performance, you send them home to fuck?"

"What?" Dwayne took a careful step backwards.

"You convinced Orlando he was stinking up the place as Romeo, and there was only one way to get things on track."

"I never suggested that." Dwayne took another step back. He felt honestly intimidated with six-foot-six Tom towering over him.

"Don't lie, Finnegan. Take a look!" He jerked his head in the general direction of Melinda and Orlando sitting on the floor, chuckling quietly to one another.

They certainly looked like lovers.

"I never told them to have sex," Dwayne whispered.

"As good as," Tom reposted. "Look at them."

"They look like Romeo and Juliet," Dwayne admitted. He actually felt pretty good about that. "Why are you so mad?"

Tom's eyes puffed wide open. His mouth opened and closed. And opened again. "Oh go eat your shorts, Finnegan." He stalked off to the other corner of the room and slunk down onto the floor, burying his face in his script.

"I guess you hadn't noticed Tom and Orlando were an item," Joan said, finishing moving the furniture into place. He looked back in the direction of his leading couple. Ry walked past them to plug in his guitar to the rehearsal amp.

"Hey, sweet cheeks," Melinda said to him from her spot on the floor next to Orlando.

"Hey." Ry sounded as emotionless as if he were imitating Joan.

Melinda looked instantly offended. She got up, picked up her belongings, and stalked off to a chair behind Dwayne and Joan, and plopped herself into it. Orlando looked perplexed. Tom looked annoyed. Ry looked oblivious, tuning his guitar.

The interweaving infatuations in this cast were more complex than Dwayne had realized.

"Ready?" Joan said. Dwayne nodded. "Act one, scene four to the stage, please," she announced. The actors got up and did that miraculous thing in which they put behind all their personal emotions and pulled themselves into their roles.

God bless them.

This was the scene in which Romeo and his friends crash the Capulets' ball. This time, when Romeo saw Juliet for the first time, the look of love bloomed on Orlando's face: *What lady is that, which doth enrich the hand of yonder knight? O, she doth teach the torches to burn bright! Did my heart love till now? Forswear it, sight! For I ne'er saw true beauty till this night.*

As Orlando approached Juliet, Dwayne saw her face open with

wonder and desire. If Melinda were at all distracted by whatever she felt for Ry, Melinda's Juliet was absolutely clear in her infatuation with Romeo. Dwayne sat up straighter and smiled with appreciation.

Romeo took Juliet's hand. *If I profane with my unworthiest hand this holy shrine, the gentle sin is this, my lips, two blushing pilgrims, ready stand to smooth that rough touch with a tender kiss.*

Juliet tilted her face up toward his and took a fast, deep breath. *Good pilgrim, you do wrong your hand too much; for saints have hands that pilgrims' hands do touch, and palm to palm is holy palmers' kiss.*

O, then, dear saint, let lips do what hands do. Thus from my lips, by thine my sin is purg'd. And he moved in slowly for their thrilling first kiss.

Absolutely beautiful.

Then have my lips the sin that they have took, Juliet said coyly, offering up her mouth.

Sin from my lips? O trespass sweetly urg'd! Give me my sin again.

As they kissed a second time with greater hunger, Dwayne sighed with satisfaction.

He did feel a little weird after Tom's accusation. He never suggested the actors make love for the sake of the show, but he *had* told them they needed to find the passion in their roles. He offered them additional rehearsal time, but they wanted to work on it alone. That was fine with Dwayne. If they decided to go have sex, it wasn't at Dwayne's suggestion.

Whatever they'd done, it certainly seemed to have worked. Dwayne's relief overwhelmed any momentary guilt he might have felt.

They now looked how Romeo and Juliet should look.

29

Monday, September 20, 2004

C haz came early to the first rehearsal of the week with Dwayne. This was to be a concentrated music and movement rehearsal to run all the scenes that included the band. Chaz brought along a camcorder to video these colorful scenes to publicize the show. However, when they arrived, they found Joan standing at the door with her arms folded looking in on the spectacle of the Indigenous Connection Church members lying side by side across the floor, chained together, with the far end of the chain locked to the steam radiator on the north wall of the room.

"It looks like they don't plan to leave," Joan said in the direction of the other side of the hallway.

"Oh my God," Dwayne and Chaz said simultaneously. Dwayne sounded deeply disturbed. Chaz, however, sounded absolutely delighted. He pulled his camcorder out of the case and aimed it at Dwayne.

"Could you tell us, Dwayne, what is supposed to be happening in this room?"

What the hell was Chaz doing? "You know very well we have a rehearsal scheduled to start in this room shortly."

"And what were you planning to accomplish?"

"Working the scenes that include live music and movement."

"A pretty important rehearsal, would you say?" Chaz asked.

"Yes! We are very close to opening night."

Chaz panned the camera to the church members chained to the floor. "And here you see the members of the Indigenous Connection Church chained together on the rehearsal floor that the theatre has rented," he narrated. "They appear to be staging a *lie-in* or something of that ilk." He moved right up to the feet of the parishioners lying on the floor and panned from face to face, down the line. One young woman had her eyes tightly shut and was writhing in place. *There's snakes on me,* she moaned. *Snakes. Snakes. Get them off.*

At the end of the line was Dan Darwood, who had locked himself as the last link of the chain and then wrapped and fastened the end of the chain to the radiator. Chaz zoomed in on his face. "Dan Darwood, could you tell us why you and your followers are chained to the radiator?" Chaz asked him.

"You do not have permission to film here," Darwood said. "Nobody is going to sign a video release. You won't be able to use that tape."

"Any comment on why your people are chained here when the Psychedelic Dream Theatre has rented this space for their rehearsal?" Chaz repeated.

"This is a sacred space," Darwood said. "They defile it, and they must be stopped."

The woman moaning about snakes had become louder and more panicky.

"Dan," Pearl called down to him. "Chastity thinks the chains are snakes."

"Give her a minute," Darwood said irritably. "Let the wisdom of Mother Ayahuasca come to her."

"Your people drank ayahuasca before you chained them to the floor of a space you claim is defiled?" Chaz said. "Doesn't that add undue stress to the drug experience?"

"This isn't a drug experience," Darwood insisted. "It's a holy sacrament of earth wisdom. This is our church. We cannot allow it to be desecrated."

Chaz panned to Dwayne who had come up behind him. "What building are we in?" Chaz asked him.

"The Chicago Repertory Arts Playhouse," Dwayne said. "This is one of the rehearsal rooms."

"So if this room and this building were consecrated to anything, it would be to the making of live theatre," Chaz said.

"I suppose, yes," Dwayne said.

"This building is on the ancient lands of the indigenous Potawatomi peoples," Darwood insisted.

"The Potawatomi drank a lot of ayahuasca, did they?" Chaz said.

Dan Darwood looked up frowning at the ceiling above him for a moment. "We honor all indigenous peoples," he said. "We imbibe the sacred Mother Ayahuasca, as per the spiritual awakening of our international tribe."

"It seems like all your people are white," Chaz said. "Is anyone in your Indigenous Connection Church actually indigenous?"

Darwood looked confused. "I think Duarte…" He gestured to a curly headed man lying on the floor below them."

"I'm not indigenous," Duarte said. "I'm Portuguese."

Suddenly Joan was at their side. "I just checked. Our theatre is vacant. I'm moving our rehearsal down there. Baring an act of God, Green has to provide us rehearsal space. I don't think these goofballs qualify as an act of God."

"We are an act of God! We are an act of God!" Darwood called. Then his whole congregation took up the chant. *We are an act of God! We are an act of God!*

Chaz absolutely loved it. He continued to videotape. He could just imagine the dollars flowing from the Darwood Foundation. And if they didn't want to pay up, he could get this on the evening news, and it'd be tremendous exposure for the show. Whichever way it went, it was a huge win. His life as an independent P.R. man was looking up. "I'm going to get some more footage," he whispered to Dwayne. "I'll meet you down in the theatre later on."

When Dwayne got to the floor below, Ingrid was arguing with Green. She'd come to rehearsal to observe the band so she could plan the sound design for the show. Joan had brought her up to speed on the chained indigenators upstairs.

"If you are going to rehearse in the performance space, you have to pay the performance space rate," Green insisted. He was wearing a formerly white tee shirt with yellow stains around the armpits. A hammer hung in the hoop on the side of his jeans, pulling them down just enough to expose a patch of pale, hairy hip bone.

"This is on you, Green," Ingrid shot back. "You have to provide a rehearsal room we can use." The bass player approached, carrying a small rehearsal amp and his bass guitar in a backpack case on his back. Ingrid waved him in.

"No, no, don't send them in there." Green said. "Unless you want to pony up a grand for this week of rehearsals."

The bass player looked from her to Green. She waved him into the theatre.

"Darwood's people are not my responsibility," Green said.

"You signed a contract with us," Ingrid insisted. "Since we can't use our rehearsal space, you are in default. We are going to finish our rehearsal run in the theatre at the rehearsal rental rate."

Green took two steps backward like Ingrid had shoved him. "You can't do that."

"You have no bookings in this theatre for this week. Next week we are in here for tech anyway. I'm not risking my people in a space that's claimed by religious fanatics who traffic in live snakes. We're moving into the theatre a week early, and we aren't paying a dime extra." She tossed back her chin-length ice-blonde hair and put her hands on her hips. She looked ready to wrestle Green to the floor.

Green noticed Dwayne approaching them. "Tell her she can't do that," he whined. "That's not in our contract."

"She's found a way for you to honor our contract despite the lunatics," Dwayne said. "Sounds like *Winner Boats Rising Together.*" He swept past them into the theatre.

"Winter boats?" Green said to Ingrid. "What are winter boats?"

"That's what I'll put you on and push it out into the arctic circle ice floes," she replied.

Joan was whizzing across the stage, taping out the set on the floor from memory. She taped in all the entry doors, the locations of stairs and platforms, the wall and balcony. If someone were to measure out the locations from the set drawing, they would find every length of tape on the floor was in its perfect location.

The band was tuning up, and all the actors had come into the space. The ones who'd witnessed the parishioners chained to the floor were describing the scene with great animation to their peers.

One voice sounded out of harmony with the rest: "No! No! No!"

Dwayne turned to see Tom and Orlando in a far corner of the audience seats in the midst of an argument, whisper-yelling at one another to avoid being overheard.

"You would have done the same thing," Orlando hissed.

"Never! I would never have done that!" Tom insisted.

"I did it for the show."

"Oh, what bullshit!"

Tom noticed Dwayne watching and stalked off backstage. Orlando sat down and put his head in his hands. The other actors had chattered on amongst themselves and hadn't noticed—all except for Ry, who looked Dwayne in the eye, plucked a note on his guitar and bent it savagely.

What was Ry's part in this triangle? Or was it a quadrilateral? Melinda was hot for Ry. Ry was playing it cool with her, but Dwayne had seen sparks fly between them not that long ago. Melinda and Orlando may or may not have delighted in one another's flesh to bring some passion to their Romeo and Juliet. Tom and Orlando had been an item recently, and now Tom was furious about Melinda.

O, what fools these mortals be!

Dwayne followed Tom backstage and found him in the men's dressing room.

"You all right?"

"What do you care?" Tom said, eyebrows arched high into his forehead. "As long as you get your *Romeo and Juliet*."

"Come on," Dwayne said. "We've been friends since high school. You know I care about you."

"Then why would you suggest they fuck?"

"I didn't suggest that." Dwayne looked up at the ceiling. "I told them they needed to find the passion. They looked totally uninterested in one another."

Tom's mouth dropped open, and he raised his hands to the sky. "See? See? You are immediately back to talking about the play. The emotional life of your actors be damned."

"Come on, Tom," Dwayne said. "Do you think Melinda and Orlando will feel peachy if they blow the chance to embody two of the greatest roles in the English language? This is about their emotional lives, too."

"Well, maybe." Tom took a deep breath and looked down at his shoes. He shook his head. "Do you know how long it's been since I had a relationship that was more than just a hookup?"

Dwayne moved closer to his friend and lowered his voice. "I'm sorry."

"I really felt like there might be something true and good between Orlando and me. But if he can't even stop himself from fucking *Melinda*, what possible faithfulness can there be?"

"If he did do something with Melinda, it was all about Romeo. I don't believe he was unfaithful in his heart."

Tom looked at him in amazement. "Did you see them afterwards? He looked like he loved it! I'm like, oh great, now you're going to want to be fucking her? Who's next? Where is the space for me?" He looked at himself in the makeup mirrors that lined the wall.

"Did you give him a chance to explain?" Dwayne asked.

"Explain what? It's obvious they were fucking. He wasn't denying it."

"Even if he did, it was just for, you know, *emotional memory* as an actor. I bet he didn't think you'd mind since he's not actually in love with her."

"Emotional memory. Oh, thanks, Lee Strasberg. You know, to play John Wilkes Booth, you don't have to actually assassinate a president."

"Of course not." Dwayne took a deep breath. "Clearly he didn't think how this would affect you."

"Well, he should have."

"Agreed. But you need to shake it off. Tonight is music and movement. I'm totally relying on you as a choreographer and performer."

"The show always comes first!" He cocked back his head and blew air out his nose.

"My artists come first. Can I buy you a drink afterwards?"

"Forget it," Tom said. "Let's just do this thing." He walked out of the dressing room and down the hall. Dwayne followed him back into the space. "Places for the top of the show," Tom cried. Joan had them ready, and they scurried into place.

Ry stepped on a pedal at his feet and a solemn organ riff began to play. He put his lips to the microphone and began to preach: "Dear loves and lovers, we gather here to tell the story of untimely death." Then he pulled his guitar neck up, the drummer and bass player hooked into a funky beat, and Ry began to play a variation on Prince's *Let's Go Crazy*. Half the actors danced onto the stage from stage right, the other half from stage left, facing each other in opposition, some with swords in hand, and Ry began to sing:

Capulets and Montagues
They want to fight.

Benvolio and lovesick Romeo danced from upstage into the center, a bouquet of flowers in Romeo's hand. A chorus dancer portraying Rosalind spun away from him.

Romeo's in love, but he can't find a wife.
Rosalind hates him.
Like Tybalt hates all.

Tybalt and Benvolio face off in the center to break into a half dance/half sword fight.

Benvolio smiles. He's pushed to the wall.
Why can't these people just release their bile?
I don't know, let's go!

The band plays as the fight continues, dangerous and athletic and sexy. Dwayne loved it. So much of what made these Psychedelic Dream productions great was Ry's music and Tom's choreography. He loved their contributions, and he wished Tom were having a better time of it. Tom was his long-time friend. Ry was more a mystery.

It was a shame he couldn't include some of this choreography for the performance at Angela's school, if in fact they were able to make that happen. He was using just four actors, but suddenly realized he wanted Ry, too. The music added so much, and the kids would love it, even if it were just the guitar. He'd have to talk with Ry.

Dwayne felt so impressed with what he was seeing onstage, he was surprised and sorry to see a scowl on Tom's face. His choreography was brilliant.

Ry finished the verse in the persona of the Prince and in the style of Prince. He broke into a Prince-like solo as more of the actors joined in the sword fight while the others backed away, dancing with horror on their faces at the danger. It was absolutely electric and amazingly funky. The music and fighting built to a crescendo and then everything stopped. With only the solemn organ beneath him, Ry declaimed as the Prince:

Rebellious subjects, enemies to peace,
Hear the sentence of your moved prince.
If ever you disturb our streets again,
Your lives shall pay the forfeit of the peace.
You, Capulet, shall go along with me,
And Montague, come you this afternoon,
To know our farther pleasure in this case,
Once more, on pain of death, all men depart.

Tom clapped his hands twice. "Okay! And from there we move straight into the Romeo/Benvolio dialogue. Thank you, everyone, for remembering your chorography so well!" He stopped and looked at Orlando. "Romeo, don't let your lovesickness throw you off the style," he said with evident distaste. "Your dancing still needs to fit with everyone else."

Orlando looked embarrassed and annoyed. Dwayne had not noticed anything wrong with Orlando's dancing.

Tom clapped twice again. "Okay! Let's move to the Capulet Ball for the dance and the first meeting of Romeo and Juliet."

They moved through all the scenes in which choreography was matched with live music. Some scenes had to be repeated to fix misremembered moves, but, overall, Dwayne was delighted. Tom, however, still looked grumpy whenever Orlando was the focal point onstage.

They moved into the final swordfight between Romeo and Paris at the graveside of Juliet, where she lies in a drug-induced coma. The young men fight, not knowing Juliet is still alive, and Romeo kills Paris.

"All right, hold it!" Tom called, interrupting the music before it could move on into Juliet's awakening and suicide. "Orlando, please remember, the feel is Prince. It's Paisley Park. Not Porky Pig."

Dwayne sat up. All through the rehearsal Tom had been calling Orlando out for this or that, usually for faults Dwayne could not see.

Orlando dropped his sword. "Porky Pig?" He looked both astounded and hurt.

"Yes," Tom insisted. "This fight is the most solemn of the fights, but it still has to vibe with the music. Your movement looks like stuttering. Like Porky Pig." He did a dismissive imitation: "Da, da, da, da, da, da, da, Dat's all folks!"

"You know what?" Orlando said, his face tightening up and his eyes glistening. "Fuck you." He turned his face away and walked off the stage.

"All right, everyone," Dwayne called. "Let's take ten."

"Ten minutes, please," Joan echoed.

"Thank you, ten," a number of the actors echoed back, sounding disturbed by what they just witnessed.

"Tom, could you join me, please?" Dwayne said. Dwayne led him offstage back to the men's dressing room, and closed the door behind them. "Whatever your personal grievance, you have to deal with them outside of rehearsal."

"He was completely off the rhythm…"

"No. Stop," Dwayne said. "We've worked together a long time, and I've never seen you treat a performer like that. If I had, I wouldn't still be working with you today. You've been calling him on stuff all evening, and I don't know what you're seeing. Nobody is performance-perfect yet. You are punishing him onstage for what you need to be dealing with in private."

Tom squirmed. "Well…."

"If you want to complete the evening, you need to apologize to Orlando. Otherwise, I just need you to work as a performer for the rest of the night, and I will run the remainder of the rehearsal."

"You can't do that!" Tom said. "This is my choreography."

"Are you ready to apologize to Orlando?"

Tom hung his head. "Okay."

However, they could not find Orlando off-stage, back-stage, on-stage or in the men's room. They came back into the theatre where most of the actors were back from the break.

"Has anyone seen Orlando?" Dwayne asked.

Melinda stood up. "After you and Tom left the space, he came back in and grabbed his backpack. He told me he couldn't take another minute of this."

"He left?" Tom said in amazement. "He's Romeo."

"I got the idea he was going home," Melinda said.

Tom ran out of the theatre without another word.

"And there goes your choreographer," Joan said dryly.

Dwayne dashed to the stairwell, but Tom was gone. What was he going to do now? Tom was supposed to work with the band and the choreography for the entire evening. He looked at his watch. Forty-five minutes of rehearsal time remained. They had done most of the choreography at least once.

"Okay, everybody," he announced. "We are going to start with right after Romeo's death scene. We'll do Juliet's death scene through the end of the show with the music."

He hoped to God that by the time they finished, his Romeo and his choreographer would be back. Otherwise, they'd all be going home a little early. Tech and opening night were next week. Dwayne prayed they'd have enough time to make this show sing. He still hadn't picked up the phone to invite Reg Camper—and showing the show to him for a possible chance at the Goodman had been his original reason for doing this.

30

Tuesday, September 28, 2004

Before Saturday's rehearsal Dwayne made sure Tom and Orlando were sorted. His antenna for trouble pulsed in every direction. What would happen next? Today they had the first costume fitting. Monday would begin tech week proper. They'd taken over the theatre a week early to avoid the Indigenous Connection Church, so that was good. Ingrid and Green had come to an agreement giving him a little bonus from the Darwood Foundation money for early takeover of the theatre. Dwayne stopped her in the hallway.

"Listen, I talked with the actors about the school assembly. Romeo, Juliet, the Nurse and the Prince are available. Friar Lawrence is not. Melinda would have to take an unpaid day from her job, so she needs a full day's pay if we are going to do it. They all expect to be paid, so how about we use some of the Darwood money?"

"Yes!" Ingrid said. "You can play Friar Lawrence and do the intro and host the Q and A. Joan is not available, so I'll come in to stage manage. Melinda's got the best day job. I'll find out what a day's wage is for her and allocate a little more than that for each of the six of us." She smacked Dwayne smartly on the side of the arm. "Let's do it!"

"Great!" He hadn't expected her to agree so readily.

"I love it! We'll get our first education offering on the books. We're going to need those when it comes to getting grants." She hurried off backstage.

Dwayne was pleased, but as he passed the larger dressing room, his trouble antenna twitched again. He heard Peaches muttering to herself inside. He went in to investigate.

"What's the matter?"

She looked at him, startled. Beside her stood the long rack of costumes the actors would try on for the first time today. In order to harmonize with the music, the costumes worn by the nobles were inspired by the 1980's-era costumes of Prince and his band: shiny brocade long jackets with tight shimmering matching pants in deep colors. Frilly white neckpieces or open shirts with frills down the center. Peaches had done a tremendous amount of shopping and sewing to assemble these.

"These look great, Peaches."

She sighed deeply and lifted one of the other costumes. The servants and townspeople had costumes that were decidedly plain. Peaches put them in homespun tunics and loose trousers that she'd originally constructed for a production of *Mother Courage and Her Children* and altered for this show. The Friar's garb was ecclesiastical but similarly plain.

Peaches looked on the edge of tears.

"What's the matter?"

"I'm afraid." She looked toward the doorway as though a pack of wolves were approaching to tear her flesh from her bones. Dwayne closed the door to give them some privacy.

"Tell me."

"Coco," she said.

"Why?" Dwayne said.

Peaches looked shocked and amazed. "Have you forgotten I had to completely rework her act one costume for *Titus Andronicus*? The show before that, she had me in tears. She's so demanding."

"She can be difficult," Dwayne admitted. "But she really believes in the work. Her body and voice are her instrument."

Peaches' eyes flared. "I know! Fitting her, I've seen her in her underwear I don't know how many times. I've had my hands in contact with her flanks and waist and..." Peaches looked momentarily abstracted into an awestruck reverie. "Every part of Coco that I've ever touched was poetry. There's only enough body fat on the woman to make her more sexy. I can't imagine the number of hours she spends in the gym. I know she didn't sculpt that form to hide it in a shapeless bag." Peaches hung her head and pulled out the costume. Shapeless bag was a fair description of Coco's Nurse costume.

"I hate confrontation," Peaches said. "I'm not even all that fond of conversation. I love sewing. I love drawing renderings of my designs. I like thrifting for costume pieces and digging through fabric stores and art supplies. I like listening when the group goes out for drinks. Going out with actors is great for me because they're happy to do all the talking."

"Would you like me to be here when Coco tries on her costume?" Dwayne asked.

"Would you?" Her face beamed with desperate hope.

"Of course. I want you to be comfortable."

He really did like Peaches, and he loved her work. She was an odd mix of attributes. Despite the fact that she liked to disappear into the background, her physical appearance was eye-catching. She dyed her hair in three shades of pastel. Her personal wardrobe appeared to be some combination of Björk, Courtney Love, and Cyndi Lauper. She favored fur-covered boots even in the summer.

Melinda came in first. She loved her costume but noticed a blonde wig sitting on a wig stand. "Say," she said enthusiastically, "do you think Juliet should be a blonde?" She snatched the wig off the stand, put it on her head, and glanced into the mirror. "I look hot as a blonde," she murmured.

"I just got that wig." Peaches took it off her and put it back on the stand. "That's for a different show."

"Humph," Melinda scoffed. Peaches finished her adjustments, and Melinda strutted out to try her costume on the stage.

Next came Orlando. He put on his costume and noticed an eye patch among Peaches' accessories. "Hey! How about Romeo in an eye patch?" He put it on and held out his arms in display.

"No eye patches for actors who sword fight," Dwayne said. "I don't want you poking someone by mistake." Orlando took it off and tossed it back among the accessories.

Peaches had just finished making a final adjustment to his costume when Coco walked in. She looked him up and down. Orlando looked good. Except for his height (much, much taller) he looked more like the rock star Prince than anyone else in the cast.

"Ooo wee!" Coco exclaimed. "Are you fly? Or are you Superfly?" Coco and Orlando chuckled.

"I am pretty, am I not?" He put out his arms and twirled once.

"All the boys going to be after you," Coco said. "Like they weren't already."

"Maybe the girls, too," Orlando said.

"Hmm." Coco pointed at him. "You learning to be ambidextrous? Your little fling with the basic white ingénue wasn't a one-time thing?"

"Coco," Dwayne warned. "Let's please eliminate *basic white ingénue* from the palaver."

She looked at him blankly but did not respond.

"I never said I had a fling with Melinda," Orlando insisted, looking truly put out.

"Yeah. Uh huh." Coco laughed derisively. She looked from Orlando to Dwayne. "Like Tommy-boy was losing his mind over nothing, right?"

Orlando looked insulted. He turned to Peaches. "Could I wear this onto the stage and try some movement?" he said harshly.

"Sure." Peaches had a quaver in her voice. She didn't like to witness conflict any more than she liked to be part of it. "Tom wants to run the show in costume today to see if there are any issues with choreography or combat."

Orlando left the room without another word.

"He touchy," Coco said. "If he's gonna to be so sensitive, he should avoid having sex with cast mates."

"Yes, he probably should," Peaches said, very quietly.

"I don't know if having sex with both genders is a plus or a minus," Coco said. "What do you think? You're polyamorous bisexual, or whatever, right?"

"I was having such a manic phase when I said that." Peaches blushed deeply red. She'd introduced herself to the *Titus Andronicus* cast with an uncontrolled blathering speech in which she included too many personal facts. She always said either too much or too little.

"Hey. We love all kinds." She looked up at the homespun gown hanging on the rack. "Oh my God. This is me?" She looked from the gown to Peaches. Suddenly the hemp-colored gown looked like a terrible insult. Peaches shrunk back. Would Coco hit her?

"Huh." Coco slid it off the hanger and held it up in front of her. She looked into the full-length mirror. "Huh." She said again. She tossed it onto the makeup table, shut the dressing room door, kicked off her sandals, and stripped off her blouse and her shorts. Dwayne was going to offer to leave the room, but she moved too fast.

Despite her fear, Peaches felt a stirring of desire. Coco was so beautiful and so beautifully formed. Peaches liked girls more than boys, though she found them both attractive. But she was so shy, she seldom had sex with anyone. If Coco took hold of her and made love to her, she would die in ecstasy.

Coco pulled the gown on over her head, and Peaches felt the pressure in her chest subside.

"I, I, I have a belt to go with that." She pulled the belt out of the accessories and gave it to Coco, who tied it around her waist. It was a simple fabric belt. It had no buckle.

"I, well…" Peaches was not sure what to say, she was so filled with doubt. Before she'd seen Coco in it, she thought the costume was right for the show, right for the overall design and right for the character. But now…

Coco turned and looked at herself in the mirror again.

"Yeah. I get it." She turned all the way around. Was she about to tear it off her body and throw it at Peaches?

"Yep. I see what you done," Coco said.

"Well, I'm not sure…" Peaches hands trembled.

"No. Absolutely," Coco said. "Slave garb. It's exactly right. You got the black slave with the all-white noble family. That's what we got, and that's what we play. So your costume for me is absolutely right on."

"Well, I'm not sure *that's* what I was thinking…"

"No. You got it, Peaches," Coco said. "You like it, Dwayne?"

"I think it's great," Dwayne said. Peaches looked at him with amazement and gratitude.

"Yeah." Coco looked from the mirror to Peaches. "It's absolutely right. I don't play some *Hattie McDaniel Mammy*. This costume gets it." And she walked out in her costume toward the stage.

Peaches felt so light-headed, she sat down in case she might faint. "I don't know how you did that, Dwayne," she said, "but thank you."

Dwayne laughed. "That wasn't me. That was you."

◆ ◆ ◆

After fitting the rest of the actors, Peaches and Dwayne joined Ingrid and Joan to watch the run-through. The actors were just finishing fight call. Every night they would run through all the fights before the show for safety.

"You always want to junk things up at the last minute," Joan said, speaking straight out at the stage.

"It's not junking things up," Ingrid said. "And I didn't propose it earlier because I didn't have the equipment. This is top quality, and it's free!"

"I would pay you *not* to use it," Joan said.

"You are a troglodyte."

"What's all this?" Dwayne said.

Ry and the band stepped out onto their platform for a sound check. The solemn organ riff began, Peaches heard Ingrid gasp, and she smiled. The band looked so much like Prince and the Revolution! They were beautiful.

"Dear loves and lovers," Ry recited, "we gather here to tell the story of untimely death." The band hooked into a funky beat reminiscent of Prince's *Let's Go Crazy*. "Capulets and Montagues," Ry sang, "They want to fight..." Some of the actors began dancing onto the stage.

Ingrid leaned in to Dwayne. "I put a smoke machine under the band platform. I want to have smoke come out, a pin spot on Ry as he starts the recitation, expand the light onto the full platform as the band kicks in, and then a full stage wash as the actors enter."

"That sounds cool," Dwayne said.

"No, no, no, no. No!" Joan said.

Dwayne and Ingrid looked at her, Ingrid with intense annoyance.

"You won't even hear the band for the coughing," Joan said, sounding unusually emotional. "Whenever an audience sees smoke, they start coughing."

"The smoke is just water vapor," Ingrid insisted. "There's nothing in it to make anyone cough."

"Pavlov's dog. They see it, they cough. It happens every time."

"This is a high-quality unit," Ingrid said. "I got it from the Goodman. We're using it for a Goodman traveling show I'm designing, but we won't need it until after *Romeo and Juliet* closes. I checked it out early. It's free!"

"When they see smoke, they cough," Joan insisted. "I'm in the booth for every performance. I know what audiences do."

"Maybe those were all cheap smoke machines, like that fluid spitter Green has," Ingrid countered. "This will look really cool. It'll totally go with the Prince thing."

"The music is loud, so that would cover a little coughing. The smoke is just for the beginning and then it's gone?" Dwayne asked.

"Right," Ingrid said. "The opening music and the fight."

"Can you make the smoke purple?" Peaches said timidly.

"Purple smoke! Ha!" Ingrid said enthusiastically. "I love it! With purple lighting, it'll look purple."

"Even more coughing," Joan said dourly. "And you know Ingrid. Once she's got it, she'll want to add smoke to every scene. It'll be a cough fest the whole night long."

Everyone sat quietly for a moment. Dwayne calculated. Two designers for smoke, one against. He thought it might look cool. *No Fears/Big Ears.* "Let's try it with purple smoke for the previews," Dwayne said. "If we don't like it, or it's disruptive, we'll cut it for opening. And this sound level is good," he said pointing at the band.

"Let's reset!" Joan called.

Ingrid made a quick change of lighting gels as everyone got in place for the top of the show. Dwayne leaned in toward Peaches. "They look fantastic. I love the costumes."

"Me, too," Joan said.

Peaches felt a wave of joy. Every one of them looked great.

As the actors played the opening scene, the purple fog really did make the introduction look like a Prince concert. Later in the action, Peaches was amazed at how antipathetic Coco's Nurse was to Melinda's Juliet. When the Nurse returned from arranging her wedding to Romeo with the Friar, it seemed most pronounced of all.

Now, good sweet Nurse,—O Lord, why look'st thou sad? Though news be sad, yet tell them merrily, Juliet said.

I am aweary, give me leave awhile, Coco's nurse said dismissively. *"Fie, how my bones ache!"*

I would thou hadst my bones, and I thy news: I pray thee speak; good Nurse.

Do you not see that I am out of breath?

How art thou out of breath, when thou hast breath to say to me that thou art out of breath?

In every other production Peaches had seen, the Nurse played this with teasing affection, but not Coco. It made Juliet come across as a spoiled rich girl with her sulky servant.

Lord, how my head aches! It beats as it would fall in twenty pieces, the Nurse said.

I'faith, I am sorry that thou art not well. Sweet, sweet, sweet Nurse, tell me, what says my love?

O God's lady dear, are you so hot?

Come, what says Romeo?

Hie you hence to Friar Lawrence' cell; there stays a husband to make you a wife. I must fetch a ladder by which your love must climb when it is dark. I am the drudge, and toil in your delight, she said, without any delight in Juliet's joy.

Hie to high fortune! Honest Nurse, farewell. Juliet exited stage right in radiant joy while the Nurse shuffled off stage left in drudgery. Peaches' choice of the homespun gown for the Nurse and the Prince-like finery for Juliet only emphasized the gulf between them.

When they got to the intermission after Romeo and Juliet had secretly married and the actors had been given a fifteen-minute break, Tom approached the group at the director's table.

"I've talked with the combatants backstage. We're all having a problem when we raise our arms for a hanging parry five or go for a moulinet head cut," he said, demonstrating the two fight moves. "The jackets are binding. The bodice of the jackets are so fitted, it doesn't allow flexibility for the arm to go overheard. Could we unbutton the jackets for fights?"

"Mmmm…" Peaches said doubtfully.

"I mean, it's not a perfect solution," Tom said. "Even open, the jackets are kind of restrictive. Or maybe we could take them off at the beginning of a fight?

"Mmmm…" Peaches said doubtfully.

"Okay, speak, girl!" Ingrid commanded.

"Their torsos look so hot in the tight jackets," Peaches blurted, and then blushed deeply red.

"True that," Joan mumbled.

"How hard is it to fight in the jackets?" Dwayne said.

"It's a safety issue," Tom said. "I don't want anyone getting a sword to the face because someone didn't get their arm up enough."

"No," Dwayne agreed. "Peaches? What do you think?"

"Well…" She stood up and walked around the table to Tom. She lifted his arm to the ninety-degree position. She ran a finger in a semi-circle under his arm pit. "I could cut the sleeve seam half-way around freeing up the whole bottom connection," she said. "No more binding. You'd see their shirts exposed here whenever they raise their arms, but I think that'd be okay. Their arms would definitely be free. What do you think?"

"Make it so," Dwayne said, doing his best Jean Luc Picard imitation. "For the rest of today's rehearsal, take off the jackets."

"*Oui, mon capitaine*," Tom said.

After the break, they continued the run. With everyone in grief over the death of Tybalt, Juliet's father promises Paris she will marry him in a few days time. Secretly married to Romeo, she refuses her father's command.

What is this? old Capulet asked. *Mistress minion you, I will drag thee on a hurdle thither. Out, you baggage! You tallow-face!* He threw his arms into the air, flapping his ample sleeves like the wings of a bird.

Good father, I beseech you on my knees, hear me with patience, Juliet begged.

Dwayne leaned over to Peaches and whispered. "What do you call those sleeves?"

"Angel sleeves," Peaches whispered back. "All that extra fabric gives old Capulet and old Montague more gravitas. It's like a bishop or a Chinese emperor."

Old Capulet swirled into the center of the stage, flying on wings of fabric into his rage.

Hang thee young baggage! Get thee to church on Thursday, or never after look me in the face. Wallace had always directed his fury in on Juliet, but today he continued to swirl about center stage, coming down to declaim his lines out over the audience, and then to swirl again, sleeves flying, to another portion of the stage.

Speak not. Wife, we scarce thought us blest that God had lent us but this only child; but now I see this one is one too much!

"I think it's possible Wallace is enjoying his costume too much," Dwayne murmured to Peaches. "He's totally changed his blocking so he can fly those sleeves around."

"Do you want me to change them?" she said tremulously.

"No. I'll talk to him."

You are too hot, Lady Capulet told him.

God's bread, it makes me mad! Wallace's Capulet thundered, throwing himself around the stage. *To have the wretched fool answer, 'I'll not wed, I cannot love, I pray you pardon me.'* He finally descended again on Juliet. *But, if you will not wed, I'll pardon you,* he said darkly. *Graze where you will, you shall not house with me. If you be mine, I'll give you to my friend; if you be not, hang, beg, starve, die in the streets, for by my soul, I'll ne'er acknowledge thee.* And he stormed off-stage.

Is there no pity sitting in the clouds, that sees into the bottom of my grief? Juliet continued as Dwayne got up and circled around to the backstage to intercept Wallace.

"I noticed you took some liberties with the blocking," he said quietly, as the action continued on stage.

"Yes!" Wallace said. "I was inspired by these, what did Peaches call them? Angel wings?"

"Angel sleeves. Right. Your action seemed less Juliet's father than Lear on the heath."

"Yes!" Wallace enthused. "I've really got the jones to play that part. I'm glad you could see that."

Saint Frances de Sales, grant me patience.

"I've never had any doubt but that you have an incredible King Lear inside you," Dwayne said. "But for now, let's stick with Capulet and his blocking, shall we?"

Wallace laughed heartily. "Oh, absolutely," he agreed. "Just flexing the muscles."

Dwayne gave a heavy sigh on his way back to the director's table. On stage, Melinda's Juliet was in deep woe.

O God! O Nurse, how shall this be prevented? My husband is on earth, my faith in heaven. What say'st thou?

Coco looked at her with a lack of interest that was devastating. *Romeo is banished. I think it best you married with the County Paris. O, he's a lovely gentleman. Romeo's a dishclout to him. I think you are happy in this second match, for it excels your first: or if it did not, your first is as good as dead, as you no use of him.*

Dwayne's heart went out to Melinda's Juliet. She looked so broken-hearted.

Speakest thou from thy heart?

And from my soul too, Coco replied coldly.

But at the end of the play when the Nurse, along with a host of others, discovers Juliet and Romeo both dead, Dwayne was amazed at how stricken Coco looked. The love she'd never shown Juliet in the course of the play was now revealed in her epic grief. He had not seen her play this moment like that before.

At the end of the night, Dwayne was able to have a word with her about it.

"Yeah, tonight I suddenly saw Juliet was almost as much a slave as me. Her dad wanted to marry her off like she's a cow to be traded. Maybe wearing that homespun costume put me deeper in that frame of mind. Suddenly Juliet's suicide looked different—more like those Africans in chains who threw themselves into the ocean rather than live as slaves. It all came home."

Dwayne was so delighted with it all—the costumes, the acting, the music—that the next day he was on the phone with Reginald

Camper. The Big Man would come to see *Romeo and Juliet* the second week of the run.

31

Saturday, October 2, 2004

Opening night! If everything went well and they had great reviews and got off to a successful run, how wonderful life would be. And next week, Reg Camper would be there! Dwayne got to the theatre early. Tech week had gone well enough. The lights, the music, the sound effects—all were in place and looking and sounding fantastic. Peaches had finished the alterations on the costumes. The men were able to lift their arms and fight and dance with abandon. The actors' performances were sharp and touching and exciting and heartbreaking. Dwayne felt wonderfully optimistic—until he got to the playhouse.

At the top of the stairs he pushed through the door marked *No Admittance* that led to the dressing rooms and backstage. In the middle of the hallway, Peaches lay facedown on the floor sobbing. One of the men's costume jackets lay on the floor beside her. An aroma of foul smoke hung in the air. Dwayne's insides contracted. What fresh hell was this?

"Peaches, what's the matter?"

She sobbed, unable to lift herself from the floor. She waved a hand toward the open fire escape door at the end of the hall. Dwayne saw twirls of smoke flutter through the opening. He hurried out onto the wrought iron fire escape that hugged the wall of the building over the alley below. Directly below him stood the row of Green's garbage dumpsters. Standing atop the middle dumpster, Dan Darwood chanted some kind of pseudo-indigenous prayer, his arms outstretched wide, the pupils of his eyes widely dilated. Below him in the alley, four women stood around a smoking, smelly fire, singing along with Darwood's prayer. Pearl took something from a stack and handed it to

Armageddon, who dropped it atop the flames.

It was one of the men's jackets that Peaches had finished altering yesterday.

"Hey, stop!" Dwayne screamed. "What the fuck do you think you're doing?" He ran down the iron stairs of the fire escape toward them. When Armageddon saw him, she tossed the remaining few costumes onto the flames and sprayed them with BBQ lighter fluid to encourage the conflagration.

The four women danced around the fire, chanting: "Too late, too late, too late." And then Darwood left off his prayer and joined them in singing: "Too late, too late, too late!" He turned merrily atop the dumpster but caught his toe on a rib in the cover top and tumbled into the dumpster next to it. Sadly, the dumpster contained a pile of corrugated cardboard to break his fall.

Dwayne got to the bottom of the stairs and grabbed Pearl. "What have you done? Those were our costumes!" Pearl looked shocked and chagrined and somewhat stoned.

"That was *all* of your costumes," Armageddon cackled. "You're just in time to see the last of them burn."

"What the fuck have you done!?!" Dwayne fought a tremendous impulse to punch Armageddon in the face.

"Armageddon had a vision!" Darwood shouted from inside the dumpster. A piece of torn craft paper stuck to the top of his head like an absurd bonnet as he stood up and looked over the lip.

The two women whose names Dwayne did not know cried out: "Purification!"

"Say it again!" Chaz leaned over the railing of the stairs, halfway down, aiming his camcorder at Darwood. "And push that hat back a little, please, if you could," he added.

Dwayne was trying to pull a jacket out of the fire, but it was too much damaged.

Darwood knocked the paper off his head. "Armageddon had a vision!"

The two women cried out again: "Purification!"

Chaz continued down the stairs to the surface of the alley, shooting with his camcorder all the time. Darwood struggled to climb out of the dumpster, made clumsy, presumably, by a healthy dose of ayahuasca. The four women looked equally impaired.

"This was *all* our costumes?" Dwayne shouted. "All of them??"

"Too late, too late, too late," Armageddon and one of the other women began to chant again.

"Um, yes, yes, all of them," Pearl said, looking guilty. "We got all the ones out of one of the dressing rooms, and we thought we had them all, but Taffy noticed they were all men's costumes. Then we found the women's dressing room and took all of those, too." Her voice trailed off. "Sorry..."

"We are not sorry!" Darwood shouted. "Never say sorry. Armageddon had a vision."

The two women cried out: "Purification!"

"I'm having a vision, too, of all of you in handcuffs," Dwayne shouted back.

Chaz sidled up to him. He spoke too quietly to be heard by anyone other but Dwayne. "Leave them to me. The Darwood Foundation is going to shower us with money."

"They need to go to jail!" Dwayne stormed.

Chaz held up his camcorder. "Not before I document everything."

"They destroyed our costumes," Dwayne fumed.

"Right," Chaz agreed, looking annoyingly pleased about it. "So you need to decide what to do tonight. Meanwhile, I'm going to generate either unbelievable publicity or very big money."

As infuriating as it felt, Dwayne did need to get back to his production team. What *were* they going to do? Peaches had worked so hard! As Dwayne climbed up the fire escape stairs, Chaz began to tape interviews with the five Indigenous Connection Church members about Armageddon's vision of purification and why they needed to burn all the *Romeo and Juliet* costumes. He started with Dan Darwood.

Peaches was no longer face down on the floor. She sat with her back against the wall, her legs stretched across the corridor. The single costume jacket lay across her lap. An array of melted eye makeup colors smeared down her face. Her multicolor hair looked in greater disarray than usual. She wore a skintight top in swirling hues and an equally colorful puffy skirt (almost a tutu) over pink leggings. She had stopped sobbing. She looked like a life-size pathetic sad-faced doll. She looked up at Dwayne, holding the costume jacket.

"This is all that's left. I took Montague's jacket home to reduce the size of the angel sleeves." In the jacket Wallace had done too much twirling. "I've hardly slept all week. I've been sewing all night long, every night. And for what?" She began sobbing again. "I tried to stop them, but that Armageddon girl pushed me down, and I hit the back of my head on the pavement. It really hurt. Another one warned me to get away because Armageddon was unpredictable. And then Armageddon picked up one of the flaming costumes and came at me, like she was going to throw it on me, with the lighter fluid can in the other hand. The nicer one tried to stop her, and I ran back up the fire escape. I started sobbing, and I couldn't stop." She held up Montague's jacket. "This is all that's left." She began sobbing once again.

"I'm so sorry," Dwayne said. "You should see a doctor. You might have a concussion."

Two of the actors stepped over Peaches' legs, looking at her with concern. Dwayne gave them a nod and waved them on.

"I don't think so," Peaches said, catching her breath. "What are we going to do?"

"Chaz is getting evidence. He's taking video. I think he's going to call the police."

She waved her hands. "No. About the costumes. We have no costumes. It's opening night. What are we going to do?"

What *were* they going to do?

Saint Jude, patron of lost causes, pray for us!

Dwayne looked at his watch. Ninety minutes to curtain.

"Are you sure you don't need to see a doctor?"

She blew air out her mouth and rolled her eyes. "I'm not nauseous, dizzy, or sleepy. I didn't hit my head that hard. Now, what are we going to do?"

"I don't know. Green has a bunch of costumes in the basement storage locker."

Peaches eyes flared open, and she sat up abruptly. "Are you kidding me? I'm going to suddenly re-costume the show with crap Green has lying around? How is that going to make any sense? And then what? I make alterations with safety pins so they don't fall off the actors?"

"Right. Right. That'll never work." Dwayne sighed. "I guess they play it in their street clothes."

"Fuck, Dwayne! Unless they all show up dressed like *Prince and the Revolution*, that's hardly going to work with the theme."

Dwayne felt pushed back by the force of Peaches' words. Of course she was right. "Well, what do you suggest?"

"We postpone the opening," she said decisively. Then she looked down, and her brow wrinkled. "Maybe I can rebuild the show by next weekend. But it's going to be expensive. I'll have to hire an assistant. Probably two if we're going to be ready by next weekend. Maybe we need to postpone for two weeks."

All kinds of wheels were turning in Dwayne's head. "We've got a full house on its way here tonight," he said. "Chaz got all the critics. We've got the Tribune and the Sun-Times and the Reader. We've got the Jeff Committee. If we send them away, we'll never get them back. Those people are booked up weeks in advance."

"All my work has been burned in the alley by those drug addicts, Dwayne! The critics will look in the program and see *Costumes by Peaches Brown*, and then they'll see the actors in their street clothes? That's completely unacceptable."

"Right. Right. Well, let's go look at the actors and see what we've got." He could hear some of them doing warm up vocal exercises in the theatre. He helped Peaches to her feet. They walked around to the front and entered through the door the audience would use.

About half the actors were on stage doing stretches and making absurd noises. Others were in the seats talking amongst themselves. Most of them were wearing jeans and a casual shirt or top. Wallace sat in the front row in slacks, a white button down shirt and seersucker jacket with a small straw fedora on his head, poring over his script. He looked like a British diplomat at Rick's Café Americain. Orlando wore snugly tailored black slacks, a fitted black organdy shirt and a cream kerchief tied at the neck. Tom wore peach bell bottoms and a paisley shirt open low down the neck with billowy sleeves. He looked like Tommy Tune in the cast of *Hair*. Melinda and Coco were clearly dressed for the after-party. Melinda looked sweet and sexy in a flowery short sun dress with push-up foundation garments beneath. Coco wore a tight little black dress that capitalized on the word *little*, with spike heels and a string of pearls that brought the eye to her generous décolleté.

"If they all dressed like they usually dress to rehearsal, that'd be one thing," Peaches hissed. "But this…" She threw her arms in the air hopelessly.

"It doesn't seem ideal…" Dwayne said. He looked at his watch. "It's already seven o'clock. Curtain's at eight. I can't send the colorful ones home to change."

"And what would that achieve?" Peaches said. "To put them all in jeans and tops? That would somehow make a better statement? No. We have to postpone."

Ingrid came into the theatre, all smiles. "Hey!" she said brightly. "We comped half the house, but the rest is totally sold out! And Chaz got all the best critics for tonight!"

"We're not doing the show," Peaches said.

Ingrid looked shocked.

"The Indigenous drug addicts burned up our costumes," she said. "We have to postpone."

Ingrid looked from her to Dwayne.

"It's true. They did," he said.

"There are so many ways we can't afford to postpone." Ingrid's eyes flared wide open. "A week's performance space rent with no income? Blowing it with all these critics and Jeff judges…"

"I agree," Dwayne interrupted. "Here's one idea: I make a curtain speech about what happened to the costumes, and we show Peaches' renderings so they can see what the costumes should have been."

"Are you kidding me?" Peaches said.

Ingrid knit her brows and nodded. "I agree with Peaches. A friend of mine is a saucier at Charlie Trotter's. He said you never tell guests that something didn't come out as you planned. It robs them of their experience. We should go forward with no apologies. Whatever the actors are wearing."

"That is *not* what I meant!" Peaches whispered. "Look around the room. Montague looks like an alcoholic expatriate in the tropics. Romeo looks like a gay cocaine user. Mercutio looks like an even gayer throwback to the 60s. Juliet looks like the girl next door you want to fuck. The Nurse looks like the bombshell you'd like to fuck but is totally out of your league. How does that come together to make sense?"

Ingrid shrugged. "Maybe the music will tie it together?"

"I designed Prince-inspired costumes! I tailored them to fit their gorgeous bodies!" Peaches fumed. "*That's* what makes sense. I totally forbid this show going forward."

Neither of them had ever heard Peaches speak so forcefully before. Perhaps no one in the world had.

"Well," Ingrid said at last, reluctantly. "As a financial matter and as a matter of the company's future ability to operate and thrive, I believe we must go ahead. That's what I say as executive director. But I understand this is also an artistic decision. Part of the show's design has been destroyed. So, in that light I think the decision has to go to the artistic director." She looked meaningfully at Dwayne.

He sighed deeply.

He looked around the room. He certainly would not have chosen to costume the show like this. He understood how much Peaches would hate to have people think this was her design. On the other hand, he knew as a director a show never came out exactly the way you intended it. That was the nature of directing. You were guiding all those talents: the actors, the designers, the technicians. They all made their contributions, and that made the show what it became. But, of course, that was nothing like having designed, constructed, fitted and perfected an entire collection of costumes and then had someone set them on fire. What would that be like? Having your entire cast kidnapped? Having your theatre burn down? Having a nuclear attack on your city?

Snap out of it, Dwayne! Make a decision!

"Okay. Realistically, how long would it take you to recreate the costumes?" he said.

"Well…" As she thought about it, she began to look stunned. "Actually, I started shopping for pieces I could alter and adapt about eight weeks ago. I hit every resale shop in the metropolitan area and cleaned them out of everything that looked remotely Prince-like. I guess I'd have to go thrift in Milwaukee, and I don't know the resale scene there. So there'd be at least three or four days of shopping." She looked more and more disturbed. "Actually, I shopped for two or three weeks here. If I couldn't find the vintage pieces I wanted in Milwaukee, I'd have to hit Minneapolis as well, which you'd think might be better since Prince lived there. Or I'd have to build them all from scratch.…" She took out a piece of paper and a pencil. She held the pencil over the paper for a moment. Her face crumbled up in a blend of deep sorrow, frustration and despair, and she broke down into tears again. "This was *so* much work, and I know all the shops here…" she sobbed. Ingrid took her into her arms and held her.

Though this whole conversation had been going on in whispers, some of the actors were now looking over at them. It was time to decide. He remembered Madeline Forthright's chapter, *Swimming with the Rats*. Sometimes *Keeping Your Eyes on the Prize* required you to abandon a disaster. You did not allow yourself to go down with a sinking ship. He couldn't let the calamity of the costumes sink the ship of the production.

"All right," Dwayne said. He put his hand on Peaches shoulder. "I'm sorry, but we have to go ahead. We can take Ingrid's idea: We present the show and make no apologies. Let the audience have their experience without excuses. Or I can explain what happened in a curtain speech and show them your costume renderings. Maybe we can find a way to project them on a screen. Whichever way you prefer."

"They'll all go home talking about the crazies who burned our costumes instead of the merits of the show," Ingrid complained. Peaches wriggled out from her arms.

"Ingrid, come on," Dwayne said. "Both ways have merit."

Peaches shook her head. "No. I'm decided. No excuses."

Dwayne stood up. "Are you sure?" His heart was breaking for

her. Swimming with the rats never felt good, even if it was the right thing to do. And he couldn't help feeling they were making a dreadful mistake.

Peaches nodded.

He called the cast together. "All right, everybody," he announced. "I've got a little news."

32

Wednesday, October 6, 2004

The apartment buzzer rang repeatedly. Insistently.

Dwayne got up from the dinner table and pressed the button for the intercom. "Yes?"

"Let me up, let me up, let me up, up, up!" squawked the voice of Chaz through the tinny speaker. Dwayne buzzed him in, unlocked the door, and returned to his plate of mostaccioli vesuvio. "It's Chaz," he said to Angela.

"I've got them! I've got them all! The three majors are out!" he shouted, coming into the apartment, waving papers over his head.

"Three?" Dwayne asked. "Which three?"

"The *Trib*, the *Sun-Times* and the *Reader*! Wow, it smells good in here." He leaned over the bowl of mostaccioli, grabbed a tube with his fingers while Angela attempted to smack his hand with her fork, and popped it into his mouth.

"Get a plate!" she shouted.

"The *Reader* doesn't come out until Friday," Dwayne objected.

"Ha, ha!" Chaz said. "I plied a certain freelance reviewer with top shelf liquor, and she gave me the final draft of her review. Let's hope they don't cut a word!" He grabbed a plate from the corner hutch and spooned on a portion of pasta.

"It's good?" Dwayne said. He got up, got another glass from the hutch, and poured Chaz a glass of Chianti.

"Oh, baby!" Chaz said. He waggled his eyebrows and lifted a typewritten sheet. "Listen to this: *Romeo and Juliet can and should be open to wide interpretations, but the Psychedelic Dream Theatre production at the Chicago Arts Repertory Playhouse is like nothing we've seen before. It's a show that is both post-modern and a throwback to the era of Shakespeare himself.*"

"Wow, Dwayne," Angela said lifting a fork of pasta toward her mouth. "You're a post-modern throwback."

"Just wait!" Chaz commanded. "*Great entertainment value rises from the work of choreographer Tom Collins (also playing a feisty, fey Mercutio) and music director/lead guitarist Ry Joodey (also playing the Prince). Joodey provides a background score inspired by the music of Earth, Wind and Fire...*"

"Earth, Wind and Fire!" Dwayne sputtered. "Has she never heard a single song by Prince? The music is so closely ripped off, I'm still worried Paisley Park might sue us!"

"I thought having a guitarist dressed like the rock star, Prince, playing Prince music, and portraying the Shakespeare role of the Prince was a little too on-the-nose," Angela said drily, "but I guess it was a bit too subtle for Chicago critics."

"Well, he's not *dressed* like Prince anymore..." Dwayne said.

"True."

"*...inspired by the music of Earth, Wind and Fire,*" Chaz continued, "*that blends with the Collins-designed funky dance moves of the ball at which Romeo and Juliet meet, as well as dancerly sword fights between the Montague and Capulet factions. These are very entertaining, and I noticed many show-goers chair-dancing to the music. The costumes take the production to a strange post-modern place, while being connected with the throwback to Shakespearean times. As Shakespeare scholars know, the Elizabethan period was an intensely bisexual time, especially for men. Shakespeare himself wrote some of his most romantic sonnets for a male lover.*"

"Scandalous!" Angela said.

"Wait for it!" Chaz replied. "*Under Dwayne Finnegan's direction, a steamy love affair between Romeo and Mercutio bubbles beneath the surface.*"

"Ooo, racy," Angela said.

"*Mercutio clearly resents his infatuation with Juliet. Both characters are played more gay than straight. And when Mercutio is killed by Tybalt, Romeo's steamy affection for his boyfriend drives him to kill Tybalt in revenge, setting in motion the final tragedy to unfold. All in all, it's a*

Romeo and Juliet *you are going to want to see.*"

"I love that last line," Dwayne said.

"Oh, there's lots of lines I can blurb," Chaz said.

"I love her interpretation of the costume choices," Angela said.

"Ah, but the *Tribune* took it even farther!" Chaz cried merrily. He opened the newspaper and scanned. "I won't read the whole thing, but listen to this: *The costume choices played up the interesting racial politics of this* Romeo and Juliet. *Romeo and Lord and Lady Montague are a black nuclear family (although the Montague retinue are, oddly, all white). This gives an interesting racial tinge to the rivalry between the black Montagues and the white Capulets as well as an interracial frisson to the romance between Romeo and Juliet. The costumes play up the racial and sexual politics. Romeo wears the garb of a contemporary black dandy, while Juliet is dressed as a fetching white ingénue. Both are charismatically attractive, but clearly come from different worlds in our contemporary scene. Meanwhile, Juliet's nurse is the only black member of the Capulet retinue and brings echoes of slavery. However, the pseudo-slave outdoes Juliet in her sexual comeliness. Coco Nesbit's Nurse is something of a bombshell, and she treats Juliet with an impertinence and resentfulness atypical of the usual interpretations of the role. Only when Juliet is dead does she finally truly regard her with sympathy. And as for Romeo, she seems to disapprove of him because he is black. Although her early lines praise him, and she assists the couple in getting married, she finally regards him with disdain.*"

"All that from accidental costuming?" Angela said. "Impressive."

"And I was going to apologize and explain," Dwayne said.

"Ingrid was right. Never undercut the audience's experience." Chaz scanned the review as he stuck a fork of mostaccioli in his mouth. "He also loved the music," he continued, speaking with his mouth full. "He was the only one so far to hear the Prince influence. He loved the choreography, the fights, the *deep pathos.*"

"Why bother to have pathos at all if it's not going to be deep?" Angela asked.

"Would it be wrong to mail copies of these to Reg Camper's office?" Dwayne asked. "He's coming to the show this Saturday."

"Maybe enclose them in a thank you note after he sees it

himself," Angela suggested.

"If he likes it as much as these reviewers—Goodman Theatre here you come." Chaz handed the *Tribune* review over to Dwayne. "The *Sun-Times* is equally complimentary, although she objected to the Montague friends not being black. She wondered why Dwayne Finnegan could not find enough talented black actors in a city like Chicago."

"It all comes down to you, Dwayne," Angela said cheerily, rising to take her plate to the sink.

"The buck stops here," Dwayne muttered, continuing to read the reviews and smiling occasionally.

"Speaking of bucks, I have even better news," Chaz said.

"If it's better than these reviews, I'll have to hear it to believe it." Dwayne still did not look up from the paper.

"I brought my camcorder for opening night audience reactions, but I lucked out when the cult burned up your costumes."

"Oh, yeah, that was a lucky break," Angela said sardonically, taking Dwayne's plate and pouring herself a little more Chianti.

"I got the end of the conflagration on tape. I got Armageddon talking about her vision. I got Dan Darwood saying *Romeo and Juliet* rehearsals had tainted their worship space. Just fantastic material! I interviewed Peaches, who could barely keep from weeping. She showed photos of the costumes from the actor fittings. We costed out what one of the downtown costume houses would charge to recreate them. It's a fortune! It's amazing how Peaches built the show on the budget you guys gave her. I edited that all together and presented the video to the Darwood Foundation. I told them our board of directors was planning to sue Dan and his church for damages and for the cost of replacing the costume collection. I asked if the Foundation might want to reimburse us for the replacement and the damages instead. In that case we could keep the whole thing out of the courts and avoid a lot of bad press. They liked that idea. They ponied up a nice six figure donation."

Dwayne set down the reviews. He regarded Chaz with wonder. "Six figure? At our current budgets, that'd pay for multiple shows. Wow, Chaz!"

"No one can say Chaz Ackersley is not one sneaky son of a bitch." Angela looked on him with admiration.

"Oh, but there's more! When I was interviewing Dan Darwood, I asked him whether his people would be picketing *Romeo and Juliet*, since it was such anathema to their worship."

"Wait a minute! You planted the idea that they picket our show?" Dwayne got right up out of his seat.

"You could see the little light bulb go on in his head!" Chaz said gleefully.

"Why would you do that?" Dwayne picked up the Chianti bottle. For a moment Angela thought he was going to hit Chaz with it.

"We get picketers harassing your little underdog theatre company, we'll be selling out every show! Remember when the Catholics picketed *The Last Temptation of Christ*? Box office gold!"

33

Saturday, October 9, 2004

Thursday and Friday's performances of the second week of the run had gone well. Dwayne was up in the light booth with Joan on Saturday when he got a text from Chaz: *It's happening. Out front. Running to get my camera!*

What was happening out front? He didn't need any complications. This was the night Reginald Camper was coming to see the show.

Dwayne climbed down the stairs out of the booth, down to the lobby, through the pre-show crowd and out the front entrance. Among the passersby on the sidewalk circled five determined individuals dressed in flowing tie-dye homespun robes: Dan Darwood, Armageddon, Pearl, and the two other women who'd helped burn the costumes. They all carried placards on sticks: *Romeo & Juliet vs. Religious Freedom. theater rots soul work. Mother Ayahuasca Says No.*

He did not need any of this.

"Hey, Darwood, what the fuck!" Dwayne shouted, but he immediately felt a hand on his right biceps pulling him away.

"No, no," Chaz said. "Let me get some footage."

Dwayne sighed and stepped back while Chaz put his eye to the viewfinder and stepped backwards through the parked cars and out into the street to get a good angle on the picketers. Dwayne screamed as he continued to step backwards right into traffic, a car hitting its brakes and horn simultaneously, coming to a full stop just as its bumper came nearly in contact with Chaz's calf. Chaz glanced at the car dismissively as it continued to blare its horn. He backed deeper into the street until he was at the very center of Lincoln Avenue and the cars were flashing by him in both directions.

The picketers continued to revolve. Armageddon perked up her posture and kept her sign turned so it could be read by the camera. Dwayne's stomach knotted. "Get back on the sidewalk," he shouted.

Chaz waved him off. Clearly, he was not coming out of danger until he got the footage he wanted. Then he carefully made his way back to the sidewalk and trained the camera on Dwayne.

"Dwayne Finnegan, artistic director of the Psychedelic Dream Theatre, what is your reaction to the picketers protesting your production of *Romeo and Juliet* now playing at the Chicago Repertory Arts Playhouse?"

Dwayne cocked his head to the side. Really? He needed to get back inside. He wanted to be ready to greet Camper when he arrived. But if Chaz was going to risk his life in the street to capture B-roll, he wasn't likely to give up until Dwayne answered his questions.

"I don't understand what these people hope to achieve," Dwayne said into the camera. "They destroyed..." He stopped. Did he want it known they'd destroyed the costumes? Critics had congratulated them on the innovation of the costumes. Once Peaches calculated that it would take her at least three weeks to reconstruct the costume collection, she decided they would stick with the actors' clothes for the run.

Before he could continue, Chaz looked up from the camera past Dwayne. His face went white. "Oh my fucking God," he squeaked. He pushed the camera into Dwayne's hands and ran into the lobby.

Dwayne turned to see behind him. Two familiar large men hurried up the sidewalk toward him. One was carrying a two-foot length of black pipe. They were the two thugs who sometimes accompanied Uncle Bull. One was an enormous bald white man with the tattoo of an eagle on the side of his head and biceps the size of Dwayne's thigh. He carried the length of black pipe in his left hand. The other was a thin, tall black man wearing a black sport coat with a bulge under one arm that Dwayne suspected was a handgun. He looked like the brains of the pair. The white man with the pipe grabbed Dwayne by the arm and shook him. "Where did he go?"

"And don't lie to us," the taller man said, "unless you want see how that pipe feels."

"He ran into the main theatre," Dwayne said, pointing in through the window toward the first-floor performance space. The two men ran in, pushed their way through the crowd and forced through the door into the main theatre. The actors doing their warm-ups on that stage would get a shock, but their show started a half hour later than *Romeo and Juliet*, so they'd have time to recover. Better they had a story to tell than Chaz get a length of pipe to the head.

Dwayne ran into the theatre and followed up the stairs in the direction he'd actually seen Chaz go. He got to the top and pushed through the *No Admittance* doorway to the dressing rooms and backstage. Chaz knew about the fire escape. He was probably intending to escape that way. However, he found Chaz faced off with Rockwell Nesbit III in the hallway outside the dressing rooms. Rocky looked annoyed.

"Listen, Bull," Chaz was saying, "I worked all this out with Rocky."

Coco came out of the women's dressing room in the little black dress that had become her costume. "Pops..." she said.

Chaz was entirely frozen to the spot, afraid to move in case Bull might grab him and pull off an arm or break a limb.

"Not your Pops, baby girl," he said, smiling, turning to her.

So, not Rockwell Nesbit III. At least not in his mind.

"Don't you worry about a thing. I just got to take care of a little *business*." His smile was a scary thing.

She closed her eyes and took a deep breath. "Pops worked all that out with him, Uncle Bull," she said with weary resolve. "You don't need to take care of anything here. It's all good. You just take your medication. Okay?"

Uncle Bull laughed heartily. "Medication," he scoffed. "That's for your old man. Not for your old Uncle Bull."

"He paid his debt with Pops," Coco insisted. "You don't need to be bothering with him."

"This boy didn't take money from your Pops. He took a loan with old Uncle Bull. My business is based on trust and reputation." He laughed heartily again. "If a man don't trust that I'm going to break his knees, how am I going to stay in business?"

Coco shook her head in exasperation. "You know what? Mama's here tonight to see the show. I'm going to let her deal with you."

Bull's eye lit up. "Yvette is here? Well, why didn't you say so?"

"You just stay right where you are," Coco told him.

"I think I'll be on my way, then," Chaz said, unfreezing from the spot.

"Nah!" Bull said. "You stay right there."

Chaz refroze.

"Don't touch him," Coco commanded. "You just wait a minute, and I'll bring Mama."

"I'd love to see her," Bull said, with a hint of salaciousness.

"Don't *you* say a thing," she murmured to Dwayne in passing. "You'd just fuck it up."

Dwayne closed his mouth. He knew the truth when he heard it. He kept Chaz's camera hidden behind his back.

Bull pulled out a little notebook and consulted it. He whistled.

"Too bad you delayed your payment," he said to Chaz. "The vig pushed your total sky high." He laughed merrily. "I hope you got a lot of money."

The *No Admittance* door reopened and a woman walked through followed by Coco. The woman put her hands on her hips. "Now who am I looking at?" she demanded.

"Aww," Bull said, cocking his head to the side and smiling slyly, "Yvette, you sexy, sexy, sexy thing."

To Dwayne's eye, Bull had an excellent point. Yvette was more robustly full-figured than her bombshell daughter, but there was a poutiness to her red rouged lips and a playfulness in her eye, even through her annoyance, that made her somehow even sexier than her formidable offspring.

Yvette sighed. "Bull," she said as though she hadn't believed it until this moment, but now she understood the bad news. "Bull, Bull, Bull. What are you doing here, sweetheart?"

"Just a little *business*," he said playfully. "You know how it is. Sometimes you got to take care of the *business*."

She sidled up to him. "And sometimes you got to take care of the *bigness*. You know where I'm going?" she asked suggestively.

202 ♦ RICHARD ENGLING

"I can't say I know where you going," he teased back, "but wherever that is, I'm going, too!"

Yvette took hold of his tie and led him, as though on a leash, down the hallway and out through the *No Admittance* doors. Chaz let his back touch the wall and slid down until he was seated with his legs stretched out on the floor. Coco looked at him.

"What kind of a naïve fool takes out a loan from a man like that?" she said.

"I thought we had this all resolved," he said.

"Sure, with Rocky. But if Pops don't stay on his meds, then you got to deal with Uncle Bull."

Chaz put his head in his hands. Then he looked startled again. "Fuck! Bull's two thugs might still be around." He got up and ran out the fire escape door.

"What's going to happen now?" Dwayne said.

"Mama will take him home. After they fuck and he has a cigarette he always comes back to himself. Then Mama can get him to take his pill."

Dwayne wasn't sure what to say. "You mean your Uncle Bull thinks he's fucking his brother's wife, and your mother..."

She held up a hand in his face. "You know what, Dwayne? Nobody's family is perfect."

34

Later the Same Day

Joan entered the hallway behind Coco. "Did I just see Rocky exit the building? I called to him but he didn't answer."

"Rocky has left the building," Coco responded. "And he won't be back tonight."

"He won't be back? Curtain is in thirty-five minutes."

"Rocky is off his meds," Coco said. "He'll probably be okay tomorrow."

"Great Caesar's ghost." Joan stared at the floor, then up at the ceiling, then looked in Dwayne's general direction. "Okay, Dwayne. Get ready. You're going on as Montague."

"What?" Dwayne said.

"What did you think would happen? You cast an actor with multiple personality disorder, and you didn't cast an understudy."

"Crap," Dwayne said. "Saint Cecilia, pray for me."

"What's she?" Joan said. "Patron saint of *the show must go on*? Never mind. I have things to do. Get ready." She turned on her heel to check that props were in place and none of the other actors were suddenly missing.

A script! He needed a script! Of course he knew all of Montague's entrances and exits, and he knew the gist of what Montague said, but he certainly did not have Montague's lines memorized. His director's script was at home, no longer needed. Where would he find a script? Many of the actors had their scripts at the theatre, but he didn't want to beg a script from any of them. It could be part of their show warm-up to go over lines and notes before the performance.

The light booth! Of course! He could look at Joan's script while she was moving around the theatre making sure every thing and every body was in place. And he could leave Chaz's camera there, which was still absurdly in his hands.

He rushed out of the backstage hallway to the upstairs lobby and up the stairs to the light booth above the audience at the back of the auditorium. He sat down at the light board and began paging furiously through Joan's prompt book. What was Montague's first scene?

Why could he suddenly not remember what happened in what order in the show? He knew the action inside and out. But now, in his panic, he felt like he was looking at the script for the first time in his life.

Saint Jude, patron of lost causes, pray for me!

He suddenly remembered Montague's biggest scene with the most lines was the very first scene of the show! Why, in God's name, had he not cast understudies? What idiocy had possessed him?

It was relatively common for new, poorly funded companies to put up a production without understudies. They cast the show, avoided the cost, and hoped for the best. But now, because of the Darwood Foundation, they had plenty of cash.

He heard steps coming up into the booth. Joan stared at him from the top of the stairs. "What are you doing in here? Get out."

"I need to look over Montague's lines. I can't even remember what scenes he's in. My mind is completely blank."

"Act one, scene one. Act three, scene one. Act five, scene three. Now get out."

"I need a script. That's why I'm in here. To look at your script." Another realization suddenly hit him. "Say, the Montague family is black. Romeo, the Lord, the Lady, all played by black actors. Do you think I should use blackface?"

Joan closed her eyes. "Have you completely lost your mind?"

Dwayne's eyes widened. "Good God. No. Right. Stupid question. Absolutely not."

"You have to get out. And you can't take my prompt book. They probably have copies of *Romeo and Juliet* in Green's used bookstore."

"Saint Dymphna, why didn't I think of that?" Dwayne leapt out of Joan's chair.

"I'll bite. Who's Dymphna?"

"Patron of dementia patients."

"Appropriate!" she called as he scrambled down the steps.

Outside the upstairs lobby Green had installed bookshelves the length of the hallway. Chicago's only theatre-dedicated bookstore had closed a few years earlier and Green had set this up to fill the gap. He didn't go the full distance of stocking new books, but he did buy used books from actors (at a pittance of their worth, of course) and sold them from these shelves. However, in the second-floor hallway no one was minding the store. An honest person would pay for a book at the box office in the main lobby downstairs. Many people were grateful that any kind of theatre-related bookstore existed again and would make the effort to pay. Others were not so scrupulous.

Dwayne scanned shelf after shelf, sweat breaking out on his face. *Holy drops from the crown of thorns!* He suddenly remembered Reg Camper was coming to this performance. Dwayne had been planning to greet him and to sit somewhere where he could secretly observe Camper's reactions. But now Camper would be watching him playing a role he'd never even rehearsed! Blood surged into his head with such fury he felt his eyes would pop.

Then he saw an entire section of Shakespeare scripts, study guides, and scholarship. There was one lonely copy of *Romeo and Juliet* on the shelf. Dwayne grabbed it and ran back to the men's dressing room. The room was filled with actors getting into costume. Some were putting on makeup. Others didn't bother with makeup since the audience was so close.

"Dwayne!" some of them shouted when he entered. He waved vaguely back at them.

"You watching the show tonight?" Orlando asked him.

"I'm playing your father," Dwayne replied. "Rocky is...not well."

"Oh." Orlando frowned and cocked his head. "Well...break a leg," he said doubtfully.

"Thanks." Dwayne sat on an open chair. He opened to act one, scene one and the old glue spine of the book cracked loudly and one of the pages came loose. It was a page before Montague made his entrance so Dwayne tossed it in the trash under the makeup table.

At the other end of the room Ry and his bass player were having a loud discussion of the pluses and minuses of finger picking vs. a plastic pick.

Focus, Dwayne!

Every actor he'd ever known had had the nightmare in which you are on stage in front of a live audience, and you don't know any of your lines. And now he would live out that nightmare, simply because he hadn't cast understudies. With Ingrid's encouragement.

We got through Titus Andronicus *without them*, Ingrid had argued. *Let's wait for the next show. Maybe we'll have more money in the bank by then.* He'd caved so easily.

He found his entrance on page forty-five. Capulet says: *My sword, I say! Old Montague is come, and flourishes his blade in spite of me.*

Shit! That's right! I enter carrying a sword! Where do I find the prop swords? He felt his entire body tingle with panic.

Focus Dwayne! The other actors would know. They would help him. He had to focus on the lines! He repeated the first one to himself several times: *Thou villain Capulet! Hold me not, let me go.*

Okay, that should be easy to remember. Then the Prince has a speech. Ry delivers it from the band platform. Then Dwayne had a line to Benvolio: *Who set this ancient quarrel new abroach? Speak, nephew, were you by when it began?*

He repeated it several times, and then it occurred to him he'd forgotten the first line and he jumped back to look at that: *Thou villain Capulet! Hold me not, let me go.* Yes, he is carrying a sword. And then the second line and then Benvolio and Lady Montague talk about moody Romeo for a few lines, and Benvolio asks me: *My noble uncle, do you know the cause?*

And I say: *I neither know it nor can learn of him.*

Okay, easy enough. I can handle it. And Benvolio asks: *Have you importun'd him by any means?*

And I reply: *Both by myself and many other friends; but he, his own affections' counsellor, is to himself—I will not say how true—but to himself so secret and so close, so far from sounding and discovery, as is the bud bit with an envious worm ere he can spread his sweet leaves to the air, Or dedicate his beauty to the sun. Could we but learn from whence his sorrows grow, we would as willingly give cure as know.*

Oh, fuck, fuck, fuck, why did I not cut some of this when I had the chance? Then after that Romeo enters and Benvolio says: *See, where he comes. So please you step aside; I'll know his grievance or be much denied.*

And I reply: *I would thou wert so happy by thy stay to hear true shrift. Come, madam, let's away.* And I'm out of there until Act Three. Mostly short lines. I can do it. I just need to run it in my head several times.

Joan stuck her head into the dressing room. "Places please for Act One."

"Thank you, places," the actors replied.

PLACES! How the fuck was it already *places?* What happened to the *ten-minute* warning? What happened to *house open?* What happened to *thirty minutes to curtain?* How had he missed all those warnings and now it was time for places? Sweat poured down his sides and blossomed on his forehead. He had to pee and to shit. Did he have time for that? The actors in the opening scene left the dressing room and went backstage. The music would start and the fight and then Capulet entered and then he entered. Why the hell had he cut all that other stuff from the opening of the show? That was insane! Ry singing a song made up for all that? Wallace had been absolutely right! You should not cut lines from Shakespeare! Shakespeare was a genius! So what if people didn't understand the jokes anymore because the puns no longer made any sense? Do we have no respect? And now his entrance was just the length of a song and a swordfight after lights went up.

Oh, the horror!

He grabbed a few tissues from a box, opened his shirt a few buttons and mopped his armpits and down his sides. His shirt was wet and clung to his skin, feeling uncomfortably cold. Did he have time to pee? He didn't want to wet his pants onstage.

Oh, never was a story of more woe than this of Juliet and her Romeo.

He rushed to the bathroom and was unbelievably relieved to find it open. He leaned forward over the horrible stained and paint spattered toilet as he peed, also feeling the pressure in his nether parts, wanting him to sit down and take a shit as well, but horror gripped him as he heard the band begin to play. Oh, sweet Jesus, they were already starting the song, and then there'd be the sword fight, and then his entrance with Lady Montague. He hadn't even talked to Lady Montague! Did she know he was covering Lord Montague today? Surely Joan would have told her. But she would be standing in place right now, wondering where he (or Rocky, if Joan hadn't told her) was. He should be in place!

He zipped up, praying his shit would stay in the tube of his lower intestine and not creep past his sphincter while he was on stage. The music was going! Ry was through his opening lyrics, and they were already into the first sword fight. The swords were clanging onstage, and he was not even in place! Oh sweet Jesus on the cross!

Christ's wounds! Did he enter from stage right or stage left? Oh, butt splinters!

Okay, he told himself. He was the one who staged this show. He was the one who gave everyone their entrances. He knew the show inside and out. It was just his panic making him forget everything he ever knew.

Now he remembered. He hurried to the stage left entrance.

Yes! There was Lady Montague, the music booming around them, waiting in place, looking around with a bit of panic in her eyes herself. He hurried to her side.

"I'm covering Montague tonight," he whispered.

"I heard," she whispered back. "But I wondered if you'd got lost."

Clearly she was annoyed.

"Sorry. Do you know where is my…" She handed him his sword. "Thanks. I was trying to learn the lines. I wasn't expecting…"

She put her hand on his shoulder. "Take a deep breath," she commanded. "You directed this play. You know it as well as anyone. Just trust yourself and have fun."

Have fun. That was rich. He was straining his sphincter closed to keep his shit in his colon. The deep funky bass lines on the music felt like they were vibrating his poops toward the exit. He feared he would not remember a single line. And his shirt was drenched with flop sweat. He would surely be an amusing sight for the audience.

When he first started acting, he would shit five times before any performance. His internal panic expressed itself in peristaltic action to the intestines. By the time the lights went up, his guts would be squeezed tight and empty, and he'd feel totally miserable. He wouldn't relax until he was onstage for ten minutes. One of the first plays he'd ever done, he was sitting on stage as the lights came up, holding a newspaper in front of him, reading. Every night as the lights came up, the newspaper rattled so loudly in his quivering hands that he was sure any octogenarian in the back row with his hearing aids off would still be able to hear it.

Over time he developed a ritual of exercises, meditation and breathing for before every performance that calmed and centered him. It transformed his experience from terrifying and miserable to something in which he could take joy. But there'd been no time for any of that tonight.

Another part of his preparation was an overabundance of time spent on memorization. The greatest fear was being up there and suddenly forgetting his lines in front of the audience and having no way to move the play forward. That was the true actor's nightmare.

Lady Montague nudged him, giving him an annoyed look. The music had come down. The fights were easing up. Right! This was his entrance. He was supposed to charge onto the stage with his sword, eager for a fight, while she was trying to slow him down.

Yes! Go!

He stumbled out onto the stage, sword in hand, Lady Montague tugging back on his arm. Wallace was already out there as his sworn enemy, Lord Capulet, yelling for a sword.

A crutch, a crutch! Lady Capulet cried, mocking him. *Why call you for a sword?*

When Wallace saw Dwayne, his eyes widened. Was he surprised to see Dwayne instead of Rocky? Had Joan not told the full cast that he was standing in for him tonight? Or was it something about Dwayne himself?

He looked down at his shirt. He'd worn an orange/pink shirt today, but all around his armpit and down his sides where it was soaked with flop sweat, the shirt looked nearly blood red.

Why hadn't he put on a sport jacket over this mess?

My sword, I say! Wallace shouted. *Old Montague is come, and flourishes his blade in spite of me.*

Wallace looked at Dwayne meaningfully. Lady Montague shook his arm. She was looking at him sternly, as well.

Oh yes! He had a line!

Thou villain Capulet! Dwayne shouted at Wallace. He looked back at Lady Montague. *Hold me not, let me go.*

Ry stepped forward on the band platform and bent a long note on his guitar, then pumped into the next section of the opening music. They brought down the volume of the music as he sang his adaptation of the Prince's stern speech condemning the feud, ending with: *You, Capulet, shall go along with me, and Montague, come you this afternoon, to know our farther pleasure in this case. Once more, on pain of death, all men depart.*

And everyone cleared the stage except for him, Lady Capulet and Benvolio.

Did he have the first line now? Or did Benvolio say something about Romeo? This part was mostly about Romeo. Oh, the silence felt too long! He was supposed to say something! His face blossomed into intense heat. He must be blushing an intense rosy red that all the audience could see!

And, oh horror of horrors, he remembered once again that Reginald Camper, artistic director of Tony-Award-winning Goodman Theatre, the hope of Dwayne's future, was sitting somewhere in this audience! Dwayne glanced around. He didn't see him in the front rows.

What my lord would ask is this, Lady Montague said pointedly, *Who set this ancient quarrel new abroach? Speak, nephew, were you by when it began?*

Yes, that was his line. Damn it! She'd had to say it for him. He had to focus! He must not think about Reg Camper! The grip of his sword hilt felt slippery in his hand. It was soaked in sweat.

Now Benvolio had a speech, and Lady Montague, bless her, had a speech, and Benvolio one more, talking about how Romeo had been seen sulking among a grove of sycamores. Dwayne listened attentively until Benvolio gave his cue: *And gladly shunn'd who gladly fled from me.*

Many a morning hath he there been seen, with tears augmenting the fresh morning's dew, Dwayne said, feeling so good to have remembered this much, *adding to clouds more clouds with his deep sighs; but all so soon as the all-cheering sun should...* (oh no! How did it go?) *in the east sky...draw shady curtains around Aurora's bed...away steals Romeo from...somewhere...* (oh God save me! Benvolio is looking at me like I'm insane) *and shuts himself in his chamber pot* (oh God, not chamber pot!) *pens himself...with the daylight outside.* Well, that was not how the speech ended, but that was as far as he could take it. Benvolio waited, and when he realized Dwayne would say no more, he physically lurched and said his line: *My noble uncle, do you know the cause?*

Dwayne had a line. A short line. *I could not learn it* or something?

No, Dwayne said. He left it at that.

Ah! Benvolio said in shock at his brevity. *Have you importun'd him by any means?*

Now what was he supposed to say? It was another longer speech, with something in it about *sounding and discovery, as is the bud bit with an envious worm.* Fuck! How did that fit in?

I have tried but failed, as so have many other friends, Dwayne said in an absolutely hideous paraphrase of Shakespeare, *but if you could figure it out, I would be forever grateful.* And he stopped. A whole long speech reduced to a single sentence that was not even close to what Shakespeare wrote, though it was sort of what Montague meant. And now Romeo was supposed to enter, off on the other side of the stage, but he was not coming, because, of course, Dwayne had said nothing remotely similar to the cue line for his entrance.

What should he do? He could not for the life of him remember the cue line. Would they just stand in silence until Romeo got the idea and entered?

And now I wonder, Dwayne improvised loudly, trying to give Orlando the hint, all the while witnessing the horrified looks on the faces of Benvolio and Lady Montague, *wherefore art my son, Romeo?*

Oh, sweet Jesus, what a horrible improvisation! To steal Juliet's *Wherefore art thou, Romeo?* What an idiotic thing to do!

However, it did get Orlando onto the stage. He was supposed to enter, oblivious to the three of them, but he could not resist a furtive, weird, and annoyed look in Dwayne's direction.

See, where he comes, Benvolio said wearily. *So please you step aside; I'll know his grievance or be much denied.*

Dwayne was supposed to say something like: *I would thou wert so happy about hearing the truth or something...* No, that wasn't quite right.

Good, he said simply and turned to Lady Montague. *Come, madam, let's away.* And they exited the stage. At least he got the last four words right.

Once they got out into the hallway, Lady Montague broke down laughing. "Oh my God," she said. "You stunk that up beyond *recognition*, Dwayne."

"Thanks," he said, his heart sinking ever deeper. *And Reginald Camper was watching.*

35

Still Later the Same Day

Dwayne had time to memorize the few lines he had for his other two scenes of the show, and he put on a sport jacket to cover his badly sweat-stained shirt. He was even able to do some of his ritual meditation before his next entrance, but he still played his other appearances as Lord Montague clumsily. Worse still, his clumsiness seemed to infect much of the rest of the cast. By Joan's assessment, that performance, witnessed by Reg Camper, was the absolute worst night of the run. The next night, the actors returned to their previous excellence.

Dwayne was so dispirited, Angela had to coach him in writing a thank you note to Camper. He could not bring himself to enclose the copies of the reviews. He felt his opportunity with the Goodman was as lost as most of the lines he should have delivered in Act One.

Chaz continued to boost the visibility of the show. His videos of the theatre picketing made it to the Channel 9 Nightly News. He wrote Op-Ed articles in two made-up identities, one complaining about the reliance on cheap sex and the debasing of traditional values in the production of *Romeo and Juliet* and the other asking what ever happened to the freedom of expression and why were religious groups attempting to shut down the immortal Shakespeare. They appeared in the same issue of the *Chicago Sun-Times*. He also wrote and placed a cheeky article about the whole controversy in the *Chicago Reader*. He was careful in all these efforts to keep the Darwood name and Dan Darwood's face out of it.

On Wednesday, Ingrid called Dwayne to the playhouse. "Tickets for Friday and Saturday are already sold out," she told him. "Advance tickets for next week and for the final week are gangbusters. Chaz, apparently, is a genius."

She led him into their performance space and pulled out a ladder.

"What are you two doing here today?" Green said, following them in.

"Expanding our seating," Ingrid said. "We're taking down the masking from the back rows."

"No, no, no you are not," Green said.

The upstairs mainstage in which *Romeo and Juliet* was performing was a 300-seat thrust stage auditorium. Dwayne's company could never sell 300 seats so they hung flats masking off the back two rows in the side seating sections plus a curtain hiding the back row in the center section of seating to bring it down to 175 seats. Having too many empty seats looked bad. They'd set it up that way for *Titus Andronicus*, and it had stayed that way.

"I can sell those other 125 seats now, Green," Ingrid said.

"The computer is set for selling 175 seats," Green said. "I'm not reprogramming the computer for 300 seats in the middle of your run. It'd crash the system."

"I got a guy who can do it," Ingrid said.

"You're not bringing in some stranger to work on my system." Green's face turned red, and he vibrated as the volume of his voice increased. "I can't have you fucking things up."

"We are taking down the masking." Ingrid set the ladder at the end of the first masking flat and climbed up.

"All four shows in this building depend on the ticketing system," Green shouted. "This is not just about you!"

"We are taking down the masking," Ingrid repeated. She pointed to the far end of the aisle. "Dwayne, go to the end and support the flat while I untie it. We don't want it to fall."

"If you want your audience to see those empty rows of seats, that's up to you," Green fumed. "But you are not changing anything in the ticketing system." He walked back out into the hall and kicked a bucket out of his way. He was sick of Ingrid Baardsen, who never ever listened to him. He didn't want to be anywhere near her.

Ingrid was already up the ladder and untying the straps that connected the first black masking flat to the pipe overhead.

Dwayne climbed up the side of the seating riser to get behind the flats. There were three large flats, side by side, clamped together behind, to give the illusion of a solid wall behind the seats, hiding the top row of seats. Dwayne began undoing the clamps attaching the first two. "If Green is not going to let us update the ticket system to sell these seats, why are we doing this?" he said.

"Oh, we'll update it," Ingrid said breezily. "Don't you worry your pretty little head about that."

There was usually no point in arguing with Ingrid. Besides that, Dwayne had felt lethargic ever since his disastrous understudy performance. It was easier to just go along. The only thing keeping him at all buoyant was the upcoming performance at Angela's school.

It took about a half hour to get the first set of flats down and stowed along the back wall of the space. They were halfway through getting the curtains down that masked the row of seats at the back of the center section when Green came running back into the space.

"What the hell did you do?" he shouted. He ran into the very center of the stage and did a strange little hop of rage. "What in the living hell did you do?" he screamed even louder.

"As you can see, Green, we've taken down one set of flats and now we are taking down these curtains…"

"What in the living fuck did you do to my ticketing system?" he cried.

"We've been in here the whole time…"

"Don't give me your bullshit!" He did another of his strange little hops. "The whole ticketing system is down. Nobody's tickets can be sold! There's no access to the records of how many tickets have been sold. To who they've been sold …"

"To *whom* they've been sold," Ingrid corrected. "It's *to whom*, not *to who*. *To who* is what an owl says."

"What did you do?" Dwayne whispered to her.

"You fucking, fucking bitch!" Green shouted. "You had your guy crash my system so I'd have to reset it? And then you figured I'd give in and add your seats? Is that what you figured?"

"I would never jeopardize the wonderful business partnership we've established and enjoyed," she said mildly.

"You think I'll reset it with your other 125 seats! Well, I won't! In fact, maybe I'll just evict you! Put you and your fucking *Romeo and Juliet* out on the street!"

"I don't think you want to do that, Green," she said, focusing on untying the final cords that held up the masking curtain. The curtain fell to the seats below. "But the way, where is the vacuum cleaner? These unused seats are really dusty."

"You're never going to use them!" Green shouted. "Never!"

"Excuse me. Ray?" Darla Conners, the box office manager had come into the space. Everyone looked at her. "The ticketing system is back up," she said. "Everything seems fine. Maybe the internet had just gone down for a minute, or something."

"Everything is back?" Green said, totally mystified.

"As far as I can see," Darla said. "I looked through the sales on all the shows. Everything looks correct."

"Well, Green," Ingrid said cheerfully. "How about that? Maybe we should go down and look. Darla had printed up our sales figures for this coming weekend for me." She pulled a printout out of her back pocket. "We can compare this to what's on the system and make sure nothing was lost."

Green looked deeply confused. "Yeah. Whatever." He did not look ready to extend an apology.

They all went down to the box office. Darla took Ingrid's printout and compared it to what was on the screen. It all matched up.

"Does it still show I'm sold out for Friday and Saturday?" Ingrid asked.

Darla looked. Her mouth dropped open. "No!" she said. "Somehow or other you now have 125 unsold seats remaining. Oops! A set of four of those just sold for Saturday."

"What the hell did you do?" Green shouted.

"I've been upstairs this whole time," Ingrid said. "I didn't do a thing."

"Don't fuck with me, Baardsen. I'll throw your lousy show out."

"Now wait…" Dwayne said.

"Shut the fuck up, Dwayne!" Green said.

"Now, now, now," Ingrid said. "Yes, I did have my guy rework the system. But first he backed up everything. He made a copy of the system and added my new seats to the copy. Then he loaded in the new system. He predicted the system would be down less than five minutes."

"It was not down very long," Darla agreed. "Raymond was standing right here when it went down, and he went running upstairs immediately."

"So, you see, everything is fine," Ingrid said. "In fact, it's better than fine, because starting this weekend we will pay the regular full price for our space instead of the discount you've been giving us. And I won't charge you anything for my guy's programming time."

Green was torn between his roiling outrage and the greed for getting full price. It wasn't easy keeping the books balanced on a facility like this, and he needed the cash. He started to say something twice, but remained flustered.

"*Keep Your Eyes on the Prize*, Green," Dwayne said. "*Winner boats rise together!*"

Green gave him a confused look, then walked away.

Darla watched him go, and then looked from Dwayne to Ingrid, still not sure exactly what had happened.

"Say, do you know where the vacuum cleaner is?" Ingrid asked.

36

Wednesday, October 20, 2004

D wayne stopped outside Angela's classroom on his way to the school auditorium. He looked in through the window in her door. The glass was reinforced with an embedded mesh of wire. Angela was up at the board, demonstrating something to the students. Most of them were paying attention. Dwayne was impressed. She noticed him at the window.

"All right, class, today you get to meet someone special," she said, opening the door. She took his hand and led him to the front of the class. "This is my husband." Most of the students made little *ohs* and *ahs* showing they were surprised and impressed, except for one boy in the front row. "Aw, come on!" he complained. "You never said you had a husband!" The other students laughed and shouted in response. Now they were all wiggling in their seats. One of them started singing: *Ms. G. and Tyrone sitting in a tree....*

"All right everyone, settle down," Angela said. "You all want to be able to go to the assembly today, right?"

"*Romeo and Juliet....*" a boy in the back voiced in a ten-year-old's impression of drippy romance and began making kissy noises.

"James...." Angela said, giving him the stern look of death.

Everyone quieted down. Dwayne thought it was semi-miraculous the effect Angela had on them, although they were still wiggling. Tyrone looked at Dwayne with suspicion and resentment.

"Mr. Finnegan directed the production of *Romeo and Juliet* we are going to see today."

Tyrone stood up abruptly. "Do you do the kissing and stuff with Ms. G?" he demanded loudly.

All the children shrieked and whooped. Tyrone sat back down, looking around mystified by the ruckus he'd inspired.

"All right, all right, all right," Angela said, using both arms to indicate everyone should settle down. The volume began to decline.

Angela put her hand on Dwayne's arm. "They're excited about the assembly," she said quietly but enthusiastically. Despite the tumult, she seemed pleased. "I'll see you afterwards."

Dwayne had prepared a few words to say to Angela's class, but he nodded and headed toward the auditorium. As the door closed behind him he heard one of the girls say: "Mr. Finnegan is *hot*."

He chuckled to himself. He and Ms. G. were the heartbreakers of the fifth-grade crowd. He'd forgotten that Angela had the kids call her Ms. G., but of course they would murder the pronunciation of Guiseppelli, so it was a natural choice.

He could hear Ry's guitar even before he entered the auditorium. Ry was onstage with his guitar plugged into the amp. Ingrid leaned out of the light booth at the back of the auditorium.

"About half that volume, Ry," she shouted down to him. "Otherwise it's going to overwhelm the actors. He rolled his eyes, adjusted the amp, and went back to playing riffs to warm up his fingers and tuning his guitar. Ingrid experimented with the light board, discovering which dimmers illuminated what parts of the stage. Then she came backstage where Dwayne was talking with Melinda, Orlando, and Coco, who had just arrived.

"Since we just had one rehearsal of this selection of scenes," Dwayne told them, "let's make all the entrances and exits to this side. I'll have the script here in case anyone gets confused about what comes next." Ry wandered over to them. "Ry, you'll remain upstage throughout the show. If we get delayed due to any confusion, you fill in with a little guitar. You can do that, right?"

"Sure," he said, looking typically bored.

"Just not too loud," Ingrid said. She pulled a prop table over by them and put four large flashlights on it. They had red gels taped over the lenses. "I figured since this is a place we hadn't performed before, you might need something to find your way around backstage. With the red gels, the audience won't see the lights, but it'll give you enough to see."

"Thanks, Ingrid," Melinda said. She was looking a little nervous. The school auditorium was much larger than anywhere she'd ever performed before.

"Before the kids get here, let's test our voices on the stage," Dwayne said. "We have to project to fill this place. Especially if the kids are wiggly."

"Hey, I can help out," Ingrid said. "If I'm not hearing you, I'll give the lights a momentary surge, very subtle, but enough to know you need to pick up the volume."

"Yeah, well, please keep that very subtle."

Dwayne had a feeling this was a bad idea. It didn't take long to find out why.

The kids filed in, noisy as could be. The principal, Fran Konacki, took the stage and quieted them. She and Dwayne gave their introductions to the show, and Ry wound into his guitar work and opening lines. However, as the show progressed, Orlando was not projecting to be heard well at the back of the auditorium. At first Ingrid gave the most subtle of light surges, but Orlando didn't seem to notice. Then the surges became more noticeable. One of the children shouted: *Lightning!* There was general hilarity while the teachers hopped up and quieted their classes. Between the efforts of the teachers and the excitement of Romeo and Juliet's first meeting at the Capulet ball, the auditorium mostly settled down.

If I profane with my unworthiest hand this holy shrine, Orlando said, kneeling and taking Melinda's hand, *My lips, two blushing pilgrims, ready stand to smooth that rough touch with a tender kiss.* Dwayne heard a sharp intake of breath in the crowd. He felt suddenly overwhelmingly proud of his actors. These children were entranced!

Thus from my lips, by thine my sin is purg'd, Orlando said. The two leaned in to one another and shared their first kiss. Sighs and giggles and a few cries of prepubescent outrage from the crowd were followed by a teacher shushing.

It was going well! However, as the scene progressed Orlando began losing volume again. As they moved into position with Melinda on a platform for the balcony scene and Orlando below, Ingrid gave another warning surge of the lights, but then all the lights went out.

Dwayne heard a strangled cry of frustration from Ingrid. What had she done?

The lights were not coming back on. Ry had the presence of mind to cover with a guitar solo. The kids had not yet realized something was wrong.

And yet the lights did not come back on.

Holy Saint Lucy, patron of blindness, what am I going to do?

Somewhere in the dark, Angela was out there with her class. All her colleagues knew this was *her husband's play*. He could not embarrass her! He would not swim with the rats! This ship must not go down. Dwayne suddenly remembered Ingrid's flashlights. He groped in the dark until he found the table, turned one of them on, tore the red gels off another two, crept out on stage, and turned the two flashlight beams, which were remarkably bright, onto the faces of Melinda and Orlando. When Orlando began his first line, it was magic:

But soft, what light through yonder window breaks? It is the east, and Juliet is the sun! Arise fair sun and kill the envious moon, who is already sick and pale with grief.

They continued under flashlight beams through their individual speeches with a spellbound audience of school children. Then Melinda said, talking to herself, unaware Romeo was listening below: "*Romeo, doff thy name, and for thy name, which is no part of thee, take all myself.*"

Suddenly the lights came back, and Orlando stretched out his arms to her as Dwayne rolled behind the balcony platform and offstage. *I take thee at thy word,* Orlando called to her triumphantly. *Call me but love, and I'll be new baptis'd. Henceforth I never will be Romeo.*

It was beautiful, just as though they'd planned it that way. For the rest of the presentation, the lights stayed on and Orlando was careful to keep his projection loud and clear.

When it came to playing Friar Lawrence, Dwayne had hidden a script inside the covers of a prayer book to which he often referred on stage. He did not fumble his lines.

At the end the kids were stunned and sad at the deaths of the lovers, and after Ry played his final riff and gave his final speech, they

222 • Richard Engling

broke into wild applause. It was fantastic.

Dwayne was chatting with his cast as the children filed out—and Reg Camper came down the aisle.

"Very nicely done, all!" he congratulated. Dwayne hopped off the stage down to the aisle to greet him. "Mr. Camper…" he stammered.

"My daughter is a fourth grader," Camper said. "I'm here as a parent volunteer. I didn't realize I'd be seeing part of your show again. I have to say, it's looking much better here than it did on Saturday."

"Thank you," Dwayne said. "Saturday was not what we would have liked." Melinda, who'd come to the edge of the stage to listen in, nodded.

"Yes. I read the *Tribune* review afterwards," Camper said. "It didn't sound like the same show I'd seen." Camper gave Dwayne a quick, friendly clap on the shoulder and turned to rejoin his daughter's exiting class.

"Well, that was nice," Melinda said.

Dwayne caught up with Angela, who was talking with Jayden, her super-buff Poet in the School. Fran Konacki swooped in. "Jayden, I'm going to need to talk with you," the principal said sternly, leading him away.

"There goes Jayden," Angela said.

"What's up with him?" Dwayne asked.

"I guess I should have reprimanded him. He was also working with one of the young new teachers, Christina Harris. Apparently, he shared his workout photo with her as well, and Christina shared it with Fran this morning. She was not amused."

Dwayne, however, was.

But the best part of the day was later at home. Angela was pleased and grateful for Dwayne's work and for making her the hero with her colleagues and principal. The lady teachers now knew her husband was both handsome and talented, which was nice. They all enjoyed the assembly and thought the actors were terrific and Dwayne was charming in the post-show Q&A. Angela particularly liked the flashlight scene. The whole event rekindled her affection, and she and Dwayne spent the most delightful night together.

37

Sunday, October 24, 2004

The extra seats Ingrid had opened in their theatre sold well. The updated ticketing system operated without a glitch. Friday and Saturday of the next weekend were totally sold out. Thursday and Sunday were good houses, too. Their fundraiser was scheduled in the space for after the Sunday matinee. Dwayne and Ingrid had been running around all weekend, collecting donated items for the silent auction and discounted liquor for the bar. The Darwood Foundation had been kind enough to donate four nights at a Darwood-owned residence in the Bahamas plus air fare. Then there were the items from Uncle Bull's *I've got a guy* guys. Knowing these were items extorted from poor debtor bastards like Chaz, Dwayne felt uneasy about accepting them. But neither did he dare to refuse anything that came from Uncle Bull, in case Bull might make a new appearance. Plus, they had dinners for two at various local restaurants, gift baskets from local boutiques, and lots of theatre tickets from companies around town.

After the matinee started, he and Ingrid would be heading out to collect a quarter barrel of beer from a nearby craft brewer and donated food from a local Noodles and Company where Ingrid knew the manager. Ingrid was positively buoyant. They were able to sell a decent number of tickets to the fundraiser. And as their Sunday night audience filed in, she was even more over the moon about how they were selling out the 300-seat house.

"I thought Chaz was kind of a jackass after he fucked around with Coco and destroyed his marriage and then lost his job during *Titus Andronicus*," she said. "But he's been a genius handling the Darwood Foundation and spinning all the P.R."

224 ◆ RICHARD ENGLING

"Well, the quality of the production didn't hurt, either," Dwayne said.

"Even great P.R. can't sell a turd," Ingrid agreed.

Dwayne stood near the entry, greeting ticket holders as they came up the stairs and into his theatre. On other nights, he'd stood at the door as people exited, too, and he'd seen how excited they'd been by the show. That was his joy. He wasn't exactly sure how much money Chaz had collected or how much they'd make after the show closed, but he felt sure they could offer everyone a bonus for this show and pay better for the next.

Maybe his career *would* go somewhere.

But what was this? Climbing the stairs he saw two of the leading artistic directors in the city of Chicago: Reginald Camper of the Goodman and R.J. Smith of Northlight walking up the stairs together.

"Mr. Camper. Mr. Smith. Welcome," he said to them. They looked up at him. He extended a hand to shake.

"Ah yes, Dwayne," Camper said, taking his hand. "After that assembly, I thought I'd give your production another look. I heard interesting things about what happened to you Saturday. Picketers, thugs with pipes, backstage threats." He smiled down on Dwayne from on high. He was tall, and his long white hair curled down at the sides of his face. He looked very smart and privately amused.

"It was a challenging night," Dwayne allowed. "Thanks so much for coming back. I'm very glad to see you both." He shook with R.J. Smith as well.

"Been hearing a lot about your show," Smith said. "Controversy sells tickets."

"That's true," Camper agreed. He smiled kindly at Dwayne and continued into the theatre.

Reg Camper and R.J. Smith in his house! When they hired a director, that director got paid a living wage. Oh, how he prayed this afternoon's show would go well.

And now up the stairs came three faces that he loved: Angela, Chaz, and Aleister. They'd volunteered to bartend for the fundraiser after the show. They already looked a bit tipsy.

Angela sidled up to him and gave him a hug and a boozy kiss.

"Brunch was delicious," she assured him.

"Did you have any food with your mimosas?"

She laughed long and hard. The other two chuckled as well.

"Oh, Dwayne," she said, patting his shoulder. "You are so droll."

"I can see you three are going to be excellent bartenders."

"Super. Absolutely super," Chaz agreed.

Aleister put a bag into his hands. "Three autographed copies of *The Soul in Grief*," he said. "For your silent auction."

Once the audience took their seats and the doors were closed, Ingrid joined him in the hallway. Inside, a funereal organ began to play. Ry's voice began the lines: "Dear loves and lovers, we gather here to tell the story of untimely death." And they broke into the music that was so much like Prince's *Let's Go Crazy*, with Ry singing:

Capulets and Montagues
They want to fight.
Romeo's in love, but he can't find a wife.
Rosalind hates him.
Like Tybalt hates all.
Benvolio smiles. He's pushed to the wall.
Why can't these people just release their bile?
I don't know, let's go!

"I just love this," Ingrid said.

"Prince was a great choice," Dwayne agreed.

"Yeah, that," Ingrid agreed, "but I mean standing outside the theatre as a show starts inside. There's all that stuff going on in there that we made happen. The audience is seeing it for their first time, and we are out here, taking a moment before we do the next thing we have to do. And maybe we can also hear a little bit of sound bleeding out from another show happening in the studio theatre down the hall." She paused for a moment, and yes, they could hear voices from that show, too. "I just love this feeling of theatre happening all around."

Dwayne considered it for a moment. Inside he could hear the combatants storming the stage and their swords beginning to ring out as the music continued. Downstairs, two more shows were playing in the first-floor main stage and studio. Four shows running simultaneously to their audiences, and he was one of the people who had made it happen.

"Yeah," he said. It *was* a good feeling.

"Okay, we better roll," Ingrid said. They headed down the stairs. "Don't forget to pick up ice to keep the beer cold. Four bags probably? They said they'd give us cups with the quarter barrel, so don't forget that." She handed him a company credit card with his name on it.

"Well, look at that," Dwayne said. "I get to spend company money."

"Of course," Ingrid said. "I've had that for you ever since I set up the account."

"Really?" Dwayne said.

"You just had to ask. Say, do you think it's okay for me to buy some gas on the company? I've been driving all over town for us."

"Of course," Dwayne said. "Fill it up!"

While the first act played, Dwayne picked up the beer and ice, and Ingrid fetched the food. They brought it all into the upstairs lobby. Angela, Chaz, and Aleister skipped the second act of the show to help them set up the bar and the food. The auction tables were already in place from that morning. And then the attendees began showing up. They were joined by a throng from the show as it ended. Chaz and Aleister were busy serving drinks as Angela circulated and answered questions about the buffet and the auction tables. Dwayne was taking a breath and enjoying a sip of Cava when Reg Camper approached him. He was smiling.

"Hello, Mr. Camper," Dwayne said, shaking his hand again.

Camper chuckled. "Call me Reg. Listen, I loved your *Romeo and Juliet*. The school assembly really opened my eyes. I'm glad I came back. The interplay between the music, the fight choreography, the dancing…really fantastic."

"Thank you."

"I wondered what you plan to direct next. I might have an idea for you."

Holy Saint Cajetan, patron of gamblers and opportunity, could he be offering me a job? At the same time, Camper seemed amused. Was he amused at Dwayne? Did he find him funny? Did he know about world-famous performance artist Laurie Anderson coming to see *Titus*

Andronicus and being turned away at the door? Did he know Dwayne's chance with the Public in New York had been blown by the stupidest of misunderstandings?

"I was considering *King Lear*," Dwayne said. "Our Wallace Proctor has the chops for Lear." They looked over at where Wallace was holding forth with a group of older lady patrons. "Coco Nesbit would make an amazing Goneril." They looked at Coco, who was leaning against the bar as Aleister poured her a glass of Cava. Camper hummed in affirmative. "Melinda, our Juliet, would be a fine Cordelia. And our Romeo, Orlando Gunn, could play either Edmund or Edgar. He's adept with both good and evil." He stopped. He suspected he was talking too much and too fast.

"So, you'd want to cast it with your ensemble?" Camper said. He looked around the room, spotting more cast members among the patrons.

Was this a trick question?

"We have started talking ideas in the company," Dwayne said cautiously. "But I'm also interested in freelance directing opportunities."

Camper chuckled again. "Of course you are," he said. "But I'm curious about your vision for *Lear*. Would you continue in the style of *Romeo and Juliet*? Prince-inspired music? Choreography?"

"Probably not Prince," Dwayne said. "It worked for *Romeo and Juliet*, but I don't hear it for *King Lear*. We've been thinking about David Bowie."

"Bowie?" Camper sounded surprised. "Tell me more."

"There's a huge range in his work. I think about *Putting Out Fire* that he wrote for *Cat People*. And the moody, atmospheric stuff he wrote with Brian Eno. There's plenty of hard driving rock for fight scenes. Maybe something from *Heroes*. Even *Fame*, that he wrote with John Lennon makes a possible theme for Lear himself."

"Interesting."

"We're still talking. Ry Joodey is the genius behind the music."

"He was your guitarist? And played the Prince?" They looked over where Ry was whispering into Melinda's ear and she was grinning happily.

"That's right."

"I saw your *Titus Andronicus* got good reviews, as well."

"Yes," Dwayne agreed.

"Do you know the Owen?" Camper said.

"I...I love the Owen."

"Wait a minute," Camper said. "We talked in the Owen, didn't we? When I thought you were a funder." He remembered and laughed.

"Yes," Dwayne said, feeling the embarrassment of that meeting again. He was still annoyed with Brad Cunningham for not making it clear to Camper that Dwayne was a director.

"So, here's the thing," Camper said. "I have an Owen slot in November/December that was set for a visiting show from *La Mama*, and they cancelled. The members of my artistic collective are all already committed during that time. I wondered if you'd like to take that slot. We'd offer production support, of course."

At first Dwayne couldn't speak at all. He felt like he might choke. Or vomit. Or never breathe again.

He barely squeezed the air through his vocal chords. "Yes, I would love to do that."

"Good!" Camper said cheerily. "Call my office Monday and set up an appointment for early in the week. We'll hit the details."

And he headed out the door, waving at someone that he knew.

Dwayne didn't get a chance to thank him, but maybe that was all for the best. He could still hardly get air to move through his throat.

He had to tell Angela. This was unbelievable.

He looked at the bar. She wasn't with Chaz and Aleister, who were pouring drinks as fast as they could. He looked at the food tables. She wasn't there. He found her at the silent auction tables, explaining to a patron how to place a bid.

He opened his mouth to speak, but still nothing came out.

"What's up?" she said.

He started laughing. He laughed for a full minute. She started laughing with him, unsure what they were laughing about, before he was finally able to speak.

And then he told her the amazing news.

38

Sunday, October 31, 2004

Except for Thursday night, the fifth and final weekend of the show was totally sold out. One thousand, one hundred twenty-nine tickets for the final weekend. Most storefront companies were happy if they sold one hundred twenty tickets on a weekend. They were all beside themselves.

Ingrid buttonholed him as soon as he came into the Playhouse lobby for the final performance. "Listen, Green can move what he had scheduled in our theatre to the downstairs theatre. We can extend!"

"Wow," Dwayne said. "How long?"

"He could give us three weeks but Orlando and Melinda are both booked after two. I checked with all the actors. They can all do two more weeks except Rocky. So you'd take over Montague. Okay? And Joan is booked, so I'd take over as stage manager. I'll shadow her today. Everybody gets a raise. We'll add a stipend for every performance of the extension. And a bonus for Joan, even though she has to move on."

"And I thought we were here to close the show."

"Isn't it amazing? You can do Montague, right? We'll do a put-in rehearsal, if you like."

"Yeah, I'll do it."

He hesitated. Should he tell her the news? So far, he'd only told Angela. He felt that spouting out about it too soon might jinx it. From what Camper said, it sounded like they'd be doing a Psychedelic Dream production at the Goodman. But he didn't really *know* if that's what it would be. Hell, did he really know it would happen? No details had been set. No contract signed.

"Did you want to say something?" Ingrid could see he had

something on his mind.

"No. I just wanted to say: Good work. You expanded our audience. You got us more dates. You really *Kept Your Eyes on the Prize.*"

"Thanks, Dwayne." She smiled radiantly, then cocked her head to the side. "Sometimes I get the impression you think I'm too pushy."

"This company wouldn't exist if you hadn't pushed." In fact, he'd been shocked and dismayed at the way she'd kept it going after *Titus Andronicus.* But he was happy now. "It's like Madeline Forthright says: *Winner Boats Rise Together.*"

"Who?"

"Nobody. Just this author I like."

"Anything else?"

They had two more weekends of *Romeo and Juliet.* He'd meet with Camper this week. There was plenty time to share news with the whole group once an agreement was actually made.

"Nope," he said. "Just happy to be working with you."

"Aww." She gave him a rib-crushing hug and rushed off to shadow Joan.

◆ ◆ ◆

The audience who believed they were there for the final performance gave the show a standing ovation. The actors basked in it, turning and bowing to all three sections of seats. Then Dwayne hopped out on stage to make an announcement before the audience could leave, letting them know about the extension and to please tell their friends to come see the show. Extending at the last minute meant they needed to work hard to get the word out.

After the audience left, Ingrid brought out the leftover booze from the previous week's fundraiser to make a toast with the cast on stage. Dwayne had a glass of wine and enjoyed everyone's high spirits. He saw Tom and Orlando hugging, so they seemed to have worked out their problems. Peaches stood off to the side, looking lost. Poor thing. Dwayne promised himself that whatever might happen at the Goodman, he would make sure that she was designing the costumes. Then the band started playing and the cast started dancing. It was all great fun, but he realized there was somewhere else he'd rather be.

All the way home on the El he shuffled the various bits of good news in his mind. He was going to meet with Reginald Camper. He might be directing at the Goodman in October. It might be his company and his production of *King Lear*. And even if not, Psychedelic Dream had money in the bank. Between the donations Chaz extorted from the Darwood Foundation, the fundraiser, and the boost in ticket sales, Psychedelic Dream had a surplus of $125,000. And if the two-week extension went well, there would be more. It was hard to believe.

He finally felt like he was going somewhere. He smiled hugely. *Winners Are Grinners.*

When he got home, he found Angela grading papers at the big table in the second bedroom.

"I didn't think I'd be seeing you," she said. "Don't you have to strike? No big closing night party until two in the morning?"

"We didn't close. We're extending for two weeks."

"Nice." She got up from the table to give him a kiss.

"The cast was having an extension celebration when I left. Drinking and dancing."

"And you didn't stay?" She leaned back with her arms around his neck. He kept his arms around her waist.

She really was the most beautiful woman.

"I just kept thinking how cute you'd look if you had a great big stomach," he said.

"Aww, Dwayne," she cooed. "You left the party to come home and knock me up?"

He smiled and nodded. The thought of filling her belly with a baby aroused him completely. His beautiful Angela, large with child, and later, with a child at her breast. Watching the baby grow. The two of them hand in hand with their little son or daughter. *Keep the Home Fires Burning.* You just had to support each other and trust in good things to come. It would be great.

"That's so sweet," she said.

"Yeah," he said. He took her hand and led her into the bedroom.

The End

Now that you have read *Romeo and Juliet Keep Their Eyes on the Prize*, please leave a review at your online retailer and/or your favorite social media. We depend on your support. And recommend it to your friends!

Find more information about Richard's events and upcoming work at www.richardengling.com and sign up for his newsletter.

About the Author

Richard Engling's writing career began in high school when his coffee shop theatre group needed material to perform, and he was elected to write it. He's spent a lifetime writing and performing, paying his bills as a teacher, truck driver, and copywriter, while performing as an actor, drummer in a jazz quartet, and working as the founding artistic director of an ensemble theatre company in Chicago. His books include *Body Mortgage, Visions of Anna*, and the first Dwayne Finnegan novel, *Give My Regards to Nowhere*. His plays include *Ghost Watch* and *Anna in the Afterlife*.

Richard holds a Masters of Arts in Creative Writing from Indiana University and he majored in Theatre as an undergraduate at Northern Illinois University. He lives in Evanston, Illinois, with his wife, Gail.

GIVE MY REGARDS TO NOWHERE

The First Dwayne Finnegan Novel
by Richard Engling

"ABSURD COMIC HI-JINX" —Chris Jones, *Chicago Tribune*

"As Carl Hiaasen does with his Florida-based satirical crime novels, Engling's gloriously silly narrative allows his readers to witness how the sausage gets made...Engling's satire on storefront theatre is thoroughly entertaining from start to finish."
–ChicagoOnStage

"a rollicking ride through the underbelly of the acting world"
–Midwest Book Review

"The chaotic shenanigans conceal a tightly constructed plot full of vivid dialogue that hones to comedy's fundamental principles: pleasure, surprise, folly, luck both good and bad, and a celebration of human ingenuity and resilience. *Give My Regards to Nowhere* reminds us that theater has always been sustained by dreamers who keep striving in the face of all the odds."
—Evanston RoundTable

Available wherever books and audiobooks are sold.
www.polarityensemblebooks.com

BODY MORTGAGE

by Richard Engling

"Fast paced future thriller."
—SCIENCE FICTION AND FANTASY REVIEWS

"This is a neat SF detective story in the Mike Hammer / Philip Marlowe / Bladerunner mold...an engaging and well-constructed thriller, very enjoyable."
— BRUMM GROUP NEWS

A gritty thriller in a nightmare America where human parts are worth more than the whole.

The big market in Chicago used to be livestock. But now it's human body parts. People can mortgage their own bodies to organ transplant companies, but it's a gristly end when they can't pay up.

Gregory Blake is a private investigator in this savage city. His first mistake is to take on a client whose body is marked for foreclosure. His second is to try to find out why the most powerful forces in town are in such a hurry to repossess. Blake thinks he knows all there is to know about the underworld. But never did he expect to be lost in the corporate corridors of perverse power—in the hell that future America has become...

Originally published by Penguin Books USA and Headline UK.

Available wherever books are sold.
www.polarityensemblebooks.com

VISIONS OF ANNA

by Richard Engling

"PASSIONATE, POIGNANT" —Elizabeth Cunningham

"Matthew Harken's urgent questions about his friend Anna's suicide and his own critical illness compel him to risk a perilous, spiritual quest. His heartrending, heart-opening journey through the interwoven worlds of memory, dream, and shamanic magic lead him not only to visions of Anna but to visions of grace. A passionate, poignant novel."
—Elizabeth Cunningham, author of *The Maeve Chronicles.*

"...a strong authorial voice, motivated characters, and a plot that propels the book... The novel's most transcendent moments occur in Matthew's flashbacks to the time he spent in Paris with Anna. Both young emerging writers subsisting on meager meals in less than modest living situations, Matthew and Anna immerse themselves in the Parisian literary scene. In recalling these memories, Matthew squires readers through a vision of The City of Light so charmed and romantic even he questions whether it truly was as magical as he believed it to be. Engling displays an enviable gift for dialogue and a painter's eye for clear detail."
—Jarrett Neal, *New City* (Chicago)

Available wherever books are sold.
www.polarityensemblebooks.com